Mistress – The Secret Desire

Mistress – The Secret Desire

Alex Magistra

Chapter One

Alexia Summers was an elegant woman with a commanding presence who took no prisoners. She was strong, sexy, and a mistress who loved dominating men and, sometimes, other women too. In fact, she was such an expert at it that her clients were willing to pay whatever she wanted to be dominated by her, and she had plenty of them to do just that.

Alexia knew how far she could go with each client and never had problems with any of them. She would almost always use her clients to fulfill her own sexual needs as part of the session, and as she was a stunningly attractive lady, they did not mind in the slightest. In fact, most clients wanted to be dominated by Alexia because of her willingness to use them as her own personal sex slaves. Her favorite saying when she was with a client was, "The mistress always comes first."

And, indeed, she did. Alexia would punish any man who dared to come before she was totally satisfied and, more importantly, until she allowed them the privilege of having a climax themselves. She would tease her clients and bring them to the brink of ecstasy, then stop what she was doing until they calmed down before doing it all over again. Alexia excelled in all aspects of her work, which was the reason she was so popular, and clients would sometimes have to book her services more than a month in advance.

However, this was not always the case. Alexia had a very troubled past that she would often relive in her mind. Oh, how different her life was now compared to how it used to be when she was young, but to her credit, she used her past troubles to help her achieve what she has today.

As a mistress, Alexia was prepared to listen to her clients and tried her best to give each of them what they wanted ... within reason, of course. She was generous when rewarding them but a bitch when punishing them if they did not please her, like Cliff, the client she was in the process of disciplining right now.

She slowly walked over to him while he was tied upright with his arms stretched out above his head, shackled to a chain that was attached to the ceiling.

"This is what you get when you do not please me," she said as she brought the whip down on the back of her tied-up slave.

"Yes, Mistress," he replied, as he tried very hard not to let her see how much the whip hurt him.

"I am very disappointed in you today. Remember, you must please me, not only by doing whatever I command but also sexually, my little slave. After all, this is why you are here, isn't it? To please and pleasure your mistress?"

"Yes, Mistress. I am sorry, and I shall try harder next time," Cliff replied.

"TRY?" Alexia screamed in an angry voice as she once again brought down the whip on his already sore back.

"OUCH!" Cliff screamed out, by now really feeling the bite of the whip.

"There is no try! You either obey and please me, or you get punished. It's as simple as that, my little slave, so don't you ever forget it," Alexia said with a serious look on her face.

"Yes, Mistress, I am sorry, and I won't forget it," he replied in a feeble voice.

"How long have you been visiting me?" she asked him.

"For just under a year, Mistress," he replied.

"Well, do you not think that by now you should have learned?" Alexia asked him as she ran her long fingernails down his back, scratching his skin as she did so.

"Yes, Mistress, you are correct; I should have by now," Cliff replied, trying not to show any pain.

"Well then, I guess my punishment is not severe enough to make you remember," she said as she dug her fingernails even deeper into his back.

Cliff arched his whole body forward from the pain as Alexia did this, telling her he was sorry and that he would make sure he never let her down again. He swore that he would remember this lesson and said that her punishment was indeed sufficient enough.

Alexia walked around so that she was now standing in front of him and reached her hand down slowly.

"I love playing with a man's balls. Are you sure my punishment is enough?" she asked, as she cupped her hand around them, and gave a little squeeze.

"Yes, Mistress, it is," he said, again trying very hard not to show the pain.

"Ok, we shall see," Alexia replied as she gently began to touch his cock in such a way that he became aroused within a minute.

"My, my, it seems you are very excited and so hard," Alexia said as she gave his hard cock a tender little squeeze.

"Yes, Mistress," Cliff replied, hoping he was now going to get a reward after the pain he had endured.

"Well, it's a shame for this stiff cock of yours to go to waste, but as you did not pleasure me well enough today and forced me to punish you, you will not be getting any pleasure from me. So get dressed, because your session is now finished. Perhaps next time, you will make sure that your mistress is well and truly satisfied," Alexia said as she unchained him.

"Yes, Mistress, thank you," Cliff said as he began to get dressed while Alexia watched him.

Oh, how he wished that he was able to please her so that she may have rewarded him, but alas, it was not meant to be, and he had to leave her house wanting.

Once he was ready, Alexia opened the dungeon door and escorted him through to the front of the house. They said their goodbyes, and then she went into the front room, where she poured herself a drink. She sat there relaxing for around thirty minutes, reminiscing, as she often did, about her past, which was a very sad one, before finishing her drink and heading off to have a bath.

Having a long soak is something Alexia always did after spending time with a client, not only for cleanliness, which she took very seriously, but also because it was very relaxing. She ran the bath, pouring in some oils which would turn to bubbles when hit by the gushing water and then undressed before settling herself into the tub. She would often just lay there for sometimes nearly an hour, having a glass of wine most times as she soaked, again, quite often reminiscing.

Whenever she felt down, she would remind herself of how lucky she was to be living the life she is and how terrible her life could have been if not for that turning point early in her past. Yes, she indeed considered herself a very lucky woman, especially doing what she loved to do, which was to dominate men.

After around forty-five minutes of relaxing in the water, recollecting the past, she showered off the bubbles, got out of the tub, put her toweling robe on, and began to dry herself. Once done, she put on a clean, dry robe and went into the kitchen to make something to eat. Alexia had around three hours before her next client was due to arrive, someone she had never met before and had only spoken to on the telephone when the appointment was made.

When there was only an hour left before her new client was due to arrive, she made her way into the bedroom and began to prepare herself. Alexia styled her hair, painted her toe and fingernails, put on a pair of black stockings, high-heeled shoes, and a dress with a high split on one side. She always made an extra effort when she was due to dominate a new client, and today was going to be no different ... or so she thought.

Little did she know at this stage that what was soon to follow would be a terrifying ordeal for her. Not only could her life change for the worse, but she could also end up spending the rest of it in prison.

Chapter Two

For most of his life, Jason Carini had always been a strong, ambitious, and dominant man who never knew when to quit or liked losing in any way, shape, or form. As he grew older, his strength and determination grew with him, as did his hunger for success. Yet, he had never forgotten about his childhood and the tragic incident that eventually helped make him the man he is today. However, things could so easily have been very, very different for him indeed.

He was now a middle-aged man who had become a very successful and sought-after criminal defense attorney, but he was not always ethical in his approach. He was not only prepared to bend the rules at times but also, if the need arose, to push the boundaries of the law to breaking point in order to successfully defend his clients. He had no problem doing this, even if he suspected that his clients were guilty, and his actions could have major implications if it was ever found out what he was doing.

He had a very shrewd mind, as well as being able to read between the lines. It was these abilities, along with his ruthlessness, that helped him to win a lot of cases that seemed to be a lost cause. In fact, this was what earned him his reputation and was the main reason he was always sought out by clients who wanted his services. Jason knew exactly what he wanted from life and was pretty much prepared to do anything needed to achieve it. He was not afraid to take risks, and his desire, ambition, and drive are the qualities that have made him the successful man he has become today. However, this was not always the case.

He had a normal childhood growing up in his younger years and always dreamed of becoming a lawyer. But he went through a very difficult and traumatic time as a teenager when both of his parents were killed in an automobile accident. Their car was hit one evening by a driver who was under the influence of alcohol when Jason was just short of his sixteenth birthday. Even though the driver was caught and prosecuted, Jason still felt anger and, as a result, he became very depressed. He could not come to terms with the fact that he would never see his parents again and understandably began to lose all perspective on life.

At the time of the accident, Jason's brother, who was called Mark, was only thirteen, and his sister, Kate, was only fourteen years old. As they were all of a young age, the three children were taken in after the death of their parents and raised by their aunt Rachel. Up until then, the three siblings were very close and did everything together. However, the tragic deaths changed all of that as Jason became a different person after losing his parents, which understandably ripped his life apart.

Jason turned into a very private person, refusing to talk to anyone about how he felt, even though he was angry and confused, becoming even more depressed as time went by. He was very distant with his siblings and aunt as a result of the tragic loss of his parents and the way his whole life had fallen apart. This once happy young man was now a shadow of himself, feeling bitter towards the world and pretty much giving up on everything that was once important to him. Unable to get through to him, his aunt arranged for Jason to be seen by a psychologist, but even that did not seem to help him.

Due to him feeling this way, his schoolwork suffered. He eventually dropped out of high school after mixing with the wrong crowd and ending up getting involved with a local gang.

His aunt tried everything she could, as did his siblings, but they found it very hard to communicate with someone who clearly did not want to be reached.

Over the next six months, Jason lived a life of crime with his newfound so-called friends where he was stealing, drug running, and getting into gang fights. However, during one of these fights, his life took a turn for the better, which eventually led to him becoming this very successful lawyer.

During his six-month crime spree, he was fortunate enough not to have been apprehended by the police, and as such, the authorities knew nothing about his crimes. However, one evening, Jason was involved in a gang fight that saw two of his friends killed, but he managed to escape without getting hurt. Frightened for his life and without anywhere else to go, Jason went to his aunt and told her everything that had happened over the last six months. Rachel then decided to send him to live with her cousin, Richard. He had also been in trouble with the police in the past but had turned his life around so that he was now a pillar of the community. She had hoped that his influence could help Jason, and over the next few months, that is exactly what happened.

With Richard's help, Jason was now in a much better place, and he had realized that spending his youth running around with a gang was not for him, especially when he remembered that he had wanted to be a lawyer not too long ago. He decided to go back to live with his aunt. Jason knew that his recent behavior towards his aunt and siblings was very wrong, so he began trying to make amends for the way he had treated and distanced himself from them. He also realized that his siblings needed him now more than ever and that it was up to him as the eldest to ensure they suffered as little as possible.

Soon after moving back in with his aunt, Jason went back to school. He also began working in a restaurant waiting tables during the evenings to help his aunt financially and support her with raising his siblings. Life slowly began to get back to normal for Jason.

Once he had finished school, he decided that he was going to try and continue with his education so that he could become the lawyer he so badly wanted to be before his parents' tragic death and when his life fell to pieces.

He began to study in the evenings by doing online courses, while now working in the restaurant during the day, so he was earning a lot more money, half of which he handed over to his aunt Rachel. As time went by and his siblings were able to get part-time jobs in a local store after school so they too could help his aunt, Jason was able to focus on his own career once again. He enrolled in a community college to continue with his education and changed his working hours in the restaurant to work in the evenings once more. This meant that he spent around fifteen hours a day either studying or working, but he felt it was worth it, and it was his way of showing his siblings and his aunt that he was a changed man.

Jason worked very hard at the college so he could get the qualifications he needed. Eventually, his hard work paid off when he was, in fact, able to get into Harvard. Again, he continued to give it his all whilst there, and during those years, he kept remembering his parents' death and the life of crime he had, which gave him that extra little push when he needed it. All his hard work had now paid off, as he was finally able to get his law degree. It was not only his hard work, his drive, and ambition that helped him achieve it, but helping his aunt to raise his siblings had also given him the strength and determination he needed to succeed in his quest.

Throughout his life, Jason always thought that his parents would be looking down on him. He liked to think that they would have been proud of the successful man he had become, even though they may not have approved of the way he achieved his success in his later years or indeed his behavior in the period following their deaths. They would most certainly not have been proud of the time when he was in the gang, but at least he had been able to move away from that life of crime before it was too late.

After he had achieved what he wanted by getting his law degree, he was offered a position working for a local law firm, where he stayed for five years, learning all he could from the more experienced people around him. At first, Jason wanted to work for the DA's office as a prosecutor, but he soon learned that the real money would be earned as a criminal defense lawyer. He so wanted to repay his aunt for her kindness in raising him and his siblings, as well as make enough to be able to help Mark and Kate as much as he could financially.

When he felt the time was right, Jason left the law firm he was working for. He had always felt that he was destined for greater things, and he finally decided that the time had come for him to move on. He set up his own small practice, and within two years, he had established himself as an up-and-coming defense attorney. As you would expect, more clients wanted his services as a result of that.

Thanks to some of his clients, he frequently began to attend functions and charitable fundraisers. Of course, he used this to his advantage to get to know some of the more influential people who attended these events and even managed to convince some of them to use his services. After all, he knew only too well that some of them must have had a few skeletons in their closets which may come out at some stage.

Jason was a smooth talker who knew exactly what to say and when to say it. He knew what he wanted and that his dream of becoming a very successful criminal defense lawyer would take a lot of strength, determination, and hard work to achieve. He also knew that he needed these high-profile clients if he was ever going to achieve his goals.

But achieve them, he did, and Jason had spent the last twelve years making his dream come true. The pinnacle of his career came three years ago when he was offered a position at Langley & Foster, one of the top law firms in New York. He did not hesitate when the position was offered, accepting it with open arms. He even convinced some of his more influential and wealthier clients to retain their services.

However, he knew only too well that he had to be very careful with his ethics and the way he conducted himself, or he could soon find his position terminated just as quickly as it was offered. Yes, things were certainly looking good for Jason at this time, but a secret desire lay beneath his smooth, confident exterior. It would, in fact, surface with his next case, which would entice him even further, and it could, if it came out, not only ruin his career but also change his life forever.

Chapter Three

Soon after joining Langley & Foster, Jason met Lydia, who was ten years younger than him, at one of the many functions he attended, and for him, it was almost love at first sight. She was a striking woman with long blonde hair, a figure that any supermodel would be proud of, and she took every care to always look meticulous in her appearance. Lydia had a seductive look about her which would always turn heads whenever she entered a room. She thrived on the attention she would receive from the men as well as the jealousy she would feel coming from the women.

Jason considered himself the envy of the room whenever he would walk in with her. He felt proud of that and thought he was a very lucky man to be with such a sexy, beautiful lady - not only when they went to these functions but also because he could make love to her whenever he wanted.

Jason was a very generous man and did not think twice about spending money on Lydia. He did so by lavishing her with gifts, taking her to the most expensive restaurants, the opera, and pretty much doing whatever she wanted so he could please her, as it gave him pleasure in doing so.

Jason used this to his advantage on many occasions by taking her to as many functions as possible so that Lydia could interact with the men there. After she spent some time talking to and even flirting a little with them, Jason would go over and introduce himself, using that opportunity to get to know some of these very influential people who were also attending. This worked well for both of them, as Lydia would do what she did best, attracting the attention she desired, and Jason would meet more people to add to his already large pool of friends and associates.

However, unknown to Jason at that time, Lydia was, in fact, an unscrupulous woman. After having received and spent a very large settlement from the divorce from her previous marriage, she was now looking to get her claws into someone new. Of course, Jason was the perfect catch for her, with his ever-increasing reputation and his position at one of the best law firms in New York.

Like Jason, Lydia also knew exactly what she wanted: money, power, and being in the limelight through socializing with the rich and famous. She did not care who she hurt in the process, and to her, Jason was simply just another rung to be used to climb up the ladder of wealth.

They got married after a whirlwind romance, and in the beginning, everything seemed to be going well for Jason. He was content enough with both his work and his personal life, but he was not totally happy. He always knew that something was missing; there was an emptiness he could not fill. Up to this point, he thought that his life was a good one, he had a wife that loved him very much, and he, in turn, loved her more than he could ever have imagined. But little did Jason know that this seemingly loving wife was anything but that, and she was already trying to figure out the best way to get everything she wanted from him.

As time passed by, things slowly began to change. Jason could see that Lydia was now not as loving or caring as she once seemed to be. Recently, she started to go out with friends more frequently without any consideration for him. As long as she was doing what she wanted and had the funds to do it, Lydia was not too bothered about the man she was meant to love. It was not long before Jason began to realize just what kind of woman he had married and wondered if their life together had just been a lie.

Things became worse in their relationship over time, and Jason began to think that perhaps Lydia had been using him all this time as her meal ticket. She certainly loved the money, the power, and the high-profile life she had, and he wondered if she had ever truly loved him. Slowly, his suspicions grew even more when Lydia began to get phone calls that she would want to take in another room, and she suddenly began to see a new friend called Valerie, whom he had never met. It finally dawned on him that his darling Lydia was not the caring, loving wife he thought she was and that perhaps he had made a mistake in marrying her. He now began to wonder exactly where she went every time she left home and, more importantly, who she really met up with.

Jason finally decided to ask one of his friends, Marcus King, to follow his wife the next time she went out so he could find out what was going on, and sure enough, his suspicions were confirmed. Lydia, his so-called loving wife, was cheating on him with a high-profile married politician. Jason was devastated about the news and his initial reaction, understandably, was to tell her exactly what he thought of her before throwing her out of his home and filing for divorce. Then his thoughts turned to the bastard she was having an affair with, and the desire to beat the hell out of him was very hard for Jason to resist.

However, Jason was a practical man, and he knew that such actions would have dire consequences, especially where his work was concerned. A scandal like this would pretty much end his career at Langley & Foster and perhaps any chance of continuing his career within the legal system. After all, Jason thought to himself, 'You simply cannot punch a politician in the face even if he *is* fucking your wife!'

Even a divorce could have the same effect, as he was not sure just how his darling, bitch of a wife, Lydia, would react to it. Lydia was the sort of person who would blow any settlement she got from the divorce within a year and then have to find another sucker to support her. Jason suspected that she would not accept a divorce quietly and would surely cause a scandal out of pure spite just to get back at him for daring to leave her.

Apart from that, Jason was damned if he was going to simply hand over a massive chunk of his wealth and perhaps even his home in a divorce settlement to that bitch. So he decided to ask his friend Marcus to keep tabs on her and find out all he could about the man she was having an affair with. That way, at least, he would have some ammunition to use if the need arose. Jason, at last, realized that Lydia had indeed used him for her own personal gain rather than loving him during their life together and thought to himself, 'Two can play that game.'

He should have seen this coming, as their sex life had been dwindling for a while now and they did not have sex anywhere near as much as they used to. Lydia nearly always seemed to feel unwell, was tired, or it was her time of the month whenever he wanted sex, but would feel just fine when she wanted it. Now he knew why, and even when they did have sex, he found it quite mundane and unfulfilling. So much so that he often thought about his past experiences with other women and fantasized about them while having sex with his wife.

Jason decided that he would bide his time and not say anything for now. He would simply live his life as normal, continue with his work, and keep track of what she was doing through Marcus. He knew it would not be easy as he still loved her, but he also knew that it was only a matter of time before those feelings would start to fade because of the way she had betrayed him.

After all, Jason was not only successful, but he oozed confidence and had an inner strength that would not allow him to feel like a victim. He knew only too well that he did not need Lydia in his life. Sure, it was nice to have her there, but the last six months had been anything but great. He had already begun to wonder if this woman really was the one he wanted to spend the rest of his life with, even before finding out about the affair. Besides, he relished the idea that perhaps Marcus may uncover something about the politician, other than the affair, that he could use for his own purposes, should he ever need to.

After all, the man was having an affair with his wife, so he thought to himself, 'Why shouldn't I use any information I've got against either of them, or for any reason, for that matter? A high-profile politician could be a useful person to have a hold over, especially in my profession.' A wry smile came over his face, hoping that Marcus would indeed find some dark secret. But he also knew that, at the very least, he could blackmail this politician by threatening to tell the world all about his affair with Lydia if he ever needed to. That would be a good hold to have over him, or her, for that matter.

Up until this moment, Jason had always been fully committed to their marriage. Now, however, the time had finally come for him to start thinking about himself and what he really wanted, rather than always thinking about his wife. Although he was sad that their relationship was all but over, he felt a sense of freedom come over him because he could finally stop suppressing the true desires that he had buried since being with Lydia. Jason did love his wife and had always been faithful to her, but there was a side to him that not even Lydia knew about. It had been hard for him to keep these feelings hidden from her.

He did not want to keep things secret, but he knew that she would not understand, so he felt it was better to suppress these feelings and just live a so-called normal life with his wife. But now, he again began to think about what he really wanted from his life, what was missing, and that finally, he could start being the person he wanted to be. After all, it was due to loving his wife that he had to put aside the life he had before he met her. Now, after finding out about her cheating, he felt that he had every right to do what he wanted and not have to be concerned about her. She did not care about him or his feelings, so why should he care about hers?

Although Jason was a dominant man with a strong character, he bent over backward to give Lydia what she asked for because he loved her and wanted to please her. He never questioned her about how much money she spent or what she spent it on, as he had pretty much given her carte-blanche due to wanting to please her.

It was Lydia who decided how to re-furnish his house; it was Lydia who chose where to go on vacation; it was Lydia who decided which parties and events they should go to, and, in fact, it was Lydia who had the final say on most things. Jason felt a sudden surge of anger and thought to himself that, from now on, he was not going to allow her to do so anymore. He would take back control of his life by making his own decisions, and if she did not like it, then she could go to hell.

It was never easy for Jason to give her that much control in the first place, as it went against his dominant nature to have decisions like this made for him. However, he allowed it due to wanting to please the woman he loved. He told himself that by letting her make these decisions, he still had control from a certain perspective. He was just glad to have realized this so early on in their marriage rather than spending the rest of his life living a lie with a woman that clearly did not love him.

What a fool he had been, what a waste the last couple of years had been, and how could he be duped in this way, he wondered. Well, no more, enough was enough for Jason, and he decided that his life would now be very different. Oh, the fun he would have now that he could be himself without having to think about that bitch. To finally be able to do what he wanted, when he wanted, and how he wanted, without having to worry about her. This made him feel so happy, and he now realized just how lost he had become in his life with her. 'Yes, life will be very different now,' he thought to himself.

Little did he know, at this stage, just how different his life would actually become.

CHAPTER FOUR

During the course of the following week, Jason lived his life as though nothing was wrong and had not let on to his wife that he knew about her affair. As usual, he went to work, went to the gym, and even acted normal at home so that Lydia would never suspect that he had learned about her lover. After spending the weekend at home, he got up on Monday morning and, as always, had a shower, ate some breakfast, kissed his wife goodbye, and off he went to work.

While driving to the office, he began to think about his life before meeting Lydia and just how much he missed it. You see, Jason was born and grew up in the Bronx. It was a hard life growing up in that area, but he could always be himself when going to a bar with friends for a few drinks. He had a bit of an attitude and was certainly one of the lads, but, of course, he had to act very differently where his work was concerned as he could hardly be and act like himself with a client. No, he would never get any work if he was that way with them, so Jason had to become a different person where work was concerned, but he never forgot where he came from.

Even when he and his wife went to functions, out for meals or even drinks with their friends, he had to be seen to be this well-spoken, educated man. But what Jason missed the most from the days before he met Lydia was the fact that he had no ties. He was able to go out with his friends anytime he wanted to, be himself, get home at any time he felt like it, and chase any woman he took a shine to.

Jason enjoyed the companionship of women, but due to a very hectic workload when he was just starting out on his own, he did not have much time for a relationship or indeed wanted any real commitment. Any women he did meet would not stay with him for too long as he was always working and too busy to spend any real time with them.

Jason decided that his career would have to come first if he was to succeed, and he would simply play the field as and when he was able to do so, even if it was only for a one-night stand. Of course, all of this stopped once he met Lydia, but he always missed the single life and, in particular, a certain lady he used to see called Selene.

It was in a wine bar where he went on rare occasions for a change of scenery, where he first saw Selene. She was a long-legged blonde sitting at the bar all alone, and he decided to go and talk to her. However, it was not too long before it became evident that Selene was, in fact, an escort. Jason had not had any sex for a while and thought, 'What the hell? No one really knows me here.' So he decided to go back to her apartment for some company and a little fun.

He had a great time with Selene and decided that since he could afford to see her, he would do so as often as he wanted. This arrangement suited Jason perfectly rather than wasting his time trying his luck with just any random woman he may have met. After all, his time was precious, and he did not want to waste it on the chase that might not lead anywhere anymore, especially now he had met this sexy escort and could meet up with her whenever it suited him.

So they began to see each other on a regular basis, having a great deal of fun together. He would often take her out to fancy restaurants, the theater, and they would even have weekends away together.

After a while, Jason wanted to get a bit more adventurous, so Selene introduced him to role-plays such as doctor & patient, police officer & prisoner, Lord of the manor & servant. But the one that really excited him was when Selene played the part of the dominant boss while Jason played an employee who was about to lose his job. If he wanted to keep it, he would do whatever his boss wanted.

Out of all the role-plays they had acted out, this was by far his favorite. It was the one he wanted to do on a regular basis, or at least any kind of role-play that involved Selene being in charge, with Jason as the submissive one. He found it strange that he liked this role-play as he was always so dominant in his everyday life and the fact that he enjoyed being bossed about was very confusing to him. But having said that, deep down inside, Jason felt that he was still in control, as he was paying Selene, and he gave her permission to dominate him. Also, due to the fact that he would always get the sex he wanted by the end of the session, Jason not only felt in total control but, in a sense, he was the master, even though he was the one being dominated.

So here was a dominant man who loved to be bossed about by this beautiful, sexy lady and pretty soon, all the role-plays they did were domination-related. She would tell him what she wanted him to do to her, such as give her pussy a good licking, massage her, kiss her feet, to name but a few things, and Jason would obey her every wish, doing anything he was told to do. In turn, she could do whatever she wanted to do to him, such as a bit of spanking, name-calling, or whatever else she wanted. After they both had some fun doing these domination role-plays, they would then have sex, and he would pay her before leaving to go about his everyday life.

Jason thought that this whole domination scenario was the best sexual experience he had ever had. Little did he know then that this so-called domination would, in fact, be nothing compared to what was to follow later in his life, when he would learn what the domination lifestyle was really all about. He would come to understand exactly what it meant for someone to be dominant or submissive in the true lifestyle of domination rather than a role-play.

He eventually stopped seeing Selene after he met Lydia, but to Jason it was as if he had lost a big part of his life. The only time he felt truly free or happy was when he was doing these domination role-plays with Selene. But he knew only too well that this was a secret he could never tell anyone about. If this were ever to get out, it would cause such a scandal that his position with Langley & Foster would surely be in jeopardy. After all, his high-profile clients would never want to be represented by a lawyer who visited escorts, which was so hypocritical considering most of them have probably done the same thing at one time or another in their own lives.

So he had to keep everything a secret, but he never forgot the good times he had with Selene and how much he enjoyed these domination role-plays that they did together. He even contemplated getting back in touch with her now that his wife was cheating on him.

'Oh well, time to think about work,' he said to himself as he neared his workplace. Upon arriving at the main reception, he was told that Mr. Langley wanted to see him immediately, and as he began to make his way to his office, wondering why he had been sent for.

Outside Mr. Langley's office, he saw a stunningly beautiful lady sitting on the comfortable couch. She had long black hair, perfectly manicured and painted nails, makeup that looked like it had been done by a professional, and a seductive look about her that would make any man take notice. She was elegantly dressed in a silk blouse with a knee-length skirt and sat with one leg over the other with her six-inch stiletto heels catching Jason's eyes.

For a minute, he wondered if she also wore any stockings to go with those heels of hers as Jason loved a lady who dressed that way. He found it very hard to pull his gaze away from her, but he had to see Mr. Langley now, so those thoughts would have to wait for the time being. He could only hope that this sexy lady would still be here when he had finished with his boss.

"Come in," a voice said from within the office after Jason had knocked on the door.

"You wanted to see me, Mr. Langley?" Jason asked as he walked up to the desk.

"Yes, Jason, I do. Please sit down."

Jason sat down, still wondering why he had been called in, and as he did so, Mr. Langley began to tell him the reason for this meeting.

"There is a lady sitting outside named Alexia Summers, and I want you to handle her case. This is a delicate matter because she is a high-class escort, and I have been asked by one of our most influential clients to look after her as a personal favor to him."

"I see," Jason replied, his heart suddenly beating faster at the thought of meeting this sexy lady.

"According to Miss Summers, a client of hers called Simon Morley was not happy with the service she provided, and he began to attack her, then tried to rape her. This is strange considering he was a client of hers, but during the struggle, she managed to break free, took the gun she had in a drawer, and shot Mr. Morley. After he fell to the floor and she saw that he was not moving, she called 911, but Mr. Morley had, in fact, died from that single gunshot wound."

"So this is a case of self-defense then?" Jason asked.

"Well, it would seem so, but the police are still looking into it, and as yet, I do not know what is going to happen. We are simply going to take a look at this case because, as I said earlier, we are doing this as a favor for one of our clients, but if she is to be charged and prosecuted, then yes, we will be defending her. However, due to her occupation, or more importantly her very influential client list, it is preferred that this is dealt with as swiftly and with as little publicity as possible."

"Of course, Mr. Langley, that's understandable," Jason replied.

"I spent some time over the weekend talking with Miss Summers about what had happened, and I have made up a file based on what she told me. I have decided to let you deal with it, Jason."

"Thank you, Mr. Langley, Jason said emphatically as he was very happy at the thought of representing the sexy lady he had seen outside Mr. Langley's office. Learning that she was an escort immediately reminded him of Selene for a brief moment, but he had to concentrate on what his boss was telling him now.

"This certainly looks like self-defense, to be honest, as you will see from the file. It seems that he got too rough with her, and she had no choice but to try to stop him in any way she could. The fact that she is an escort could make this case a bit tricky, but I expect a quick and discreet resolution to this matter. I want your full commitment on this, Jason, and I will reassign the case you were due to take to another attorney."

"Yes, Mr. Langley, I shall get right on it," Jason replied as he got up from the chair.

Jason's heart was pumping like a giddy schoolboy at the thought of spending some time with this stunning beauty, but he knew only too well that he had to remain professional in his approach. 'Oh, if only I had met this woman in a bar or at a fundraiser rather than outside my boss's office,' he thought to himself.

Jason left Mr. Langley's office and walked over to the lady sitting on the couch.

"Mrs. Summers?" Jason enquired as he looked at her.

"It's **Miss** Summers, actually." She replied in a well-spoken, educated English accent even though she was, in fact, not English but an American. She stood up and shook Jason's hand, asking, "And you are?"

"My name is Jason Carini, and I will be looking over your case, Miss Summers. I have only just been given your file, so I do not yet know the full details, but I will read through everything we have during the course of the day, and I will be in touch with you to arrange another appointment."

"Thank you very much, Mr. Carini, and I would appreciate your discretion regarding what you read about," Alexia said with a pert smile.

"Please, call me Jason, and you can rest assured that I will be very discreet," he replied with a smile of his own while gazing into her eyes for a few seconds.

"Very well, Jason, I have a prior engagement shortly. I would appreciate it if we could round things up here for now, and I shall await your call."

"By all means, Miss Summers. As I said, I will review all the details of your case today, and my secretary will telephone you to arrange an appointment for tomorrow morning."

"Thank you very much, Jason, and I shall see you tomorrow then. Goodbye," Alexia replied as she turned and walked elegantly to the elevator.

"Goodbye, Miss Summers," Jason replied without being able to take his eyes off her. He watched as she pushed the button for the door to open, entered the elevator, and pushed the button for the door to close behind her.

"Wow," he murmured softly to himself as he turned and began to walk to his office. His thoughts had now suddenly turned back to Selene, and he dared to wonder if Miss Summers also offered the same services that Selene did. 'Ok, stop it,' he thought to himself as he remembered that she was a client and he had to remain professional. He made his way to his office and began to read her file, but every so often, thoughts of her being an escort and, more importantly, exactly what services she offered would creep into his mind.

In the meantime, Alexia arrived back home after her busy afternoon. After taking off her shoes, she poured herself a glass of red wine, sat down on the couch, and began to wonder about what may happen to her regarding this incident, as well as her life in general. She started to recall the memory of how she became the person she is today. Alexia had been a strong-willed, confident, and dominant lady for the last twenty years, but her earlier life was very different. Without realizing it, the horrific memory of what happened to her in her teens came back to haunt her and brought tears to her eyes.

She leaned forward and took a large sip of her drink before sitting back on the couch, where she began to have a flashback of when she was young and the terrible ordeals she had suffered.

CHAPTER FIVE

Alexia had a happy childhood for the early part of her life with her parents. However, her father left Alexia and her mother for another woman when she was only thirteen years old, and although he would send her mother money, he never really bothered to visit them. Alexia did not have any other family, and as she did not know where her father was anymore, she lived a lonely life with her mother. She was always a strong-willed child and had a good head on her shoulders, but she had to grow up a lot sooner than a child should due to her father leaving them, especially as her mother took to the bottle soon after he left them.

Her mother, Vivien, began drinking and going out more often, and within six months, she began dating Kevin Moran, a local maintenance man who also liked his drink. As the drinking became worse, Vivien began turning up late for work, sometimes still drunk and, on occasions, even missing complete days. One day Vivien turned up at work so drunk that she did not even realize where she was. Her employer had no choice but to tell her that he had to let her go, as he could not have any of his employees coming to work drunk.

Running out of money and unable to pay the rent, Vivien and Alexia were on the verge of being evicted when Kevin suggested that they move in with him, and they decided it was the best thing to do. Things were not too bad, to begin with, but as the drinking became worse, so did the neglect of Alexia. By the time she was fifteen, not only did she pretty much have to fend for herself, but she also had to clean the house, cook, do the shopping, and anything else that had to be done.

It got to the stage where Kevin would slap Alexia around if she was ever late with the dinner, if he had no clean clothes to wear for work, or if she ever dared to stand up for herself. Her mother was no help as she was drunk more often than not, and it was obvious that she did not give a damn about her own daughter.

One day, Kevin told Alexia that if she wanted to keep living there, she had to get a job after school to help pay the rent. Alexia, who loved her mother, despite the way she was being treated, did as she was asked and managed to get a job working in a convenience store after school. To make things worse, Alexia had to hand over all her salary to her mother's boyfriend. He would give her some money back for the food shopping, but the rest he would keep for himself to feed his and Vivien's habits.

It got to the stage that more money was being spent on alcohol and cigarettes than was actually being spent on food, and Alexia would then get the blame for there not being enough food in the house. This went on for a couple of months, and Alexia was getting so fed up with it all that she contemplated running away from home, but where would she go?

She had no other family as she did not know where her father was, and she was only fifteen years old, so there was no choice for her but to stay put. Apart from that, she mainly wanted to stay there for her mother's sake as she did not want to leave her behind. Her sad life continued, as usual, going to school, then going to work. By the time she got back home after work, it was time for her to cook dinner and then time for bed. As time passed, she became depressed, wondering if this was all that life had to offer and thoughts of suicide entered her mind on a number of occasions.

One evening after Alexia came home from work and found her mother passed out on the couch, as usual, she made dinner then went upstairs to have a shower. After washing she went into her bedroom, dried herself off, put on her nightgown, and got under the covers to listen to some music.

Around ten minutes later, Kevin opened the door to her bedroom, went inside, and closed the door behind him.

"What are you doing coming into my bedroom without knocking?" Alexia asked him.

"It's my apartment, and I will do whatever the fuck I want, so just remember that," Kevin replied.

"And what about my privacy?" she asked.

"Oh, shut up, you little bitch! You and that drunken mother of yours would be living on the streets if it wasn't for me, and don't you forget that," Kevin said in an angry voice.

"Ok, but what do you want?" Alexia asked nervously.

"I have been watching you for a long time now, and you are becoming a pretty little thing," Kevin said, looking at her up and down.

"I'm not sure I understand what you are saying," Alexia said as she looked deep into his eyes, feeling very uneasy.

"I mean, it's about time you showed me some appreciation for everything I have done for you," he replied as he took a couple of steps closer to her.

"What do you mean? What do you want?" she asked fearfully.

"I want **you** because that passed out, drunken mother of yours is no good to me, and I have my needs," Kevin said with a cold smirk on his face.

Alexia suddenly realized what Kevin was insinuating and looked at him in utter shock and disgust as she called out for her mother.

Kevin looked at her and laughed out loud; then, with a big grin still on his face, he coldly said, "You can call out as much as you like, but that stupid drunk will never hear you."

"If you lay a hand on me, I will go to the police," Alexia cried out.

"No, you won't because it will be my word against yours, and who do you think the police are going to believe? Besides, if you tell anyone or do not do what I want, I will kick you and your mother out of my apartment, and you will both end up on the streets. Is that what you want?"

Alexia then realized that if he did kick them out, they would have nowhere to go, and with her mother always so drunk, it would not be safe for either of them on the streets. Kevin saw the defeated look in Alexia's eyes and moved closer towards her, pulling back the covers.

"No, please don't," Alexia begged, but deep down, she knew that there was no escaping what was about to happen to her.

"You and your mother will remain safe living here as long as you do what I want when I want it and keep your mouth shut. It's not like you are a virgin because I know about the boyfriend you had last year. Now, take off your nightgown!"

Alexia did as she was told as she knew that she could not refuse, and Kevin got on top of her and began to fuck her, which, fortunately for Alexia, did not take too long. After he had finished, he simply left the room without saying a word.

Once he had left, Alexia began to cry until she eventually sobbed herself to sleep a few hours later.

Alexia woke up the next morning and waited until Kevin had gone to work before deciding to tell her mother what had happened the night before. She began to tell her what Kevin said and did, but Vivien, who was still worse for wear with a hangover and a splitting headache, seemed to care more about getting another drink than listening to what her daughter was telling her.

"ARE YOU LISTENING TO ME?" Alexia shouted out as she began to cry.

"Don't shout, for god's sake, I have a bad headache. What are you saying?" her mother asked.

Between sobs, Alexia told her mother about the events of the previous night when Kevin went into her room, but Vivien found that hard to believe and accused her daughter of making it up.

"I AM *NOT* MAKING IT UP!" Alexia screamed before she continued. "I called you, but you were asleep drunk on the couch as usual, and he said that if I did not have sex with him, he would kick us both out of his apartment."

"Kevin would never do that; he has been good to us. Why are you saying these things?" Vivian asked

"But he did, Mom, I swear to you," Alexia said, crying while holding her mother's hand.

"Ok, I will talk to him and see what he has to say about it tonight," Vivien replied, moving her hand up to her head.

"Well, he will deny it, but ok, fine, ask him anyway," Alexia said, shaking her head.

Alexia then went back to her bedroom instead of going to school, upset that her own mother did not believe her, and waited there until early evening when Kevin came back home from work. She then listened through the slightly open door to hear what her mother would say to Kevin, but there was no mention of it. Unsure of what to do now because of the threats that Kevin had made about kicking them out, Alexia waited for a few minutes. She then decided to go into the other room where Kevin and her mother were.

As soon as she opened the door and went inside, she noticed that her mother was barely coherent with yet another drink on the coffee table in front of her and cuddled up to her boyfriend. Kevin then looked at Alexia with a smirk on his face, and she knew that her mother would be of no help to her as she could barely stay sober anymore.

Alexia then went back to her room and resigned herself to the fact that there was nothing she could do to stop Kevin apart from going to the police. She thought for a few minutes and realized that if her own mother did not believe her, why would the police do so? It would be her word against his. She could not rely on her mother for support and did not want to take the chance that they would both end up on the streets if Kevin followed through with his threat.

From that night onwards, Alexia gave no resistance whenever Kevin went into her room and did whatever he wanted so that at least she and Vivien had a roof over their heads. The hardest thing for Alexia to accept was that Vivian was totally oblivious to the sacrifice she was making, but she loved her mother so much that she felt she had no choice. This abuse went on for a few months, and Alexia, who had just turned sixteen, was able to switch off whenever she spent any time with Kevin. Little did she know during that time that worse was to follow.

One evening after Alexia had finished work, she began her usual fifteen-minute walk home, which took her through the park. The subway was not an option as it would have taken her longer to walk there than it would for her to walk home, and avoiding the park would have put an extra ten minutes on her journey time. This was a journey that she had done every evening when finishing work without ever having a problem. However, on this particular evening, just a few yards from the park's exit, which led to the street her home was in, she heard footsteps behind her which made her turn. She saw a man walking around ten yards behind her.

"Excuse me, sorry to bother you, but I seem to be lost. Can you tell me how to get to the nearest subway, please?" the man asked as he quickened his pace to catch up with Alexia.

"Oh, sure," she replied as the man neared. "If you take the path on the right over there," pointing to it as she spoke, "then when you get to the exit, turn right, go straight till the next block, then turn left, then turn right at the next block and you will find it."

"Thank you, but that sounds very complicated, and I am not very good with directions. Could you not show me the way? Once there, I will pay for a cab to take you home, as a cute thing like you should not be walking through the park especially as it is getting darker on your own," the man said in a caring way.

"No, sorry, besides, I am nearly home now anyway," Alexia replied as she continued to walk again towards the exit, feeling very uneasy about this stranger.

"Oh, come on, no need to be scared of me; I won't hurt you," he said as he began to follow behind her.

"No, really, I have to be going," she said, quickening her pace as she approached the exit.

Suddenly, the man grabbed Alexia, putting one hand over her mouth to stop her from screaming and picking her up with his other arm, carrying her further into the park where there were some trees. He then let her go, slapped her on the face a couple of times until she fell to the ground, and pulled out a knife.

"No, please don't," Alexia begged him as she tried to get up.

"Stay down there, you little bitch," he said to her as he began to unzip his pants.

Alexia began screaming and tried to get up, but the man kicked her in the abdomen and then knelt over her, putting one hand around her neck and pointing the knife at her with the other.

"I **always** get what I want, so shut the fuck up unless you want to die," he said in a chilling voice while staring her in the eyes. Fearing for her life and crying, she did as he said and simply lay there while the man pulled up her dress, pulled off her panties, and raped her.

"I told you, I **always** get what I want," he said as he stood up, then simply ran off and left the park.

Alexia just laid there in tears shaking and in a state of shock. After a few minutes of lying there crying, she managed to get up, then made her way back through the park to the road. She began to walk without really knowing what direction she was headed in.

A few minutes later, three ladies came around the corner, chatting and laughing while they headed for a night out, and saw Alexia staggering along. It was clear to them as they neared her that something had happened. They could see the blood around the mouth from the split lip her rapist had given her, and her hair was disheveled, as well as the fact that she was crying and was obviously distressed. They asked her if she was alright, but all she could do was just stare at them in a state of shock without saying a word. One of the ladies called 911, and they stayed with her until the paramedics arrived, followed by the police a few minutes later.

Alexia was taken to the hospital, and the police followed to try and ascertain what had happened to her, even though they had a pretty good idea. By the time they got there, Alexia had begun to gather her thoughts and was able to talk to them. The first thing they did was to ask what happened and then where she lived so that they could contact her parents. One of the officers called in the information, and a unit was dispatched to her home while the doctor asked Alexia for permission to do a series of tests regarding her rape.

As the tests were being carried out, the police went to her home, and although her mother answered the door, it was clear to the officers that she was so drunk that there was no way she could comprehend what they were saying. The officers had no choice but to leave and said they would return the following day.

By this time, the tests had been carried out. Apart from the obvious bruising around her abdomen where she had been kicked, there was also some vaginal tearing and semen found inside Alexia, a sample of which was given to the police for forensic testing. The doctor arranged for Alexia to be admitted into hospital for the night at the request of the police, as there was no one in a fit state to look after her at home. They said they would return in the morning to have another chat with her.

The following morning, the police officers went back to Alexia's house, and her mother answered the door. This time, she was not as drunk as she had been the night before, so the officers told her what had happened, offering to take her to the hospital to see her daughter.

Meanwhile, a detective was at the hospital talking to Alexia about what had happened the night before. She told the detective everything she could remember about what had taken place and what the man said. Although she tried to give the police a description of the man, she could not do so as it was getting dark and she kept her eyes closed most of the time. The only thing she clearly remembered was his piercing eyes as he stared at her during her ordeal and the words he spoke to her about always getting what he wanted. By now, her mother had arrived at the hospital. After a short while, the doctor discharged Alexia, and they took a taxi home.

Over the next few days, Alexia spent most of the time in her bedroom, not returning to school or work and pretty much not doing anything. For the first few days, she was not asked to cook, clean, or go to the shops, and it was almost as though both her mother and Kevin actually cared for her, even though Vivien continued to drink. The only good thing was that Kevin seemed to have lost interest in having sex with Alexia since she was raped.

However, it was not long before everything went back to normal. Again the complaints began about why she was not cooking dinner, cleaning the house, going to work, or doing the shopping. She was "becoming not only lazy but also a waste of space," as Kevin would say.

This went on for the next ten days. Even though Alexia would try and do as much as she could, she could still not face going to school, work, or even doing the shopping. Never mind the fact that she was raped only two weeks ago; all they cared about was dinner not being cooked, her bringing no money in for food, alcohol, and cigarettes, and that she was not pulling her weight around the house.

Then one night, while she was in her room, she heard Kevin shouting up the stairs to her.

"Come on, you little slut, I'm hungry. It's ok for you to go out and get laid, but what about my dinner?"

"And start going back to work because there is not enough money coming in, and we are running out of drink," her mother shouted out.

All Alexia could do was cry all over again after hearing those comments. She now realized that her mother did not give a damn about her. It was bad enough that Vivien did not believe her about what Kevin had been doing, but how could her mother be this mean to her after she was raped and beaten, she wondered. 'How could my own mother be so heartless,' she thought to herself, 'now that I need her the most?' She expected no less from Kevin, but her own mother being so uncaring really hurt her.

Alexia sat and cried for a short while and decided that it was time for her to leave, as it was obvious to her that she was no longer loved. She got up, got dressed, went into her mother's bedroom, and opened the drawer where they kept any spare money that had not yet been spent. 'Why not take it?' she thought. After all, it was her money that she was taking back. She worked for this money, but she never got to spend any of it on what she wanted. It was always used to buy more alcohol and cigarettes, but never for anything that Alexia wanted.

She then packed a few of her things and some clothes in a bag and shouted out as she went down the stairs, "I'm going to the shops now."

Of course, she had no intention of going to the shops, but instead was leaving home and had decided she would never return. Alexia had thought about doing this for quite a while but never went through with it because of her mother. Now she knew that it was time for her to leave.

It was frightening for her to do this, but Alexia could no longer stay living at home as it was clear her own mother did not care if she was raped or even believed her. She wondered what would the neighbors, school friends, and work colleagues say or think if she was being treated this way by her own mother.

Here was a sixteen-year-old girl, who was recently raped, had a drunk for a mother, and was slapped around and sexually abused by her mother's boyfriend. 'What kind of life would be in store for me if I stayed there?' Alexia thought to herself. She knew she was doing the right thing but was understandably afraid of what lay ahead.

Alexia then took the subway, and without really knowing where she was going, she got off and began walking for what seemed like hours, until she ended up in Queens. She only had just over $200 on her and knew that it would not last too long. She also knew that she needed to find some work and somewhere to live, which was something she did not even consider when she left home.

Alexia began going into the stores nearby to see if they could offer her some work, but no one was going to hire a young girl coming in off the street. After a few hours, she was tired and hungry. She decided to get a sandwich and just leaned against a wall while eating it, trying to decide what to do next. She knew she could not give up and also knew that getting a job was the most important thing as she would need the money to be able to live.

She went back out to the stores and continued asking for work, but it was no use. By now, it was already dark, and most of the stores were beginning to close. She sat down on the floor in front of a closed store and stared at the ground, wondering how her life had become the way it was. Alexia suddenly realized the enormity of the situation she was in.

Here she was, with no job, nowhere to sleep for the night, and no hope, but she would rather die than go back home to an uncaring mother and her abusive boyfriend. She spent the next few hours just wandering around without really knowing where she was going. All she could think about right now was how terrible her life had become. The hurt she felt about the way Vivien had been treating her lately was, in fact, worse than the rape and sexual abuse she had suffered. She could not understand how any mother could be that way towards her own child.

"Are you ok, missy?" a woman's voice asked.

"Yes, I am, thank you," Alexia replied as she looked up to see who it was.

"You don't seem it, my dear. Should you not be at home?" the woman asked in a calm and caring voice.

"I don't have a home. I came here hoping to get a job, but I have had no luck so far," Alexia replied, looking down to the floor.

"Oh dear, do you not have anywhere to stay?" the woman asked as she crouched down.

"No, I have nothing," Alexia said tearfully, wondering if she should have just stayed at home.

"Well, you can't spend the night on the streets, my dear; it's not safe. Come with me. I'm Alice, by the way, and I know someone who can help you. He will offer you some work and a place to stay if you are interested. What's your name?"

"I'm Sally," Alexia replied, which was, in fact, her real name at that time, before she legally changed it to Alexia later on in life. She paused for a minute to wonder if she should go with this lady that she had only just met, but as Alice looked like she was in her fifties and seemed really nice, Alexia felt safe enough.

"Ok then, Alice, thank you," she said in a very polite manner.

Alice and Alexia took a cab ride, until they came to a doorway that was just to the left of the main entrance to a club. Alice paid the can driver and once inside, they went up the stairs into a large room where Alice introduced her to a man called Bruno, telling him that she had found her wandering the streets and she needed work and somewhere safe to stay.

"So you want to work for me, do you?" Bruno asked, looking at her up and down.

"Yes, please, I would love to get some work," Alexia replied.

"Well, I know quite a few men who will pay well for someone young like you." Bruno said.

Without answering him, it suddenly dawned upon her that Alice and Bruno must have been running a brothel, and the work he talked about was obviously about her becoming a hooker. 'Oh my god,' she thought to herself, 'What have I gotten myself into?'

"I'm sorry, Mr. Bruno, but there has been a misunderstanding; I am not a prostitute, and I don't think I can do this," Alexia replied, remembering what had happened to her just a couple of weeks ago. 'There is no way I could do anything like this,' she thought.

"Oh, really, and what are your alternatives? Living on the streets, hunger, danger? Besides, I am not running a brothel as such; I run the strip and lap-dancing club downstairs. Yes, I will admit that my girls will at times have sex with some of our regular clients, but at least you will be in a safe environment for this to happen in," he said to her.

"I don't know, Mr. Bruno. I have not thought this through very well, to be honest," Alexia replied, feeling very nervous.

"Look, I will give you a place to sleep here, and you will work for me at the club where you will earn money. I will deduct the rent from the money you earn, plus my commission, and you will get to keep the rest of the money you make. How much you earn will depend on how much you do and indeed what you are prepared to do," Bruno said in a gentle voice.

"I'm sorry, but I don't think I can do that. Thank you for the offer, though; goodbye," Alexia said as she began walking towards the door.

"Listen to me, my dear. Why don't you think about it tonight? We will be happy to let you stay here for one night while you make your mind up, won't we, Bruno?" Alice asked as she looked and winked at him.

"Yes, of course, she can stay here, but only for one night."

"Oh, thank you both very much," Alexia said, unsure if she should dare to stay, but she knew her only other alternative was a night on the streets. Alice then took Alexia to one of the ten rooms above the club. She told her that this would be her room for tonight and that she could lock the door if she felt the need to. She then said goodnight to Alexia and went downstairs, where Bruno was waiting.

"Ok, so what are you playing at, Alice, and why are we letting her stay here tonight?" he asked quite angrily.

"Leave it to me, Bruno. By the morning, she will want to stay," Alice replied in a very confident manner.

Bruno and Alice were partners running this club, and they both knew that they could make a lot of money from Alexia's youth. Although Alice did not need to work herself as an escort anymore, she did have some regular clients from the old days that she still met, not only because of the money but also because she enjoyed doing it.

Later that evening, Alice knocked on Alexia's door and asked if she could go in.

Alexia opened the door, and Alice entered the room, saying she was tired and wanted to check in on her before going to bed. Alexia thanked her again for letting her stay, and just then, Alice pulled out a thick wad of money from her bag.

"Look what I earned tonight from just a couple of my regular clients," Alice said, looking at Alexia and waving the money around with her hand. Alexia looked on in amazement at the money and thought there must be at least $700 there.

"Not bad for a couple hours of work, is it, my dearest Sally?"

"No, that's really great, Alice," Alexia said, still gazing at all that money.

"Well, I will leave you now to get some sleep. Please do think about our offer; goodnight, Sally," Alice said as she got up and walked to the door.

"Goodnight, Alice," Alexia replied as she got up and closed, then locked the door after Alice had left the room.

Alexia spent the next couple of hours thinking about the money she could earn before finally falling asleep.

Chapter Six

Alexia woke up the next morning still feeling tired from the previous day's events. Her first thought was of how her mother was doing, but then her thoughts turned to the matter at hand and what she was going to do. She thought about the money that it was possible to earn, but then she also wondered if she could actually do anything like that. She remembered all the times that Kevin would go into her room and have sex with her, so the sex itself was not a problem. However, doing it with a stranger night after night was something she was not sure about, especially after what had happened to her only a couple of weeks ago.

It was not the sex that bothered her so much about her rape ordeal, as she was used to being forced by Kevin to do things she did not want to do, but instead, it was feeling helpless that really bothered her. It was also the fear of dying at her rapist's hands that really scared her, but she knew that a decision had to be made about what she was going to do.

"Sally, are you awake?" Alice asked as she gently knocked on Alexia's door.

"Yes, I am," Alexia replied as she got up and opened the door to let Alice in.

"How did you sleep, my dear?" Alice asked her as she put a hand on Alexia's shoulder.

"So-so, but I do want to thank you for your kindness," she replied.

"You are welcome, my dear. Have you made a decision yet?"

"I really do appreciate the offer, but I'm not sure if this is for me, to be honest. I am going to try and find some work today," Alexia said in a hopeful way.

"Well, if that's what you want to do, that's fine, but remember this: work is not always easy to find, and how are you going to survive without any money until you do?" Alice said in a kind and caring voice.

Alexia thought for a minute, then realized that Alice was right, as she had no job and nowhere to live except on the streets. How was she going to survive without any money?

"I'm sure I will find something, Alice," Alexia replied.

"I hope you do, my dear. But remember, at least here you will have a roof over your head, money to buy what you need, and you'll be safe as you won't be out on the streets; just think about that for a minute. And perhaps in time, when you have earned some money, you could then go out there and get somewhere to live and try and get another job," Alice said, trying very hard to get Alexia to stay there and work for them.

'That does sound like good advice,' Alexia thought to herself. 'If I only do it for a short while, maybe it won't be so bad. It's not like anyone else gives a damn about me.'

However, the thought of some stranger touching her brought back the memories of not only her rape but also Kevin.

Looking into Alice's eyes, she said, "I'm just not sure if I can let a stranger touch me."

"Well, there is a little trick to help you with that. Have you ever had a boyfriend, Sally?"

Alexia paused for a moment, then said, "Yes, I have had three boyfriends over the last couple of years."

"And did you have sex with them?"

"Yes, I did," Alexia replied, wondering why Alice was asking her these personal questions.

"Well then, whenever you are with a man, you simply close your eyes and think that you are with one of your boyfriends, and it is he that is doing things to you and you to him," Alice said, looking in Alexia's eyes, suspecting that she must have been through some kind of hardship recently.

"Will that really work?" Alexia asked.

"Well, let's see, shall we? Let's try something, but you must be relaxed and, most importantly, trust me," Alice said in a reassuring voice.

"Ok," Alexia said in a nervous way.

"Now, I want you to close your eyes and think of your boyfriend. I will touch you gently, but I want you to imagine it is your boyfriend touching you. Can you do that for me, please?" Alice asked.

"I will try," Alexia replied, feeling very apprehensive.

"Good, my dear. This may very well feel strange to you because I am another woman, but in your mind, I am your boyfriend, and that's all you must think about. It is not me touching you; it is him, ok? Now close your eyes and imagine."

Alice gently touched Alexia on her shoulders, then ran her hands down the length of her arms and back up to her shoulders again. She then very slowly leaned forward and gave Alexia a kiss on the cheek, followed by a second one and finally a kiss on her lips. Alexia's reaction was to move her head away a little, but Alice calmly told her to relax and kissed her on the lips again.

"Just relax, my dear," Alice said in a gentle voice as she put her hands on Alexia's cheeks and again very gently kissed her lips.

"Now that wasn't too bad, was it?" she asked.

"No, I guess not, but it feels wrong," Alexia replied nervously.

"I know, my dear, but just relax and think of your boyfriend. I will not do anything you are not comfortable with, so please just trust me. Now let's try and do a little more, Sally. I am going to kiss you in a sexier way now, so please just relax."

Again Alice put her hands on Alexia's cheeks and kissed her lips, then used her tongue to lick around Alexia's lips. She slowly moved her hands from Alexia's cheeks, then ran them down the length of her arms and back up again before placing one hand on her breast. Alexia's reaction was to flinch a little, but again Alice told her gently to relax and think of her boyfriend. Alice then used her tongue to part Alexia's lips so that she could kiss her properly and, at the same time, gave Alexia's breast a gentle but firm squeeze.

Alexia pulled back and said she was sorry and that it felt strange. Alice explained that it was natural for her to feel like that. She told Alexia that if she could do this with her, then doing it with a man would be a lot easier because, in Alexia's eyes, it would be more natural. However, she also said that there would be times when she would have to entertain ladies as well as men. Alice told her to close her eyes again and try it one more time, and Alexia did as she was asked, really thinking that it was an old boyfriend that she was with.

Alice once again began to kiss Alexia's lips, parting them in the same way. This time, Alexia opened her mouth ever so slightly, and Alice was able to slip her tongue inside her mouth and began to kiss her passionately. She now moved her hand to the front of Alexia's blouse. Alice unbuttoned two of the buttons, slipped her hand inside, and began to caress her breast over her brassiere before putting two fingers inside of Alexia's brassiere and gently squeezing her nipple.

Alexia gave a little moan at this moment as her nipples hardened from her touch. She gave no resistance as Alice then put the rest of her hand inside Alexia's brassiere and began to massage her breast while kissing her even more passionately. Alice could tell that Alexia was still very nervous about all this, but to her credit, she was going along with it.

Alice then took out Alexia's breast, leaned her head down to put her mouth around it, and very gently sucked her nipple. At the same time, she trailed her hand down the length of Alexia's leg and then back up again, caressing her inner thigh inside of her skirt until her fingertips were touching Alexia's panties.

"Oh, Alice, no," Alexia said, but Alice once again told her in a soft voice that it was ok and for her to relax, imagining it was her boyfriend. Alice continued to suck on her breast while now rubbing Alexia's clit with one finger over her panties for a few minutes before slipping two fingers inside them, feeling just how wet Alexia had now become.

"Does that feel good, Sally?" Alice asked as she continued to pleasure her with her fingers.

"Yes, oh god, yes," she moaned and, within two minutes, began to come as she had never done before. Alexia was surprised at just how amazing the orgasm she just had was because she had never felt like this before, neither with her boyfriends nor when she played with herself.

"That was not so bad, was it?" Alice asked.

"No, I guess not," Alexia replied, confused that she was able to come like that with another woman touching her, and there was also a part of her that was intrigued. The fact that Alice was being so nice and gentle with her helped, as it actually calmed Alexia, and she thought how nice it felt for someone to treat her that way.

"Now, why don't you show me what you can do, Sally, and make me come?" Alice said.

Alexia looked at her with a shocked expression as she never suspected that Alice would ask her to do anything like this.

Just then, Alice looked her in the eyes and said, "If you give me a good orgasm, I will give you $50. I'm sure you have played with yourself, my dear, so just play with me the same way."

"I don't know if I can," Alexia replied in a very nervous, almost terrified voice.

"I'll tell you what, my dear, just simply touch me, that's all. Just touch my pussy for now," Alice said with a smile on her face.

Alice stood up, lifted up her skirt to her waist, then sat back down on the bed again. She then took Alexia's hand and slowly moved it to the top of her thigh, guiding it up and down the length of it.

"There, that is not so bad touching my thigh, is it, my dear?" she asked.

"No," Alexia replied, still very nervous and feeling unsure, yet in a strange way excited about what was happening.

"Now run your hand up and down my thigh by yourself, my dear," Alice said to Alexia. After a moment's pause, she did as was asked, slowly moving it a few inches up and then back down again continuously.

"That's it, my dear, you are doing so well. Now, why don't you run your hand on the inside of my thigh?"

Alexia again did as was asked, and after a couple of minutes, Alice took hold of Alexia's hand.

As she put it between her legs, she said in a gentle voice, "Now rub my pussy."

Alexia's reaction was to try and pull her hand away, but she found she was unable to.

"No, my dear, leave it there; you can do it," Alice told her, using a little force to keep her hand there.

Alexia looked into Alice's eyes for a few seconds, then slowly began to move her fingers ever so slightly over her clit.

"Oh, that's it, my dear, that feels so good. Please don't stop," Alice said in a soft voice.

Alexia continued to rub her clit with her fingers, slowly beginning to move them a little faster, which actually started to turn her on. The thought of doing anything like this with another woman had indeed entered Alexia's mind in the past, but she never dreamed that she would ever do it. It was, after all, just teenage curiosity when the subject came up, and she talked with her school friends about sexual matters. Doing anything for real had never entered her mind, but here she was doing exactly that.

After a few minutes, Alice, who was feeling like she was succeeding with Alexia, said, "That was very good, but let's try something a little more exciting, shall we?"

Alice stood up, removed her panties, and then sat back down on the bed. This time, she lay right down so that her back was on the bed, but her legs were over the side of it with her feet on the floor.

"Come, my dear Sally, let's see if you have what it takes to work here. Do the same again without my panties in the way."

Very nervously, Alexia put her hand on Alice's thigh and slowly moved her hand up so that her fingers were almost touching her pubic hair.

"That's it, Sally. Keep going and think of all the money you are going to make. Did I not give you a good orgasm, and do I not now deserve the same back?" she asked.

Alexia moved her hand a little bit further up and began to rub Alice's clit very gently to begin with, but Alice then said, "Faster, Sally, rub my clit faster."

Alexia did as she was asked, knowing that Alice was enjoying it by the way she was moving her hips and moaning, and thought to herself that this was not so bad after all. At that moment, Alice told her to put her fingers inside her, and Alexia did as was instructed, moving them in and out while Alice was getting more and more excited.

"Now, I want you to use your tongue on me," Alice urged.

Alexia was stunned at what she had just heard, and a look of shock appeared on her face.

"Come on, Sally, you can do it," Alice said in a gentle voice as she put her hand around Alexia's head and slowly pushed it down.

Hesitantly, Alexia leaned forward the rest of the way and began to lick her clit. Alice began to move her hips as Alexia moved her fingers faster, while still licking her. Then Alice began to moan, as she thrust her hips up and down. Suddenly she gave out a big long moan, squirting a little, as she began to come. It really surprised Alexia at how much satisfaction she felt having made another woman come.

After a minute of just lying there without saying a word, Alice sat up on the bed, reached over for her bag, pulled out $50, and gave it to Alexia, saying, "There you go, my dear. That wasn't so bad, was it?"

"No, I guess not," Alexia replied.

"So, are you going to stay with us, my dear, or not?"

Alexia thought for a brief moment and then said, "Yes, I will stay and try it."

"Good girl, but you have to convince Bruno as well. I will go get him, and then you two can have some fun together. Just remember, think of him as your boyfriend, do what comes naturally, and you will be fine," Alice said as she got up and put her panties back on.

"Ok, Alice, thank you," Alexia said, feeling both apprehensive and excited at the same time.

Alice went to Bruno and told him that Alexia was going to work out ok, as long as they were patient with her. She then told him to go and fuck her but to not overdo it so as not to frighten her away.

Bruno went up to Alexia's room where, even though Alexia was still very nervous, they had sex, and she finished him off with a blow-job, but taking his cock out of her mouth before he shot his load, so that his cum was over her hand rather than in her mouth.

A little while after they had finished, Alice went back up to Alexia's room and sat with her for a while, asking how she felt and if she was all right. After they had chatted for a short while, Alice said she was going to take Alexia shopping for some new clothes, sexy lingerie, and makeup and that she would deduct the cost of these items from the money she would be making.

"Oh, and by the way, if anyone should ask, you are twenty-one, is that understood?" Alice asked.

"Yes, I understand, Alice," she replied.

Alexia again began to think that perhaps she should have stayed at home and was not really sure which place was best for her. At home, she would have an uncaring drunk for a mother with an abusive boyfriend, or here, where even though she would have a roof over her head, she would have to have sex with strangers. Either way, she would have to have sex, but at least here, she would get paid for it, whereas Kevin would get it for nothing. It was a very difficult decision for her to make, and she wondered which one would actually be for the best.

Alexia went for a walk to think and then used a payphone to call the police precinct to find out what was happening with her rape case. She was first told by the detective in charge that even though they had his DNA, there was no match in the system, and without it, there was no way to know who he was. He then asked where she was and that she had to return to the precinct as he wanted to talk to her.

"What do you want to talk to me about?" she asked.

"We can discuss that when you get here," the detective replied.

Alexia was not sure why he wanted her to go and see him or why he could not talk to her now and wondered if he knew that she had run away from home.

"Just tell me what you need to talk to me about," she asked again.

"Your mother is worried about you, that is all," he replied.

Alexia knew that this was a load of rubbish as her mother had not cared about her for a long time and only really cared where the next drink was coming from.

"No, she isn't; all she cares about is alcohol," she replied.

"Ok, but please come and see me anyway," the detective continued.

"No, not unless you tell me why," Alexia said in an angry voice.

The detective paused for a brief moment and then said, "You have been accused of stealing your mother's money, and we just want to get to the bottom of it."

"But that was money that I earned, my money, and it's not stealing if it is my own money," Alexia snapped angrily down the telephone.

"Well, we can discuss that when you get here, but by not coming to see me, it is going to seem that you are guilty. So, please do the right thing and come see me so we can talk about it."

Alexia thought for a minute and then told the detective that she was not a thief as it was money that she had earned, but it was obvious that no one was going to believe what she said. She then told him that she was never going back home and then put the telephone down.

Alexia now realized that her decision had been made for her because she could not go back home now even if she had wanted to. The fact that her own mother would tell the police that she had stolen that money told her exactly how little she thought of her and that all she cared about was money and alcohol.

Alexia knew that, yes, legally, she did take that money without anyone's knowledge, so she could see how the police would classify that as theft, but it was money that she had earned all that time working, so she had every right to take it. Nevertheless, she was now branded a thief by her own mother, and there was no way that she would go back home now. She realized that staying with Alice and Bruno was her only choice right now, but told herself that it would only be for a short while until she could find other work.

Over the next two months, Alexia was given well-chosen regular clients by Bruno and Alice, who they knew would be gentle with her, and before too long, Alexia had become one of the most popular girls there.

However, she began to realize that she was not making as much money as she was expecting to and one day decided to ask Alice about it. Alice told her that she had to pay back all the money that was spent on her clothes, lingerie, and makeup, as well as having to pay rent for living there.

"Oh, but I did not know that I would have to pay so much rent," Alexia said.

"Oh, really? Did you think that you would be living here on the cheap while earning money? Anywhere you go, you will have to pay rent, my dear, and here is no different. We are, after all, running a business here, you know," Alice explained.

"Yes, I understand, but I just thought that I would be earning more money than this," Alexia said, who knew very well that she had paid for those clothes ten times over and was being charged far too much for this so-called rent.

"Well, my dear, if it's more money you want. then that is not a problem, but you will have to do a lot more than you have been doing to earn it."

"What do you mean?" Alexia asked.

Alice thought for a moment and decided the time had come to use Alexia for the purpose they had groomed her for while she was there.

"Well, my dear, certain clients have certain tastes or fetishes, and they are prepared to pay very well to satisfy those desires. If you would like to earn more money, then you have to be willing to do what they want," Alice said in a gentle voice while smiling at her.

"And what is that exactly?" Alexia asked curiously.

"Well, you will find out soon enough, my dear, but for now, just run along and get yourself ready as it is nearly time for you to start work," Alice replied with a big smile.

Suddenly Alexia was beginning to think that she may have made a big mistake and that maybe she should not have started doing this, but she was here now and did not really have much choice other than perhaps ending up on the streets.

'Anyway, surely things can't be that bad, regardless of what fetishes my clients have,' she thought to herself ... or could they?

CHAPTER SEVEN

Over the next few months, Alexia was given some of the more fetish-minded clients, which also included a few ladies, as well as certain clients who had a thing for younger girls. Although she was not too happy at first doing some of the things they wanted, she soon got used to it. By now, she had already made up her mind that since the money she was earning was now so much more, she would leave this life behind in a year or so as she would have saved enough for a new start.

On Alexia's seventeenth birthday, Alice went up to her room to wish her a happy birthday. She told her that she was taking her out to her favorite boutique to buy her some new sexy lingerie and that it would be her treat as a birthday present. Alexia was excited because the shop where Alice bought her own lingerie was very, very expensive, and it was not somewhere Alexia could afford to buy from.

After they returned from shopping, Alice asked Alexia to try on the items she had bought for her so she could see what they looked like. When she did, Alice told her that she looked amazing in that lingerie set, along with sheer seamed black stockings and high heel stiletto shoes.

"You really do look so hot, you know, Sally," Alice said, eyeing her up and down.

"Thank you, and thank you for buying these for me," Alexia replied with a happy look.

"You are welcome, my dear, but do you think you can now do me a little favor?"

"Sure, what is it you want?" Alexia asked.

"I am feeling so very horny looking at how sexy you look in that set, so why don't you come on over and lick my pussy?" Alice suggested as she pulled up her skirt and lay down on the bed.

Alexia, thankful for the lingerie, did exactly that by kneeling down in front of Alice. She moved her panties to one side with the fingers of one hand, felt how wet she was, then began to rub her clit with one finger for a few minutes before lowering her head and beginning to lick her. She then inserted two fingers of her other hand inside her and began to lick her clit faster. Within a few minutes, Alice had come and she thanked Alexia before getting up from the bed.

Alice told Alexia that she wanted her to wear that lingerie set tonight, as two very special clients were coming into town. She said she would have to make sure they were kept happy and wanted her to look her absolute best for them. Alice then told her that she would see them in the special room, which was in the basement where a deluxe suite had been built especially for the top clients to use, and that they would be her only clients for tonight.

Alexia had used this suite on a number of occasions, and it was usually when she would have to do things she did not enjoy too much. However, never had she been with two men at the same time before, but two clients meant double money.

Later that evening, Alexia got dressed and waited until she was called for by Alice as the clients had just arrived. The two men were introduced to Alexia, and they had a few drinks together before being led to the basement by Alice.

"Have fun," Alice said as she left them to go back upstairs.

Alexia, feeling a little anxious that she was alone in the basement, away from all the other rooms and with two men for the first time, asked them what they wanted to do. They told her just to let things happen naturally.

It all started well enough with the usual things happening, Alexia playing with them, giving them a blow job, and they in turn played with her. After around twenty minutes, one of the men told her to get on her knees as he was going to fuck her from behind and she would suck the other man's cock, while he was lying on the bed.

"Ok, let me get you a condom," Alexia said.

"Oh no, we don't use those; we like it natural," one of the men said.

"No, I'm sorry, but I don't do that," Alexia replied politely.

"Shut up, you little slut; you will do what we want," he shouted as he slapped her around the face.

The other man got up and pushed Alexia down on the bed, holding her arms down, before handcuffing them behind her back.

"No, please stop!" she shouted.

"You can shout as much as you want, you dirty whore, but have you forgotten that this room is soundproof, or did you not even know?" he asked while they were both laughing.

Alexia suddenly realized what Alice had said about certain tastes and fetishes and why these men would pay so much more for such things. Not wanting to do this, she tried to get off the bed, but with her hands cuffed she was not able to. She spent the next two hours in that room with these men, who beat her, called her names, fucked and sodomized her again and again until they were both satisfied.

Then one of the men got on top of her and began to fuck her, while the other one knelt by her head and forced his cock inside her mouth. They did this until they had both shot their cum inside her.

Once they had finished, they got dressed, went upstairs, and gave Alice $2,000 and the key to the handcuffs, leaving Alexia crying in the basement, feeling violated and in a state of shock.

Alice then went down to the basement, released Alexia from the handcuffs, and said, "Here you go, Sally. Here is $500 as payment for your little session. I told you that you can earn better money with certain clients."

"Do you know what they did to me?" Alexia asked in an angry voice.

"You are the one that wants to earn more money. Or did you think that you would earn it without going out of your comfort zone?" Alice asked.

"No, but I did not expect this!" Alexia replied as she put her head in her hands.

"I know, my dear, I know, but look at this money. You made $500 for a couple of hours' work. Is that really that bad for letting them do what they did?"

Alexia looked at Alice in shock, realizing that the new lingerie set was not really a birthday present, but instead, it was for those two bastards she had just spent two hours of hell with. Alice did not give a damn about her, just the money she could make from her. Without saying a word, Alexia took the money and went upstairs to her room, where she decided that she was not going to do this anymore.

She did not mind having sex for money but did not want to get beaten and forced to do things she did not want to do, such as having sex without a condom, or having men's cum inside her pussy and in her mouth. She packed some of her stuff in a small bag, took all of the money she had hidden in her room, and sneaked out before anyone would miss her.

It was now around 9 pm, and most places were closed, but as she had nearly $7,000 in cash on her, from the money she was saving up, she decided to book herself into a hotel for the night, and she would decide on her future tomorrow. For now, Alexia just wanted to lay in a hot bath to soak and try to erase the last few hours, have something to eat, and almost certainly a drink.

However, with her face beginning to bruise from the beating she had been given, no one at any of the hotels she tried allowed her to book into them, and they even threatened to call the police if she did not leave. They took her for some tramp because of the way she looked and figured that even if she had money to pay for a room, she must have stolen it.

This was a better part of town where the hotels were of a higher quality. If she had found one of the sleazier ones, she would have a place to stay for the night, but none of those hotels were anywhere nearby.

For a minute, she thought about calling the police to tell them about what had happened, but of course, she could not do that. She herself would be arrested, not only for working there but also for the fact that she was being accused of theft by her own mother and her boyfriend.

So here was Alexia, back on the streets with nowhere to sleep for the night, even though this time she had the money, but had no one in the world who gave a damn about her. After wandering around for the next two hours, she began to wonder if she did the right thing by leaving Alice and Bruno. At least there, she had a roof over her head, food to eat, and all she had to do was allow herself to be used by anyone who paid enough.

This is not what she wanted from her life, but what could she do? She was now so tired from all the walking she had done for the past hour that she just needed to rest for a bit. She came across a few homeless people who were just sitting around, so she decided to do the same.

During the course of the night, she learned just how bad life is if you are homeless and knew that she had to do something as she could not go on like this.

Alexia hardly slept all night but got up the next morning and headed off to the nearest subway. She used the facilities to freshen up a bit, do her makeup and make herself look a bit more presentable before heading off to try again. She again intended to try and book into a hotel to stay for a short time while looking for somewhere to rent and then also look for work.

However, things were not as easy as she thought they would be. She was constantly asked for some type of identification by the hotels, not only due to the way she looked with her now very bruised face but also because she was indeed in a more upmarket area. These hotels did not just randomly allow someone to book a room without having a credit card to go on file, which she did not have, even though she had the cash to pay for the room.

She had spent all day trying to get a room, with no luck. It was now early evening, and once again, she found herself in the same boat with nowhere to go for the night except to just wander the streets as she did the previous night. Alexia could not bear the thought of spending another night sleeping rough and was not sure if she wanted to go back to Alice's either. She was in such a state that thoughts of ending her life began to surface, and she wondered if that was not the best thing she could do.

As she walked along, she realized that she was now not in the nicer part of town, and she came across a few street prostitutes trying to wave down drivers. She realized that she could end up like that if she wasn't careful, and then, who knows what could happen to her? She walked on a bit further before deciding to sit on a wall to rest her aching feet and gather her thoughts on what to do next.

During the hour or so she was there, a few men approached her for some business as they drove by, but she kept telling them she was not on the game. Eventually, she got so fed up with it that she decided to move somewhere else to sit. She began walking again without having any idea where she was going or what she was going to do.

After a few minutes, a car pulled up beside her moving very slowly. As the tinted window from the rear seat went down, Alexia turned towards the car and screamed at the top of her voice, "I'M NOT FUCKING INTERESTED!"

"That's ok; I am not asking," a lady's voice said from the back seat of the car, in an elegant, well-spoken English accent.

"Oh, I'm so sorry," Alexia replied, falling to her knees and crying.

"That's quite all right. Please don't cry; no harm done," the lady in the car said.

"I have had a really bad couple of days, well, a bad year in fact, and I am so sorry for shouting," Alexia said, trying to force a smile.

The lady in the car paused for a brief moment and then said, "I gathered that, as I have been watching you for the last hour from my car. I could see that you did not go with any of the men that approached you."

"Why were you watching me? Did Alice or Bruno send you?" Alexia asked angrily.

"Oh, please, do not tell me you work for those two?" the lady asked.

"Do you know them?" Alexia asked fearfully.

"Only too well, my child, only too well. I used to work this very street a great many years ago until I was found by Alice and began working for them. However, there were times when I thought that I was better off working on the streets rather than for those two. But then one day I was saved from this life … and them," the lady replied, looking at Alexia with sadness in her eyes and then giving her a little smile.

"I was working for them until last night, but I left because of something that happened there. I don't want to go back, but I may not have a choice," Alexia said tearfully.

"There is always a choice. Come get into the car and let me tell you about my life, and you will see," the lady said as she opened the car door.

Alexia was very reluctant to get into the car, but the lady said she would be happy to give Alexia the car keys to hold while they chatted and that the chauffeur would wait outside of the car. Alexia hesitantly agreed, getting into the car after she was given the keys and the chauffeur exited.

"My name is Veronica; what is your name?" the lady asked.

"I'm Sally," Alexia replied.

"Well, Sally, a very long time ago, I was in your very shoes and was heading nowhere fast, until one day, one of my elderly clients, a wealthy English gentleman, who regularly traveled between the UK and the states, saved me. This gentleman, who enjoyed me dominating him very much, told me one day that he was in love with me and wanted to take me away from this life. At first, I thought he was joking, but he asked me to live with him, and once there, I never looked back."

"Oh my god, are you serious?" Alexia asked in amazement.

"Oh yes, Sally. He told me that I could stay there for as long as I wanted rent-free, and I could have whatever I wanted: jewelry, clothes, cars, anything I needed would be mine. All he wanted was for me to stay with him and be his mistress, and by that, I mean his dominatrix, not his bit on the side, as they say. Of course, I agreed, and we spent nearly twelve fantastic years together in his fabulous house where I was his mistress, and he was my slave. During that time, he educated me, taught me how to be a lady, and we kept moving between England and the US, where he had a house on Long Island. In all honesty, we ended up loving each other so much, and when he died ten years ago, he left me everything he owned. I decided then that I would never love another man. I also continued my role as a mistress and have since built up a very large list of clients."

"Wow, you were so lucky, Veronica," Alexia said.

"Yes, I was, Sally, but I never forgot where I came from. That's why I sometimes come back here to remind me of what

I once was and why I now want to help you," Veronica said with a smile.

"Help me, but why me?" Alexia asked curiously. "I'm nobody."

"Yes, Sally, and I was nobody all those years ago when he chose to help me."

"Well, thank you, Veronica, but how are you going to help me?"

"Are you fed up being used by men for their own sexual gratification? Would you like to have men eating out of the palm of your hands instead, Sally?" Veronica asked.

"Oh, you bet I would, but that's not going to happen," Alexia said as she looked at the floor of the car.

"I can make that happen if you want me to. I will train you, educate you, teach you how to be a mistress, how to dominate men, and how to use them for your own pleasure. And they will love you for it, just like he did me," Veronica replied as she took Alexia's hand in her own.

"So they would do whatever I wanted instead of me doing what they want?" Alexia asked excitedly.

"Yes, my child, you will have all the power, and they will be your playthings."

"Then yes, I want that power; I want men to suffer for what I have been through. Please help me, Veronica," Alexia said with a big smile on her face.

"I will, my child, I will," Veronica replied.

Veronica spent the next few years teaching Alexia how to command respect from men, how to treat them, punish them and leave them wanting more. She taught her when to be forgiving, merciless, and kind, how to use men for her own sexual pleasure, and when to be rewarding to them. She explained to her the different types of domination there were and the different ways she could administer punishment as well as pleasure. In fact, Veronica taught Alexia everything she knew.

After those years of training, Alexia was ready to take the role of a mistress. Of course, she would help Veronica with her clients for some hands-on experience, but until now, Veronica was always the mistress, with Alexia being her helper.

During her training, Veronica enrolled Alexia in university so she could study psychology to help her understand a person's mind during her sessions. At the end of the course, Alexia had gained her degree and was a fully qualified sex therapist and psychologist. This meant that she could understand a client's sexual preferences even better, which really helped her to deal with her clients in a way that most mistresses could not, and they loved her for it. Not only could she get the most out of the physical side but also the psychological side of her clients, and it was this that made her so good at what she did.

Now that her training was over and Alexia was going to be the mistress, Veronica thought that Sally was not a very good name for a mistress and decided that Alexia would be a much better name. Veronica then arranged for Sally to legally change her name to Alexia Summers and arranged for the money that Alexia had taken from her mother's room to be repaid with interest. She also arranged via one of her influential clients within the legal system for all charges against Alexia to be dropped.

For the first time in her life, Alexia felt in total control of her own destiny and had the strength to ensure she would never be used again by another man. Oh yes, Alexia had told Veronica everything that had happened to her, including the rape, the so-called theft, her drunk mother, and her mother's abusive boyfriend.

Veronica wanted Alexia to have a new start in life without anything hanging over her head, and Alexia was now the happiest she had ever been. She not only thought of Veronica as another mother but one that actually cared.

As time went by, Alexia came to realize just how lucky she was and that this newfound life she was living was just so perfect. However, one morning, Veronica called Alexia into the study and asked her to sit down as she wanted to talk to her.

"I'm leaving," Veronica said in a sad tone of voice.

"What do you mean you are leaving?" Alexia asked, surprised.

"My child, when I say I am leaving, I mean that I am dying. I have been ill with cancer for a long time now, which I kept from you. The doctors say it is my stubbornness that has kept me alive for so long. I say it was my desire to help someone the same way I was helped that has kept me going for so long, and it was the reason I chose you that day on the street."

"No, Veronica, please, you can't go; you can't die," Alexia cried out in a tearful voice.

"No, my child, please don't cry. I have had more than twenty happy years living here, and now it is your turn," Veronica said with a smile.

"What do you mean?" Alexia asked.

"I mean that I have left everything to you in my will, including my clientele, so this will all be yours soon," Veronica said, reaching out and taking hold of Alexia's hands.

"No, Veronica, I don't want all this. I want you to stay with me."

"I wish I could, my child, but my time is nearly up, and I will rest in peace knowing that I have left all this to you and that I was able to give you your life back. Now be a dear and go make me one of your nice cups of tea, will you, Alexia?"

"Of course, I will," she said tearfully as she got up and headed into the kitchen.

Veronica stayed in the house for the next three months until one evening when she died in her sleep. Everything then passed over to Alexia, who swore not to let Veronica down. She was determined to be the best mistress she could possibly be and to make Veronica proud of her.

Alexia spent the next eighteen years being a mistress, as well as writing books about it and building up a very large and influential client list. She had become a very wealthy woman. The only reason she was still a mistress was that she actually enjoyed the lifestyle, especially the power she had over her clients and the way men were more than happy to bow at her feet and carry out her every wish.

Chapter Eight

Alexia had fallen asleep a short while after having her flashback. She eventually woke up during the early hours of the morning with a tear in her eye, remembering her past. She decided to make herself a strong cup of tea and wondered what would happen now and whether or not this would, in fact, go to trial. Yet again, she began to think of her life with Veronica and how her life of being a mistress started.

She thought of how much she missed Veronica, who she thought of as the mother she always wanted. Suddenly she found herself drifting back to the time when Veronica saved her from that other life. When Veronica took her in that night, Alexia's life changed completely, as she was treated by Veronica as though she was her own daughter. Veronica never had any children of her own, nor did she have any siblings, which is why she treated Alexia the way she did.

Veronica was an amazing English lady, who had a large home both in the states and in England, plus a large clientele in both countries. She would spend a few months in England, then return to the states for a few months, before going back to England, and so on. This, of course, meant that Alexia would always travel with her and help with the domination of her clients over the years, both in England and the US.

But more importantly for Veronica was that Alexia was now being taught how to speak the Queen's English by an English tutor, the way that a Lord or Lady in England would speak it. Veronica was very well-spoken and wanted Alexia to be the same way, as she found that a lot of her clients actually loved the way she spoke.

Not only was Alexia being taught how to speak, walk, and stand, but also how to behave in an elegant and aristocratic way. The better Alexia got, the happier Veronica was with her progress.

Veronica herself was, in fact, a normal cockney girl who grew up in London's east end area of Bow, far from the elegant, sophisticated lady she was now. She came from a broken home which she left in her late teens after managing to get herself a job in a store. However, she struggled to make it on her own as the rent, food, and amenities all became far too expensive for her to afford, so she ended up as an escort to help her survive.

Oh, she tried to get a different job, but she did not have any qualifications, and as such, she was unable to get any decent, well-paid work. She fell into debt and was facing eviction when she decided to become an escort for a short while - until she could get back on her feet.

At first, she told herself that she would only do it for a few weeks, which then became a few months and eventually became a few years. Within a few months of being an escort, she gave up her job and signed up with an escort agency, which she stayed with for three years.

Over those years, Veronica learned from the other girls there. She found that a few of her clients were into domination, which she enjoyed very much. She learned as much about domination as she could and soon became the number one choice for clients looking for that lifestyle.

After she had earned a little bit of money, Veronica decided that she wanted to change her life, so she moved to New York to try and do that. She had found herself a job before flying out to New York and had also arranged to rent an apartment, but before too long, the money began to dry up. Her job was not paying nearly as much as she was making as an escort back in England, and within a few months, she found herself getting into debt all over again.

She liked living in New York and did not want to return to London, so she began to work the streets, trying to earn some extra money. After all, this was the life she was used to, so it was no big deal for her to do it again for a short while.

However, it was during this time that Alice found Veronica walking the streets, just like she had found Alexia. Of course, she convinced Veronica to work for her rather than working the streets. Veronica, just as she did in London, gave up her job and began working full time for Alice and Bruno until her life changed.

It was here that she met Harold Fielding, the man who would eventually whisk her away from this life. It was clear that, from the very first time they met, there was a connection between them. He would see her frequently, and they became closer with each meeting.

Harold, a very wealthy man, who had never been married, pretty much spent most of his life on his own. However, he had fallen in love with Veronica and was seeing her every week, sometimes twice a week. Eventually, he told her that he wanted to take her away from this life and asked her to go and live with him. He said it did not matter if she loved him or not because he loved her enough for the both of them. He said that she could still be a mistress but would only have one client ... him.

Harold went on to tell her that she would not want for anything. She would have the freedom to live her life any way she wanted, as long as they also spent a lot of time together. Unsure what to make of this at first, Veronica said she would think about it. After a week, she told Harold that she would go and spend a week with him to see how it went.

Well, she never looked back. He was the kindest, most generous, loving man she had ever known, and it was not too long before they began their life together. They enjoyed vacations, visits to the theatre, fine restaurants, and pretty much whatever she wanted. They lived together as a couple, with just one exception; when it came to sex, she would dominate him because that is what he wanted.

Over the years, their relationship became far more intense and loving. They spent many nights making love together, but domination was still a big part of their lives which they did two to three times a week, making love as a couple the rest of the time.

Harold taught her how to be an elegant lady, how to speak and behave, just like she was teaching Alexia now. Within six months of them moving in together, Veronica fell in love with him. She now loved him as much as he loved her. Her heart was eventually broken when he died from a heart attack after they had spent twelve amazing years together. She knew then that she would never love another man.

Harold left everything he owned to her, which made her a very wealthy woman, but she would gladly have given it all away to have her man back in her arms. Veronica knew that Harold had a rare heart disease. In fact, the doctors did not expect him to live as long as he did. Eventually, he died in his sleep in her arms one night.

A few days before his death, as though he knew it was coming, he told Veronica that he did not want her to waste her life after he was gone and that he wanted her to enjoy it. He said that she had given him so much pleasure and fun in the time they spent together. He wanted her to carry on with her domination because he knew just how much she enjoyed the lifestyle.

Veronica absolutely loved being a mistress, and Harold knew that which is why he did not want her to stop. All he asked from her was never to forget him. Up until her dying day, she never stopped thinking about him or loving him and always went to the church and lit a candle for him on his birthday.

As much as she loved the lifestyle of a mistress, she would have given it all up in an instant for Harold. She only continued with it because it was his dying wish. Veronica eventually told Alexia all about Harold and the life they had spent together. She told her that one of the reasons she stopped the car that day when she saw Alexia for the first time was so she could do for Alexia what Harold had done for her. Veronica knew that if Harold was looking on, he would have been very proud of the way she had helped Alexia.

Alexia's thoughts eventually came back to the present. She had a tear in her eye from thinking about Veronica's life, the time they spent together, and, of course, her own past. As strong as

Alexia had become, there was always a sadness and weakness whenever she thought about Veronica. She wished more than anything that she could see her one last time, if only to say thank you once more.

"Oh, Veronica, I miss you, but as you always used to say, life goes on," Alexia said out loud as she got up to go upstairs for a shower and get ready for the day to come.

CHAPTER NINE

Meanwhile, Jason had begun to read through Alexia Summer's file. The more he read, the more it seemed like it was self-defense, but questions kept popping up in his mind. There were things about what he read that made no sense to him. He had questions such as, why would Simon Morley try and rape her if he was there to have sex with her anyway? After all, he was a paying client, and she was an escort.

During all the time he spent reading her file, he could not stop thinking about how sexy Alexia looked and, more importantly, he wondered how good she was in bed. This was unusual for Jason, as he had never thought of a client in that way before, but there was something about Alexia he found irresistible, and he could not take his mind off her. His thoughts once again turned to Selene, and the domination role-plays they did together. Again, he wondered if Alexia would be just as good, if not better than her. After all, Alexia was not only elegant but much more beautiful and sexier than Selene was, and he was sure that she would be much more exciting in bed.

Jason found it very difficult to concentrate on the file and decided that he needed a drink to help him get a grip on the matter at hand. He poured himself a large whiskey, sat back down in his comfortable leather chair, and took a large sip of his drink before picking up her file to continue reading it. Over the next half an hour or so, he slowly sipped his drink as he continued to read through the file, trying very hard not to think of Alexia, but it was very difficult for him not to.

After all, he was reading about her, so how could he not think about her? Deep down inside, he knew that this was going to be a very difficult case for him. He almost felt how a lovesick teenager would feel with his first love, but he also knew that he had a case to concentrate on and a job to do.

He continued reading through her file, and before too long, he read that she advertised herself as a mistress on her website. 'So she does do domination role-plays,' Jason thought to himself. He was even more intrigued now than ever before, as once again, he began to wonder just how good this lady was. Jason had not had sex for quite a while with his wife, and on the odd occasion when they did have sleep together, it was not exactly memorable for him. The more he read, the more he thought about having sex with Alexia. It got to the stage where he was becoming aroused at just the thought of doing something with her, especially if it was going to be a domination role-play.

Once again, he had to remind himself that he had a job to do. He got up from his chair and poured himself another drink before sitting back down again, taking another large sip of whiskey, then continuing to read the file. The more he read, the more he realized that it really was a case of self-defense. However, that nagging question of why Morley would try and rape her stayed in his mind as he simply could not understand it. He could see no reason why anyone would try and rape an escort when that is the whole purpose of them meeting up in the first place - for them to have sex. He knew this was a question he would need Alexia to clarify for him, but apart from that, it was a clear case of self-defense.

However, it would be a difficult one to prove without any witnesses, as there was only her account of what happened. The saving grace was that Jason did not have to prove anything. It was the prosecution's job to prove she was guilty, rather than the other way around. Jason knew that it would be difficult for the prosecution to prove it was anything other than self-defense, as there were no witnesses to say it wasn't. Still, the fact that Alexia was an escort could have an impact on the way the jurors saw her, and this was going to be the big problem he would have to overcome.

As he continued to read her file, it was evident this was the first time that Simon Morley had met Alexia. He got in touch with her after coming across her website, which advertised her as a mistress. Simon told Alexia that he had been with a few mistresses in the past and that he wanted to be dominated by her. It seems that he was not satisfied with the way things went or what he got for his money and wanted more than Alexia was prepared to offer. He then began to get rough with her, slapped her on the face, demanded his money back, and when she refused, he tried to rape her.

During the struggle, Alexia managed to scratch Simon's face. As he released his grip on her to put his hands up to his face, in a natural reaction, Alexia was able to break free of him for a few seconds. She ran over to where she kept her gun, opened the drawer, and took the gun out. As he came after her again, she pointed the gun at him, and fearing for her life, she pulled the trigger and shot him. Alexia then called 911, and before too long, both the police and the paramedics had arrived. It was at this moment that it became evident that Simon Morley had died. 'This was certainly a case of self-defense,' Jason thought to himself, and although he did not know Alexia, his instincts were telling him that she was a truthful person.

Jason's instincts were always good when it came to his cases, and he believed everything he had read in her statement without any shadow of a doubt. The problem was how he would tell this story to the jury if this case were to go to trial. The one thing that always concerned him, and that would be on the mind of some, if not all of the jurors, was why Simon would try to rape

Alexia when he was there to have sex with her anyway. Why would he not be satisfied spending time with someone who did this sort of thing for a living? After all, if Jason himself thought this, then it was obvious that the jurors would do so as well. This could be just enough for them to side with the prosecution.

Yes, at first glance, it was clear that the members of the jury would wonder about this very question. It could cast some doubts in their mind as to what had actually happened that night. Jason's instincts were at it again, and he felt that something was missing from her statement. As hard as he tried, he could not understand the reason behind the attack.

There was something not quite right here, but he could not put his finger on it. Jason wondered if Alexia, through her ordeal, had forgotten anything when she gave her statement to the police or, indeed, had left something out intentionally.

'Perhaps this is not going to be as clear cut as I first assumed,' Jason thought to himself.

He would have to find a way to explain this to the jury. However, he could not do this when he did not even know the answer to that nagging question himself. It was something he would most certainly have to get an answer to from Alexia when they next met.

Jason finished reading her file and then went to see his boss to give him an update regarding his opinion about what he had read. He told him that everything pointed to this being self-defense, with the exception of that yet unanswered question as to why Simon tried to rape her. His boss totally agreed with Jason, and they both said that this was something that Alexia would need to clear up before they could even consider what would be their next move regarding her case. They knew that this could be a big stumbling block for them if she was indeed charged. It would certainly be a question the prosecution would be asking her in front of the jurors to hear.

'Yes, this is something I need to discuss with her during her appointment the next day,' he thought to himself as he left Langley's office and made his way back to his own.

Once there, he asked his secretary to telephone Alexia and arrange a time for her to come in and see him early in the morning. Then he went into his office, sat in his chair, leaning all the way as far back as it would go, and looked out of his window, staring at the sky.

This case and Alexia especially really seemed to be getting to him, and he could not quite put his finger on why. She was just another client he did not even know, so there was no reason at all for him to feel this way, but he did feel strange, and it confused him greatly. There was an undeniable attraction to Alexia which intrigued him as he was not used to feeling this way - especially with someone he had only met for a few minutes. He had never felt like this before, and for the first time in his life, he did not know what to do. Nor could he explain why this particular woman could have such an impact on him. Yes, she was a very attractive and sexy lady, but Jason had been with such women before without feeling like this, which made him question it even more.

'Anyway, enough of this,' he thought to himself.

He still had a few things to take care of, yet throughout that afternoon, he would occasionally think about Alexia, especially knowing that she would be returning the next day, which he looked forward to very much.

But it was now time for him to go home to Lydia and pretend everything was fine. For the first time, he really wished that she would not be there anymore. He felt sad that this woman he loved was cheating on him, but at the same time felt angry that she had taken him for a fool, or more to the point that he did not see through her act.

'Oh well, enough of this feeling sorry for yourself,' he thought as he left his office.

Jason got into his car and began to drive home, reflecting on what his life would now be like and what was in store for him going forward.

CHAPTER TEN

Jason woke up the next morning, followed his usual routine, and then went to the office, where he waited for Alexia to arrive for their morning meeting.

After a short while, his secretary, Martha, buzzed to tell him that Miss Summers had arrived, and Jason told her to show Alexia into his office. He got up from his seat as the door opened. Alexia was directed into his office by his secretary, who then closed the door behind her.

"Good morning, Miss Summers. How are you today?" Jason asked as he walked over to Alexia and shook her hand. He could hardly keep his eyes off her because she looked very sexy again today in a low-cut knee-length black dress that was tight in all the right places and very high-heeled red shoes with a matching handbag.

"I'm very well, thank you, Jason, and how are you?"

"I'm very good, thank you. Please, take a seat. Would you like a drink?"

"No, thank you, Jason. Were you able to read through my file?" she replied, quickly bringing up the matter at hand and taking control of the conversation.

"I did indeed, Miss Summers, but I would like to hear from you in your own words exactly what happened. I am going to be asking you some personal questions. Please be very honest with your answers so I can get a clear picture of everything." Jason said in a calming voice.

It was not only for the case that Jason wanted her to be honest about everything, but he also wanted her to be explicit for his own personal reasons so that he could ascertain exactly which services she offered. Even though he knew it was wrong to think of Alexia in that way because she was his client, he did not care. Here was a very beautiful, sexy lady in his office, and even though he was there to defend her, should this go to trial, all he could think about was having sex with her. He was, in fact, besotted by her, more so than any other lady he had ever met, which was a very strange feeling for Jason as he was normally a very strong person.

However, this was not the time nor the place for that, and he needed to get on with the matter at hand.

'Besides, I can always pay her a personal visit once this is all over, considering my marriage is not going to be an issue now,' he thought to himself.

"Now, please take your time when answering, Miss Summers, and please be very specific about all the details. I need to know everything that happened."

"Actually, I will have that drink, please, if I may, Jason?" Alexia asked politely.

Jason asked her what she wanted, then poured a drink and put it on the desk next to her before finally sitting down.

"Ok, Miss Summers, from what you have said in your statement, it sounds like a good case of self-defense, but one thing is puzzling me."

"Do you not believe me, Jason?" Alexia asked quite sharply.

"Yes, I do, Miss Summers, but it's not about whether I believe you or not. It's whether the jury would believe you if this case were to go to trial, " he quickly responded.

"But is it not your job to convince the jury that I am telling the truth?" she asked in a firm tone of voice.

"Well, yes, it is, but it is not always that simple," Jason replied, taken aback by her obvious strength of character, which he was not used to.

"And why not?" Alexia asked in an almost frustrated way.

"Well, Miss Summers, please forgive me for being blunt, and I mean no disrespect, but some members of the jury may wonder why Mr. Morley, a respected businessman, would have the need to attack and rape an escort he was there to pay and have sex with anyway."

"I AM NOT AN ESCORT!" Alexia shouted out angrily as she slapped her hand on the desk.

"I am sorry, Miss Summers. I did not mean to offend you, but I am simply stating what is in your case file. I don't understand: you have a website offering your services, and you get paid to have sex with your clients. I am slightly confused, so can you please clarify that for me, Miss Summers?" Jason asked, beginning to wonder if there was more to this case than he first thought.

"First of all, Jason, I am **not** an escort; I am a mistress! Secondly, I do **not** have sex with my clients; I *fuck* them if I decide to," Alexia replied in a firm, commanding way.

"I am sorry, Miss Summers, but I still do not understand what the difference is between having sex with them and - excuse my language but, as you put it - fucking them. You are still getting paid for doing that, are you not?" Jason asked, trying to understand.

"I see that you know nothing about what I do, Jason, and please accept my apologies for snapping at you, but I do not like being called something I am not. Allow me to explain," she said in a polite manner.

"Please do, Miss Summers," Jason replied.

Alexia took a moment to compose herself, then took a couple of sips of her drink before taking a deep breath and continuing.

"Ok, Jason, as I said, I am not an escort; I am a mistress. An escort gets paid to pretty much do whatever the client wants, within reason, of course, and to have sex with them … I do not!"

"I see," Jason said as he continued to listen.

"As a mistress," continued Alexia, "I get paid to dominate men in any way I choose, but I do not get paid to have sex with them, toss them off or give them a blow job. However, sometimes a client may have been a good, obedient slave, deserving of a reward. If this is the case and if I am in the mood, then and only then, I may choose to get on top of them and fuck them or even give them a hand job. But it is my choice, not theirs."

"I see, Miss Summers, but I still do not understand the difference between having sex with them and, again, please forgive my bluntness, fucking them."

"Well, Jason, an escort has sex with her clients because it is a mutual thing between them. It is for both of them to enjoy and get pleasure from, although it is generally the client that gets the most pleasure. As a mistress, I do not give my slaves that right, and it is not a mutual thing. When I fuck them, it is solely for my pleasure, not theirs, and I do it for as long as it takes for me to be satisfied. A slave is there for my satisfaction, not their own, plain and simple! Do you now understand the difference between having sex with a client and fucking them, Jason?" Alexia asked him.

"Yes, I am beginning to," Jason replied, as his mind swayed for a brief moment to the domination role-plays he had with Selene and realized that there was more to domination than he had experienced before. Without thinking straight, which was not normal for Jason, he said to Alexia, "I need to explore this whole domination scene in much more detail with you to see how you dominate a man."

"Oh really, Jason?" Alexia asked, surprised.

"Oh, please forgive me, Miss Summers. I didn't mean it in that way; I simply meant that I need you to go into more detail so that I may understand it better," Jason replied, seemingly flustered.

Of course, there was a part of him that really did mean it in the way that he said it, as this was beginning to intrigue him, but he could not let Alexia know that.

"That's quite alright, Jason, I understand," Alexia replied, realizing that Jason was a bit out of his depth here.

"The members of the jury will probably not understand the difference between an escort and a mistress," continued Jason. "If this does go to trial, it will be my job to try and explain it to them, which is why I need to know all about your lifestyle, the domination, and how your clients are with you. Only with that knowledge can I be prepared enough to go into court, should this go that far, and explain it to the jury."

"I understand, Jason," Alexia said as she took another sip of her drink.

"Now, before we continue, Miss Summers, I would like to ask you a few straightforward questions. Do you always see your clients in your home?"

"No, Jason. I do not allow any of my clients to visit me at my home, nor do they even know where I live. I have another house with its own dungeon, which is where I meet all my clients."

"Oh, I see, and by dungeon, you mean … ?" Jason asked, becoming even more intrigued.

"I mean, it is where all the items I need for all kinds of domination are kept and where I administer any punishment my slaves deserve," Alexia said with a little smile on her face.

"I see, and do all your clients know exactly what services you offer?" he asked.

"Yes, they do, or at least up to now, they have done so. My website clearly states that I am a mistress, and I also tell any new clients during our initial conversation that I am a mistress and not just another escort," Alexia replied, feeling quite at ease.

"And did you tell Mr. Morley that you were a mistress and not an escort?" Jason asked.

"Yes, I did, and he kept saying that it was ok and that I was not the first mistress he had been with. It soon became clear that he had never met a real mistress before and the other ones he had been with were probably escorts offering domination role-plays," she replied.

"I see, and why did he attack you then?" he asked, trying to find out if there was more to her story.

"Things began well enough, but it soon got to the stage where he just wanted me to give him pleasure and have sex with him. I reminded him that I was a mistress and not an escort, but he got angry and said that other mistresses had done these things to him, and so should I. Again, I explained to him I was not an escort, and I was not prepared to do what he wanted, and that is when he began to attack me," Alexia replied, unhappy that she had to relive that moment.

"I now understand the reason behind the attack. He wanted something that was not on offer, and he would not take no for an answer, does that sound about right?" he asked her.

"Yes, Jason, that is exactly what happened," Alexia replied in a relieved tone of voice.

"Very well, Miss Summers, but for me to fully understand what services you offer and, more importantly, exactly what happens between you and your clients, I would need to see where all this takes place. Perhaps I can visit this house with the dungeon to see for myself?" he asked her politely and with a little smile.

"Yes, of course, you may, Jason, but the forensics team has only just finished looking over the house, and I have this morning arranged for the carpet to be changed on Wednesday due to the blood. I will call you once that is done," Alexia replied, returning the smile.

"That's perfect, and we can continue this conversation while we are there. Here is my business card with my office number, and I will write my cell number on here, just in case you need me outside of office hours," Jason said as he began to write down his number.

"Very well, Jason, I shall speak to you soon then. Goodbye for now," Alexia said as she got up and began to walk towards the door, pausing for a moment so that Jason could open the door for her.

"Thank you, Jason," she said as she walked out of the office and headed toward the elevator.

"You are welcome, Miss Summers," Jason replied as he stared at her slim sexy figure as she walked away from him.

Chapter Eleven

As Alexia left the building and made her way home, she realized that Jason was intrigued and perhaps even interested in her. It was almost as if he lusted after her, and this brought a wry smile to her face.

Alexia had been a mistress for a very long time. She had a way about her that made most men want to worship the ground she walked on, and she loved every minute of it. She was able to make them obey her every whim without even having to try, and she truly enjoyed the power this gave her. She knew exactly what to say to them and how to say it. More importantly, she knew how to command respect from them, and she could have them eating out of the palm of her hand if she wanted to. Oh sure, there was the odd person who had no idea about the whole mistress and slave relationship and who just wanted sex as though she was an escort. However, she soon put them in their place, and in general, she had no problems with men's behavior.

Alexia was not a mistress for the money, as she was a wealthy woman in her own right. Veronica had left her a small fortune, but she had also made plenty of money herself from this lifestyle in the past. Additionally, she had written a number of books on the subject that made her a lot of profit. She still had the lavish detached home on Long Island and the country home in England that was left to her by Veronica, plus her house in Manhattan that she saw her clients in.

She really did not need to do this for a living. In fact, she only did it because it gave her pleasure to treat men in this way and watch them grovel before her and obey her every command. For some reason, men just loved being treated this way by her, and they were more than happy to pay her for the privilege of being her playthings. She knew exactly when to be stern with them, when to punish them, when to be gentle with them and when they deserved it, to reward them.

Her clients, or slaves as she preferred to think of them, were mainly wealthy gents, businessmen, celebrities, politicians, a few high-profile gentlemen from within the legal system, and even a few very well-known ladies. Adding Jason to that list appealed to her as she was attracted to him and would love to get him into her dungeon so that she may use him for her own pleasure.

Of course, he was her lawyer, but she noticed the way Jason had looked at her during their time together in his office, and she suspected that it would take hardly any effort on her part to entice him into her little world, although she would need to put this to the test. She knew that she would have to train him up slowly, as it was clear he did not truly understand too much about the reality of this lifestyle, but the training of her slaves was something she excelled in.

Alexia was experienced enough with men, and with her psychological background, she was able to know what kind of a man someone was just by spending a short time with them. She could tell that Jason was a strong-willed, confident man and had a commanding presence about him, but she also knew that he would be no match for her. In fact, the stronger and more dominant a man was, the more she enjoyed the challenge of breaking them down and turning them into her playthings, with Jason being no exception. She suspected that he would not be as easy to train as most of her slaves, but this gave her an even bigger excitement as she looked forward to the challenge with great anticipation.

She was more than confident in her abilities, and the fact that she noticed he could hardly take his eyes off her was the telling factor in whether he would become obedient or not. Now all she had to do was play her part, like she had done countless times before, and watch as Jason would fall prey to her charms and dominant nature, just like the hundreds of slaves before him had done.

On Wednesday, after the carpet had been fitted, she thought she would test the water to see just how compliant Jason would actually be by inviting him over. During the course of the evening, Alexia would know if, indeed, Jason was the kind of person that could become one of her slaves or not.

Alexia picked up the phone, dialed Jason's number, and after a few rings, the call was answered by his secretary, Martha.

"Good afternoon, Mr. Carini's office. May I help you?"

"Good afternoon, this is Alexia Summers. May I speak with Mr. Carini, please?"

"I shall check if he is available. Hold the line, please," Martha replied as she called through to Jason to inform him that Alexia was on the line.

Jason picked up the phone and said, "Good afternoon, Miss Summers. How are you?"

"Very well, thank you, Jason. I am calling to arrange for you to visit me at my house as we agreed."

"Wonderful; when are you available?" Jason asked, his heart beating quicker than normal.

"Unfortunately, I am very busy during the daytime and also over the next few days, so I was wondering whether you would be free to come round this evening, Jason?" Alexia asked him.

Jason paused for a minute as Alexia had taken him by surprise. He quickly thought to himself, 'What excuse would I give to Lydia, and what would she think?'

Lydia had always wanted to know exactly where Jason was, who he was with, and what he was doing, even though she did not afford him the same courtesy.

Of course, the reason Lydia wanted to know this was so that they would not end up bumping into each other when she was out with her lover. But then he thought to himself, 'Why should I give a damn what she thinks? After all, it is her that is cheating!'

"Yes, that would be fine, Miss Summers. Can you let me have the address, please?" Jason replied.

Alexia gave Jason the address to the house and they arranged the time to meet, before saying their goodbyes.

Jason was overjoyed at the prospect of going to see Alexia at her house and, more importantly, her dungeon, as he was very curious about what was there. It was evident that this would be unlike anything he had experienced with Selene in the past and the thought of it alone was enough to get him excited. Now he had to call his wife and tell her that he would not be home till late this evening, but he wondered what he could say so as not to make her suspicious. He could not say he was working late in case she decided to call him at the office, plus the fact that she knew his co-workers and employers would make it too risky.

After giving the matter some thought, Jason called Lydia and told her that he had bumped into an old friend from when he was at Harvard and that he would be going out for a drink with him. Lydia, who had already arranged to meet her lover, said she did not mind if Jason went out as she was going to go out for a drink with her so-called friend, Valerie. Besides, while Jason was having a drink with his friend, there would be no chance that they would bump into each other as she was meeting her lover in a plush hotel on Fifth Avenue.

'Well, that went easier than expected,' Jason thought, but he knew that as long as Lydia was meeting her lover, it would not have been a problem for him not to be at home tonight. His thoughts now turned to the evening ahead, and he could only dream of what could happen when he met with Alexia later that night.

He let out a big sigh as his thoughts turned back to reality because he knew that the chances of anything happening were very slim. Sure he could approach her as a client would, but the fact that he was her lawyer could make things very difficult, and he could not be sure exactly how she would react.

He was almost certain that it would not be a problem because, after all, this is what she did with her clients, but what if Alexia thought that he would not be focused enough on the case if he was a client of hers? If this was the case, she might complain to his superiors. Jason could not only find himself out of a job but also even disbarred for his unethical behavior. He had worked far too hard for a very long time to get to where he was in his life to let something like this destroy it. Although he would really enjoy being able to have a session of some kind with Alexia and to find out more about her services, he knew it would be a step too far for him to do so.

He was simply not prepared to risk everything he had built up for a bit of fun, and of course, there was nothing to stop him from seeing her once this case was all over. 'Yes, perhaps it would be wise to wait until she is no longer my client before approaching her,' he thought to himself.

However, he could not get the thought of this sexy beauty dominating him out of his mind, and even in his wildest dreams, he could not begin to imagine that Alexia had already set her sights on making him her next sex slave.

Chapter Twelve

The next few hours would feel like an eternity for Jason as he waited for the time to pass so he could go to Alexia's house, but he could not take his mind off the fact that she was a mistress. Just the thought of her dominating him was very hard for him to put aside, even though he had already decided that he would not approach her in that way until she was no longer a client of his. However, it was still very difficult for him not to think about her in that way.

He did as much as he could to keep himself busy enough to avoid thinking of her, but it was almost impossible. He could not understand why he felt this way about someone he hardly knew and wondered if it was in some way connected to his wife having an affair. Perhaps this was his way of playing the same game as his wife. Maybe subconsciously, he did not need to remain loyal to her anymore because of her infidelity. Whatever the reason, he realized that it was almost time for him to leave work and make his way to Alexia's house, so he began to get ready.

In the meantime, Alexia was taking her time getting herself ready, not only to welcome Jason to her house but also hoping to entice him into her world of domination. She had a long soak with bath oils so that her skin felt really soft to the touch. She then styled her hair, applied her makeup, and put on her lipstick before painting her toe and fingernails in a bright red glossy varnish that matched her lipstick color. She wore sheer black seamed stockings with a suspender belt, a black lace bra, and an above-the-knee-low-cut-red dress that matched her lipstick and showed off her cleavage, finished off with very high black stiletto shoes.

She was dressed to impress in the most seductive way anyone could ever possibly imagine, and she was sure that Jason would be unable to take his eyes off her, which is exactly what she had planned. She had no intention of actually allowing anything major to happen tonight. Instead, she wanted to see Jason's reaction to the way she was dressed, just to see if he was indeed interested and perhaps for her to tease him a little.

This was how she would treat any new prospective slave, and Jason would be no different from the others. 'Make them really want it, to the point of no return, before you give it to them,' was her motto when training any new slaves.

Alexia poured herself a drink while she waited for Jason to arrive, and before long, she heard the doorbell ring. She did not go to the door straight away but instead waited for

Jason to ring the bell a second time before going to open it for him. This was all part of teaching her slaves patience and that they had to wait until she was ready to do something and not them.

She opened the door and welcomed Jason in. After exchanging pleasantries, she showed him into the living room. 'This doesn't look much like a dungeon,' Jason thought. It was just like a normal house and did not look as he had expected.

"Please, sit down, Jason. Would you like a drink?" Alexia asked with a smile.

"Yes, please. I would love a whiskey if you have any," he replied, smiling back at her while his eyes explored her from top to bottom.

"Of course I do, Jason," Alexia said as she poured them both a drink. She then placed his drink on a little coffee table in front of him, making sure that she bent forward as much as she could so that his eyes were level with her cleavage.

Jason could not help himself, and he looked directly at her breasts which were being pushed up by the bra she was wearing. He continued to look at them as she began to straighten up before heading towards the couch directly opposite Jason. She sat down on the couch and placed one leg slightly over the other one, making sure that she sat at an angle so that Jason could see the top of her stocking through the split on the side of her dress. Jason did indeed notice this, much to the delight of Alexia, who saw him looking at the top of her thigh. Before he knew what was happening, he began to become aroused.

"Is everything all right, Jason?" Alexia asked him.

"Umm, yes, yes, it is," Jason replied as he quickly took his gaze away from her thigh and looked into her eyes.

"So, this is where it all happened, is it?" he asked, trying very hard to take his mind off Alexia's stockinged legs and busty cleavage.

"Yes, we had only been here for a short while before he began to get angry that he was not getting what he wanted," Alexia replied.

"Ok, and can you tell me exactly what happened then, please?" Jason asked her.

Alexia took a sip of her drink and then began to tell Jason what had transpired that day. She told him that Simon Morley had arrived at her house as expected, and after inviting him in, they sat down and began to talk for a bit. Alexia then spent a few minutes trying to explain to Simon exactly what she did, but he kept interrupting her, saying that he had done this many times before and he knew what would happen.

Alexia knew straight away that he did not know as much as he thought he knew regarding domination, but it was going to be her pleasure to teach him some respect because, after all, no one interrupts the mistress!

The session got underway in the living room because she did not take any slaves into her dungeon on their first visit, and certainly not until she knew they were ready for that. She had a large cabinet against one of the walls in which she kept a few items such as a crop, whip, handcuffs, and vibrators, to name but a few things, which she would use when dominating her slaves in the living room.

The dungeon was for the heavier type of domination, such as bondage, full feminization, and punishment which she sometimes administered to her slaves, among many other things. But she would quite often use the living room and bedroom for things such as spanking, light humiliation, and of course, her favorite one, sexual domination.

This was what she had planned for this evening with Simon. It all began according to plan, with her taking the payment first from Simon, which was usual. However, after the session had been going on for a while Simon began to get frustrated and angry that she was getting all the pleasure and not giving him any.

He told her that it was his turn for some fun and that he wanted her to give him a blowjob and then have sex. Alexia obviously refused and again tried to explain to him that she was a mistress and not an escort that did whatever the client wanted. Simon told her that he had paid her for sex, and he expected to get it.

Alexia then told Simon to leave because she was not an escort and would not be told what she was going to do in her own home. However, after a few minutes of arguing and insulting Alexia, Simon decided he was not going to leave without getting what he came for. He slapped Alexia, grabbed her by the hair with one hand, then grasped and ripped the top of her dress with the other one and tried to force himself on her.

It was at this moment that Alexia scratched Simon's face. She broke free, ran to the desk where she kept the gun, took it out of the drawer, and as Simon rushed at her again, she fired and ultimately killed him.

Jason listened in silence while Alexia told him what had happened. When she had finished, he said, "Well, Miss Summers, you certainly acted in self-defense and used justified force to defend yourself. However, the fact remains that the police only have your side of the story and may or may not decide to take further action."

"But this is what happened," Alexia said in an angry voice.

"Yes, I know, Miss Summers, but the police may not just take your word for it. But don't worry too much because, if this does go to trial, it will be my job to try and convince the jury that you are telling the truth," Jason said in a calming voice.

"Thank you, Jason. I shall put my faith in you," she replied as she looked him in the eyes.

"By the way, Miss Summers, how much do your clients pay you or, more importantly, how much did Mr. Morley pay you for your services?" Jason asked.

"Well, Jason, that depends on how long I spend with them and who they are. However, I do have a select few clients who I consider my own personal slaves, so I regularly see them at my home rather than here for my own reasons, but I do not charge them for my services. As for Simon, he paid me $1,000."

"I see, Miss Summers. Now, in order for me to fully understand exactly what you do and how things work, would you mind showing me around the house, the dungeon, and perhaps go into more detail about what exactly it is that you do with your clients?" Jason asked.

Although he wanted to know this for the case, he also wanted the information for his own personal benefit in case he decided to pay her a visit at some stage in the future. Plus, he wanted to know what he could expect to get from her as a client.

"Yes, of course, Jason, but not the dungeon, as I have a slave in there right now," Alexia said as she got up from the couch, walked over to the large cabinet, and asked Jason to go with her. Alexia opened the door to the cabinet, and Jason could hardly believe his eyes when he saw all the items in there. There was a whip, paddle, crop, handcuffs, various vibrators, dildos and strap-ons, gimp masks, blindfolds and a lot of other sexual items, most of which could only be used to cause pain.

"What do you think of my collection, Jason?" Alexia asked him.

Jason turned and looked at her without being able to say a word for a short while, and then finally, he replied, "Well, I, umm, I don't know what to say, Mistress – sorry, I mean, Miss Summers," Jason blurted out.

"No, Jason. You were correct the first time. In here, I **am** the mistress. I expect anyone I bring here to remember that," Alexia snapped.

"I shall remember that in the future," Jason replied both nervously and excitedly.

"Good, now let's go back and sit down Jason," Alexia commanded, and Jason followed her where they both sat back down, taking a sip of their drinks.

Alexia again sat with one leg crossed over the other one, and then Jason asked her, "So what is the difference between this room and this dungeon of yours?"

"Only my most loyal and obedient slaves are allowed to enter my dungeon. The ones I know can handle whatever I choose to happen in there and who have every confidence in me. It would take a long time for anyone new to be allowed to be dominated in my dungeon, and they would first have to get used to the idea of being my slave. They would have to be totally under my command before I would ever consider taking anyone new in there," she said to Jason, sensing that he was curious about himself.

"I see, Miss Summers, and how long does it usually take for you to consider taking someone new into your dungeon?" he asked.

"Well, it takes as long as it takes. First of all, I have to be sure that the person is suitable. To do that, I dominate any new slaves either in here or in the bedroom upstairs. Once I have their obedience, and I feel they are ready to go into my dungeon, then and only then will I take them there." Alexia replied as she slowly ran her hand over her thigh and ever so slightly raised the split of her dress so that now there were a few inches of her naked thigh visible above the stocking top.

"And how exactly would you dominate someone in here?" Jason asked excitedly as he was now very aroused.

"Why, Jason, is that a professional question or do I sense that you are becoming quite excited and fascinated by my little world?" Alexia asked as she looked him straight in his eyes.

"Oh, I am sorry, Miss Summers, I did not mean ..."

"Stop, Jason," Alexia demanded in a stern voice, not allowing Jason to finish his sentence. "I am not a fool, and I can tell when someone is interested because I have been doing this for a very long time. If we are going to continue this conversation, then I need to know that you are going to be completely truthful with me."

"Of course, Miss Summers, I am sorry," Jason replied, feeling extremely horny.

"I have seen how you have been looking at me, so again, I ask you, was that a professional question or a personal one?" she asked in a demanding way.

"Perhaps a little bit of both, Miss Summers," Jason replied nervously.

"Yes, I thought that was the case, Jason, so why not be honest with me?"

'Wow, can this really be happening?' Jason thought to himself. Was this sexy lady really making this first move? Could he really be about to get what he had wanted all along, he wondered.

'Should I really let go now and let this happen, or should I wait until the case is over?' he asked himself in his mind. His heart was saying to let things happen and to hell with the fact that he was her lawyer, but his head was saying the opposite, thinking about his career with Langley & Foster. He thought for a brief moment before speaking.

"Ok, Miss Summers, I am sorry for not being honest, but yes, it probably was more of a personal question. However, I feel it may be better to wait until after this case is over before anything happens just in case."

"Oh, my dear Jason, you really have no idea, do you? *I* decide *if* and ***when*** anything is going to happen, ***not*** you. If *I* want something to happen right now, then it **will**, and if **I** want to wait, then we will wait. It is as simple as that, really: you can do **exactly** as I say, or you can leave - the choice is yours. But that is the **only** choice you will ever have in my world as far as we are concerned. Do I make myself perfectly clear?"

"Yes, Miss Summers," Jason replied in a very low voice, unsure of how he should now behave.

"**Mistress**, you will call me **Mistress** from now on. Is that understood, Jason?"

"Yes, Mistress," Jason replied in a sheepish voice, not really knowing how it all became so intense all of a sudden. He was not complaining, though, as he was now more aroused than he can remember being in a very long time.

"Good, now tell me if you have ever had any past experiences in domination, Jason," Alexia said. She sat further back on the couch, her dress now lifting slightly higher up than before, revealing even more of her thigh for him to see.

Jason began to tell Alexia about Selene and what they had done, going into detail about their so-called domination role-plays. Once he had finished, Alexia told him that what he considered to be domination was, in fact, nothing of the sort. She explained that there was a big difference between a domination role-play, where the client pretty much gets what he wants, and her style of domination, where the mistress gets whatever she wants. She told him that in her world, any slave of hers would have to be thankful for any pleasure she decided to give them. They should not expect anything other than being there to please her. She told him that he would have to forget what he thought he knew about domination and learn from the very beginning.

Jason was fascinated by this and by Alexia herself and agreed to do whatever she wanted.

"Do you like my legs, Jason?" Alexia asked while stretching one leg out in front of the other and running her hands up the full length of her leg, lifting up her dress even more as her hands neared the top of her thighs.

"Yes, Mistress," Jason replied, unable to take his eyes off them.

"Good, well, come here and kneel by my feet," she commanded, and Jason did exactly what he was told.

There was a part of him that was trying so hard to resist, not only because he was her lawyer but also because this went against his dominant nature, but he found himself unable to refuse.

"Now, start at my feet and slowly kiss all the way up to my thighs, kissing both legs at the same time," she told him.

Of course, Jason obeyed, thinking to himself that he must be dreaming and that he was going to wake up at any minute. He had kissed both legs all the way up to her stocking tops. Now, from the position he was in, he could see her lacy panties while kissing her thighs just above her stockings. He thought that it would be a pleasure to be told to lick her between her legs.

"That's far enough; now stand up in front of me," Alexia commanded.

Jason did as he was told. As he stood in front of her with his stiff cock creating a bulge in his pants, which was about the same height as her face. He wondered if he was going to get some pleasure now. 'This is not so different from the days with Selene,' he thought to himself, and he wondered what would be so different with Alexia.

"Did you enjoy kissing my legs, and were you hoping to go a bit further?" Alexia asked.

"Yes, Mistress," Jason replied as he felt Alexia's hand push against the bulge in his pants.

"Oh, yes, you did, didn't you, Jason?" Alexia said as she squeezed his stiff cock through his pants a few times. "I love it when my slaves get excited at pleasuring me," she continued.

With that said, she got up and told Jason that his training was over for the night and it was time for him to leave as she was going home. She told him that if he had any questions regarding the case, he could call her tomorrow; otherwise, she would call him when she was ready to continue with his training.

Jason, unsure of what had just happened, asked if there was anything wrong and why she had stopped. Alexia reminded him that she was the one who was in control and that things would happen as and when she wanted them to happen. His duty was to obey without question; otherwise, he could forget the whole thing and go back to his Selene.

"Yes, Mistress," Jason replied as he began to gather up his things. He said goodbye, got in his car, and began to drive home.

While driving, he was thinking about everything that had just happened, and he still had an erection. The fact that Alexia had suddenly stopped just like that both confused him and excited him at the same time. 'This had never happened with Selene,' he thought to himself, but he had also never felt so excited either. All he could think about was kissing Alexia's legs and her hand on the front of his pants, squeezing his cock, which pulsated even more in his briefs now.

Oh, this was too much for him to bear. It would be at least thirty minutes before he would be home, so he decided to pull over in one of the side roads. He then unzipped his pants, reached in and took out his very hard cock and began to play with himself until he climaxed.

He could not believe that as a mature man, he had just played with himself like a teenager would do, and this excited him even more now, much more.

He could also not remember the last time he had such a climax, and even after he had finished, he still had a hard cock. He could only imagine just how wonderful things could be in the future and how good Alexia could make him feel, especially if a little thing like what just happened could get him so aroused. He could not wait until their next session. He used a tissue to wipe the cum from his hand, before driving off again.

Chapter Thirteen

Jason finally reached home, and as expected, Lydia was not home yet. He went into the living room, poured himself a large whiskey, sat down on the couch, and began to relive what had happened earlier that evening. He could still not believe that this sexy beauty had instigated it all and that it was almost too good to be true. Again he found himself surprised at the way Alexia suddenly stopped it all and once more found himself thinking about his sessions with Selene and how different things were between the two women.

With Selene, he knew that he would get the domination, but he would also get the sex and anything else he wanted. However, it seemed evident that he would get no such thing with Alexia, at least not unless she wanted it to happen. He would get very excited with Selene and have very good orgasms with her, but to have such an amazing one while relieving himself after only a short session with Alexia was mind-blowing for him. How could he get so excited when so little happened, he wondered? He almost felt like he was a virgin having sex for the first time.

Jason sat on the couch for the next hour, having a drink and thinking about every detail of what had happened earlier. It did not take long for him to get aroused again. 'Oh, I could sure do with a fuck right now,' he thought to himself, but that was not an option he had.

At that moment, he heard Lydia's car pulling into the drive. He knew that his wife would be coming in soon enough, but would she notice the bulge of his hard cock through his pants? Should he quickly go and jump into a cold shower, he wondered. Jason was suddenly struck with the urge to grab Lydia as she walked into the living room, to bend her over and take her right there.

He could not believe that he just had that thought, as she had obviously just had sex with her lover. However, he could not help the fact that he still found her very sexy. On another occasion, he might very well have acted out that thought, as he was feeling very horny indeed right now.

Before he could make a decision about going upstairs, Lydia opened the door and walked in with a smile on her face, put her bag down on the floor, the keys on the stand, and simply said, "Hi, honey."

"Hi, yourself. Did you have a nice evening?" he asked her, staying seated with one leg over the other so that she would not notice the bulge he had.

"Yes, it was good, thanks; we had a good laugh and a couple of drinks. How was your evening, honey?" she asked, without really caring if he had a good time or not.

"Oh, it was ok," Jason replied, thinking to himself, 'If only you knew.'

Again, Jason had this urge to grab Lydia and fuck her, especially the way she was dressed. Lydia always took pride in the way she looked and dressed, with tonight being no exception. She was sexily dressed in an above-the-knee skirt with a semi-see-through blouse, high heels, perfect hair, and makeup, and she looked like she had just come back from a photoshoot.

One of the things that Jason always found hot about Lydia was that she always wore stockings, never tights, always stockings, and tonight was no different. 'She is certainly looking hot,' Jason thought to himself. If only she had not been with her lover, he would most certainly have had some fun tonight and would not take no for an answer, especially as he was feeling so turned on.

"Why are you looking at me like that, Jason?" Lydia suddenly asked.

"Oh, I was thinking you look so hot tonight," he replied without actually thinking about what he had just said. 'What are you doing, you idiot?' he thought to himself.

"Why, thank you, Jason," Lydia replied. "Could you pour me a drink, please?" she asked.

'Oh great,' he thought to himself, knowing that he would have to get up to do so. He tried to get up so that his bulge would not show.

"What would you like to drink, dear?" He asked as he walked over to the cabinet where the drinks were kept.

"I'd like a large glass of red wine, please," Lydia said as she took off her earrings, placed them on the table, and then sat down on the couch.

Jason had poured her wine and now had to take it to Lydia, but he would be walking directly towards her. 'Damn,' he thought to himself, 'What was he going to do now?' He still had an erection, and he was sure that Lydia would notice how aroused he was and would surely ask questions. He wondered why he did not run straight to the shower as soon as he heard her car pulling up.

Normally, she would go upstairs, get changed and take off her makeup as soon as she got home from a night out, but tonight it seemed as if she had decided to sit and have a drink with him. Oh well, there was nothing Jason could do now and just turned around and began to walk towards Lydia quickly and simply hoped that she would not notice.

"Come, sit down and tell me about your evening," Lydia said, tapping the couch with her hand as if to indicate for Jason to sit next to her. As Jason neared, he noticed that she was staring at his crotch with a surprised look on her face. As he put the drink on the table, she reached out and put her hand on the bulge in his pants.

"Jason, what have you been doing or thinking about?" she asked, surprised.

"You look so sexy tonight, darling; it just got me excited," he replied as he sat down beside her. 'What an idiot,' he thought to himself again. 'What a stupid thing to say; what was I thinking?'

But that's just it; he wasn't thinking, at least not with the right head. Sure he was feeling horny, he wanted sex, and yes, Lydia was looking very hot and sensual tonight. However, at least the saving grace was that he knew that nothing was going to happen as she had just been with her lover.

He could not believe how strange and unlike himself he was feeling, and it was all due to that short time he spent with Alexia. No woman had ever had this effect on him in his entire life, and it was a very weird feeling for him to understand. This normally confident, dominant man was anything but at the moment, and it was a feeling he was not used to. For most of his life, he had been in control of every aspect of his it and his feelings, but now, somehow, he was feeling so confused.

"Why, Jason, do you really find me so irresistible tonight?" Lydia asked with a sparkle in her eyes.

"Yes, I do," he replied, wishing he had just kept his mouth shut. Well, it's not like he could say anything else; otherwise, he would have a lot of explaining to do. He suddenly had a terrible thought that she may actually want to have sex with him. Although he was feeling horny and wanted a fuck, the thought that she had been with someone else disgusted him. What was he going to do now if she really did want to do something, he wondered to himself, terrified at the prospect that she may want sex.

Without knowing the truth, Lydia was flattered that he would get so aroused just by looking at her and began to get quite turned on herself now. 'So what if I had sex with another man less than a couple of hours ago?' she thought to herself. 'It's not like Jason knows about it, and besides, I had a shower before leaving the hotel.'

She reached out her hand and ran it up Jason's thigh before placing it on his crotch and squeezing his hard cock. Jason did not know what to do now. Sure, it felt so good, her doing this, and normally he would jump at the chance of some fun, but she had just been with another man, and he could not get that thought out of his mind. If he turned her down, there would really be some questions to answer, but the thought of doing anything with her right now was sickening.

He and Lydia had not had made love for a few weeks, and it was the first time he had found himself in this position or had even dared to think about sex with her since finding out about her affair. 'What am I going to do?' he wondered to himself. Yes, he was feeling horny and wanted sex, but he could not bear the thought that another man had been inside her tonight. He could not believe how he was feeling at this very moment; on the one hand, he wanted so badly to fuck her, but on the other hand, he was put off doing anything due to her being out with her lover.

He was both excited and disgusted at the situation he found himself in. Lydia was not making things any easier as she was now gently rubbing his cock through his pants. She leaned forward and began to kiss Jason, and without really having much of a choice about it, he kissed her back.

'Oh my god,' he thought, as it just dawned on him that she must have had her lover's cock in her mouth earlier, and he was now kissing her. He suddenly felt sick and he stopped kissing her, but as he pulled away, she unzipped his pants and put her hand inside and began to wank him.

Jason could not believe what was happening or the fact that he was actually doing this. He was now so excited that he did not care anymore and forgot about the disgust he just felt. Lydia's hand was now moving at a much faster pace, and Jason just tilted his head back and allowed himself to enjoy it.

She now bent down and took Jason's stiff cock in her mouth, licking and sucking him, and within a couple of minutes, Jason decided that he was going to get the fuck he so wanted. He grabbed her hair, lifted her head, and told her to get up, then he bent her over so that her knees were on the couch, and he stood behind her. He lifted up her skirt, pulled down her panties, spread her legs and pushed his throbbing cock inside her, moving his hips fast and hard.

He suddenly realized that this was only happening because of Alexia and what had happened earlier that night. He was now imagining that he was indeed fucking Alexia instead of his wife.

Lydia was also deep in thought, thinking that she had just had sex with two men within a couple of hours of each other. It turned her on so much that she had multiple orgasms within a few minutes of Jason fucking her. Jason, hearing his wife moan and groan, excited him even more, especially as he imagined it was Alexia that had just come. Within a minute, he, too, began to come, thrusting himself deep inside her again and again until he shot out every last drop of cum.

After they had finished, they both sat back down on the couch for a short while and continued to drink their wine without talking about what had just transpired. They then went upstairs, had a shower, and went to bed, automatically turning their backs on each other, deep in their own thoughts. Lydia was ecstatic about the fact that she had been with two men that evening, and Jason was happy to have finally had the sex he was lusting for.

Chapter Fourteen

After a good night's sleep, Jason woke up before Lydia and lay there thinking about what had happened the night before. He again felt sick at the thought that another man had been with his wife before him and so got up, had a long shower, then said to himself that he had to avoid this from ever happening again. He went back into the bedroom where, by now, Lydia was awake.

As he got dressed, she said, "I may have lunch with Valerie today, honey. What have you got planned?" She simply wanted to know where he was likely to be to ensure she was nowhere near there.

"Oh, I have a very busy day today, so I'm going to be stuck in the office all day," Jason replied, thinking to himself that at least everything seemed to be back to normal, and hopefully, there would not be a repeat performance tonight.

He then kissed his wife goodbye and left the house to go to work. He spent the whole time while driving to work thinking about Alexia and wondered how to proceed from here. Should he contact her, or should he wait for her to contact him?

There was nothing more to discuss about the case as he did not know if this case would even go to trial, so the only reason he would contact her would be for his own personal agenda. However, he did not want to appear too pushy, plus he did not even know how Alexia would react to him calling her, as she made it clear that she was going to be in charge. This was all very new to Jason, and he found it very difficult to come to terms that he was not in control of this situation.

A few days had passed by, and Jason had not heard from Alexia. He wanted to speak to her so much, but he remembered that she told him only to call her if he had any questions regarding the case. He then decided to review all the information he had to see if he could come up with any new queries.

However, he could not think of anything else to ask her, so he decided it was now time for him to try and find out what the situation was regarding what the district attorney would do. He asked his friend Marcus to telephone one of his friends in the police force, asking him to look into it.

After a couple of days had passed, Marcus told Jason that the police had passed all the information they had onto the DA's office, and it was now in their hands. Wondering what the DA would do about it, he asked Marcus to try and find out what was going on as soon as possible and report back to him.

* * *

Marcus King was an ex-police officer, a detective no less. On a late summer's evening five years ago, during a few days of vacation from work, he had accidentally hit and killed a pedestrian with his car while under the influence of alcohol. As a detective, he knew only too well what the consequences would be, and rather than face what was to come, he went to his friend Jason's house. He left the car in an adjoining road, walked the rest of the way, then told him what had happened and asked Jason for help.

After a few hours of discussion regarding the best way to handle this situation, they decided to drive the car somewhere remote and leave it there. They would then go back to Jason's house, where they would both say they spent the night there having a drink together and that the car had been stolen.

The next morning, Marcus made the call to the police, telling them that his car had been stolen from outside Jason's house. Two days later, when Marcus was back at work after his vacation was over, he was told that his car had been found damaged, with a few specks of blood on the bonnet and a cracked windscreen.

Marcus continued with his work as normal until a few days later, when he was informed that the bloodstains found on his car were actually a DNA match for a hit and run victim that was found a few days previously. He was also informed that his car was now evidence not just in a case of car theft but also for a murder investigation, and he would not be able to get it back or indeed repair the damage to it. This was not the news Marcus wanted to hear, and he had not even realized that there was any blood on his car on the night of the accident.

Over the next few weeks, Marcus was questioned a number of times, as was Jason, about what happened the night the car had been stolen and if they had seen or heard anything. Of course, they both said no as they were inside having a drink and watching television.

As time went on and due to the fact that forensics could only find traces of Marcus in the car and nothing of the so-called car thieves, a couple of the detectives involved with the case had suspicions regarding whether they were both telling the truth. Many people knew that Marcus liked a drink at times; however, nothing could be proved as Jason, a lawyer no less, was Marcus's alibi for that night.

As the next couple of months passed, Marcus, who felt guilty about what had happened, realized that some of his colleagues were being a bit different with him. It seemed that they may even have suspected he was actually involved with the hit and run.

One day, he finally decided that it was time for him to leave the police department, and after resigning, he began his own business as a private investigator. As such, Jason would often use Marcus to help him with some of his cases, but they decided that it would be best if not too many people knew about that, just in case anyone began to ask questions.

Marcus still had many friends and contacts both within the police force and also outside of it, which he had made over the years, and they came in handy for helping Jason out as and when he needed it. After all, Marcus owed everything to Jason and knew that without his help, he would not be living the life he had been doing so for the past few years. Instead, he would probably be in prison on a manslaughter charge at the very least.

Marcus, who still had friends within the DA's office, found out and reported back to Jason that no decision had been made yet regarding Alexia's case. They were due to meet with the detectives in charge to review all the information and then decide whether or not to charge her with manslaughter.

Even though it seemed like it was self-defense, they only had her word for it, and the fact that they saw her as just an escort, they wondered if things really did happen the way she said they did.

Jason was not happy about this news, but he could not yet say anything to anyone as he was not meant to know anything about this. Instead, he had to wait until they had made their decision and see if, indeed, they would ask the police to arrest and charge Alexia. At least he had a heads-up for now and could start planning what his next move was going to be, just in case she was indeed arrested and charged.

He told Marcus to keep his ears open about any information regarding Alexia through his contacts and inform him of anything he found out. Jason was unsure about what he should now do and wondered if he should contact Alexia with this news or should he wait till he knew for certain what was going to happen.

If she had been just another client, he would have waited, but due to what had happened between them, he wanted to tell her but was not sure if that was for the best.

'What if she then tells someone about this?' he wondered.

After all, his boss had been asked by one of their very influential clients to look into this and to take good care of Alexia, so she must have told someone else what happened to her that evening.

'This person must be a client of hers,' Jason thought to himself while pondering what he should do next. During the course of the day, he picked up the phone to call Alexia at least half a dozen times, but then put it back down again.

For the first time in as long as he could remember, he was stuck and did not know what to do for the best, which was such a strange feeling for him. He knew he should not call her with this information. However, as he had not seen her for a few days, he so wanted to call her for personal reasons, but he knew it was not the right thing to do. He knew that if he did, in fact, call her, he would end up telling her what he had found out. This could result in her telling this influential client, whoever he was, and in turn, they could tell Mr. Langley, who would then want to know just how Jason knew all about what the DA and police were doing, which could and probably would cause problems. Jason decided that, for now, he would not call Alexia, and as it was now time for him to go home anyway, he decided that he would think about what the next move would be during the course of the evening.

Jason went home to the usual routine: having dinner with Lydia, chatting, and watching some television together for a while before she would get up and spend the rest of the evening on the phone with various people. This suited Jason because while she was on the phone, he could think about Alexia and how to deal with the situation at hand. Of course, the best thing was that while Lydia was busy, there was no chance of them having sex again.

Chapter Fifteen

The rest of the week had passed quite slowly for Jason as he had not spoken to Alexia in what seemed like ages, but it was now finally Friday evening. After having had dinner with Lydia, followed by the usual chit-chat, it was time for their nightly ritual. Jason would settle down in front of the television while his wife would be on the phone in the adjoining room for a good part of the evening.

A short while later, his cell phone rang, and he answered it with a quick hello as he would normally do.

"Good evening, Jason. This is Alexia. How are you?" came her reply.

"Miss Summers," Jason replied in a surprised voice. "I'm fine, thank you. How are you? Is everything ok?"

"Yes, it is, Jason. I have not heard from you in a while, and I thought I would call and see how everything is. Is that a problem?" she asked in quite a forceful way.

"No, not at all, Miss Summers," he said, pausing for a moment before continuing. "I do not have any new information about your case, though."

"That's ok, Jason. I was not really calling about that, to be honest. I was calling to see how you were feeling, considering what we did the last time I saw you."

"Oh, I see. Well, I enjoyed what happened the last time we saw each other very much, Miss Summers, and I have not stopped thinking about it," Jason replied in a soft voice in case his wife overheard.

"Well then, call me Mistress, not Miss Summers, and why are you talking quietly?"

"I am at home, and my wife is here, Mistress," Jason said, still in a quiet voice.

"I do not really care. Jason. If you want to speak to me, you will do so the way you would normally do. If you need to, go into another room, but I want your full attention and your obedience. Do I make myself clear?" she asked in a very demanding manner.

"Yes, Mistress," he replied as he got up from the couch and made his way up the stairs to the bedroom out of earshot of his wife.

"Very good. Jason. Now, tell me what you enjoyed the most from the other night and what else you would have liked to have happened," Alexia said seductively.

Jason went on to tell her what he enjoyed, which was pretty much everything that happened, even though it was not a great deal. He also told her that he was hoping a lot more would have happened.

"All in good time, Jason. But remember, you are here for my pleasure and not the other way around," she replied, this time in a much firmer voice.

"Yes, of course. Please forgive me, Mistress; I didn't mean to imply anything. I was simply answering your question with regards to what I would have liked to have happened."

"Very well, Jason, as long as we understand each other. Now, I have a very important question to ask you. I want you to listen very carefully to what I am going to say, so do not interrupt me until I have completely finished and think very carefully before you answer. Is that clear?"

"Yes, Mistress," he replied, feeling a little nervous at what she would ask him.

"Good! If we are to continue with this, I need to know that you will do everything I say. I will call you whenever I want, and you will answer. I will visit you at work any time I want, and you will make yourself available to me. Do not worry as I will never visit you at your home, but if I call you and tell you to come over, you will do so. I will not put you in a position where it will cause problems as far as your work and marriage are concerned, but I do expect you to be very flexible. If the occasion should arise that you cannot comply with my demands because you have a legitimate reason which is unavoidable, then I shall understand, but you will still have to be punished." Alexia paused for a brief moment before she continued.

"If, on the other hand, you do not comply with my demands and do not have a good reason, then this will all soon come to an end. I will not be messed about, and I take this very seriously. I only want dedicated and committed slaves who will put me and my needs first and foremost. If you feel you can do this, then very well, but if you cannot, you need to say so now. As for payment, you will arrange for $500 to be transferred to my bank every single week, regardless of how many times we see each other, if indeed we see each other at all, just to prove to me that you are serious about this. Once this problem I have is all over and finished with, I will then decide on what course our relationship will take and inform you. Who knows? I may even decide to make you one of my personal slaves if you are worthy. So my question to you, Jason, is, and please think carefully before you answer, do you still wish to continue with this?"

Jason stayed silent for a moment, thinking about all that Alexia had said. Not only was he very intrigued by it all, but he was also very aroused just at the thought of being dominated on a regular basis by this sexy lady. This was going to be so different from what he was used to doing with Selene, but $500 per week was something he did not take into consideration, even though he could easily afford it. Besides, he was certain that it would be worth it and that he would love every minute of it, or at least was hoping that he would.

However, he still could not understand how this woman could make him feel so helpless, weak, and submissive. He would never have thought that anyone could make him feel this way, and he had never allowed anyone to have this much control over him. This went against his better nature, and it was a feeling he had never experienced before.

Nevertheless, without much resistance, he simply looked at himself in the mirror and knew exactly what he wanted: Alexia. He did not even care about becoming this submissive man because he could feel that this is what he felt had been missing in his life for a long time and was prepared to grab the bull by the horns, so to speak.

"Yes, Mistress, I do want this. I will do my very best to please you and do everything you want," he replied in an excited but nervous voice.

"That's very good to hear, Jason, and I look forward to training you. There are a few rules you always need to follow, and I will teach them to you as we go along, but for now, always remember to be obedient and respectful to me. Never lie to me about anything and never, ever say no to me or argue with me because I am always right. Good personal hygiene is a must, as is the way you dress and present yourself to me. Is that clear?"

"Yes, Mistress, it is," he replied, questioning himself as to whether he was doing the right thing in allowing her to have this much power over him.

"Good! Now, on certain occasions when I have something specific in mind, I will tell you to abstain from having any kind of sex with your wife for at least three days prior to our meeting, and I would expect you to obey me. I will know, Jason, if you disobey me. And one more thing, do not ever dare to have sex with anyone else other than your wife, is that very clear?"

She commanded in such a way that Jason replied in a very sheepish voice, "Yes, Mistress. I promise you I won't."

"Very good, Jason. I can see this becoming a very good and fulfilling relationship between us as long as you obey my rules. I do not have many, but the ones I do have must be obeyed at all times and without question."

"I understand, Mistress, and I will do my best not to disappoint you."

"Excellent. Now tell me, Jason, are you hard yet?" she suddenly asked, as though she already knew the answer.

"Yes, Mistress, I am. But how could you know?" Jason asked, very surprised at the question and the fact that she seemed to know he had a hard on.

"I'm very glad to hear it, Jason. I will always know these things, but you cannot do anything about it. You cannot have sex with your wife, and you cannot play with yourself either.

You will have to suffer for tonight, and remember, this is **not** a request," she demanded.

"Yes, Mistress," Jason replied, feeling so turned on at this moment. Even though he knew he would not be having sex with his wife, he had just been thinking about relieving himself again. He really did feel like a love-sick teenager where Alexia was concerned, and until recently, when he left her house, he had not played with himself for many, many years.

"Just remember, I will know if you ever lie to me, Jason. You never know when I am likely to turn up at your work or call you to come round and then see just how much jizz comes out of you. I have been doing this for a great many years, and I can tell if someone has done anything or not."

"Ok, Mistress, I will not do anything tonight," he said, quite taken aback by the comment she had just made. Again, he found himself questioning everything about this relationship, or whatever the hell it was that he was allowing himself to get into.

"You are doing very well, Jason. Now, one last thing before I leave you with your thoughts. Do you have a webcam on your computer at work?" she asked.

"No, Mistress, but I have one built into my laptop here at home. Why do you ask?"

"Do **not** forget your place so quickly, Jason, and do **not** question me. I will ask you whatever I want, and you will simply answer me. Is that clear?" she snapped.

"Yes, Mistress, my apologies," he replied humbly.

"Good, then make sure you either take your laptop in to work with you every day or simply buy a webcam for your computer at work. Either way, I expect you to have a webcam at both your work and your home for whenever I want you to use it," she commanded.

"Yes, Mistress, I will order one when I get into work tomorrow and will take my laptop in with me until it arrives," Jason replied, wondering exactly what Alexia had in mind but did not dare to ask her.

"Very good, Jason, and now I am going to go. I will speak to you or see you soon."

"Goodbye, Mistress," Jason said as Alexia put the phone down.

Jason could hardly believe the conversation that had just taken place and wondered what would happen during these sessions. It was all getting so very exciting for Jason, and he could not wait to see what would happen next. He so badly wanted to have sex right now, but there was no way in hell he was going to do anything, as he did not want to disobey Alexia. He still could not believe how a confident, dominant man such as himself could be so controlled by this lady, and it was scary that she could hold such power over him.

Well, there was only one thing he could do now, and that was to take a cold shower and get into bed before he was tempted to do anything. Jason prayed that he would fall asleep quickly so that tomorrow could come round sooner and hoped that Alexia would actually arrange to meet him again so that she could carry on with his training.

CHAPTER SIXTEEN

Jason woke up the next morning and wasted no time getting to work in the hope that Alexia would be there waiting for him. Alas, that was not the case, and he was quite disappointed as he half expected her to be there. As soon as he got into his office, he went online and ordered a webcam for his computer; then, he set up his laptop just in case Alexia telephoned to tell him what she wanted him to do.

The time seemed to drag on forever, hardly being able to concentrate on anything he had to do. After a couple of hours had passed, he realized that Alexia may not even call him today. He decided that he would try and find out if Marcus had any more information regarding what the DA was going to do, so he telephoned him to find out if he had any news. Marcus told him that he had not heard anything else, but he would see if he could find anything out, and he would call him later.

During the course of the day, Jason kept himself busy, trying very hard not to think about Alexia. He caught up on some telephone calls he had to make, and then went to see Mr.

Langley to give him the update he had asked for earlier that morning.

After his meeting with his boss, Jason went out to one of the nearby restaurants. He wanted some lunch but also to gather his thoughts as he needed to get a grip on his life and get some perspective. He still had a job to do as well as a life to live, he told himself, and that this thing with Alexia could not overtake everything else. After all, he still had to earn a living. He had to make sure that his mind was where it needed to be, not just for Alexia but also for everyone and everything else. Sure, he was really excited about what may lay in store for him where she was concerned, but he also knew that everything else was just as important.

He had a couple of drinks with his lunch, managed to gather his thoughts, and began to think clearly again before heading back to his office.

Later that afternoon, he got a call from Marcus, telling him that the DA had still not decided what he was going to do. However, he had just brought in a new prosecutor called Roy Emerton this week, and he had now been given Alexia's case.

"WHAT?" Jason shouted out. "Did you say Roy Emerton?" he then asked.

"Yeah, I did. What is it, buddy?" asked Marcus, unsure of why Jason reacted this way.

Jason stayed silent for a brief moment as this was not good news for him. He and Emerton had crossed paths while at law school together, and they were not exactly on friendly terms. In fact, they did not even like each other very much and were always competing against one another at law school about everything.

Jason always thought that Emerton was jealous of him and that he always tried to go one better than him. Whatever Jason would do, Emerton would try and do better, and it was always personal for him. The main reason for this animosity was because, while they were at Harvard together, Emerton's girlfriend, who he had hoped to marry, broke up with him and began to go out with Jason. This infuriated Emerton, and his bitterness towards Jason intensified and led to the feud between them.

"A bad name from the past, my friend. I need to think for a minute. I will call you back shortly," Jason replied eventually.

"Take your time, buddy," Marcus said, knowing that this news struck a chord with Jason.

Jason knew that there would be no love lost between them and this really was not what he had hoped for. The only saving grace for him was that Emerton did not yet know that Jason would be defending the case if, indeed, it went to trial. Had Emerton found out that Jason would be Alexia's lawyer, then he would almost certainly take this to trial just to try and get one over on him.

Jason now had to decide which course of action to take regarding this news. After some consideration, he called Marcus back and told him to use his contacts to find out everything he could about Emerton. He told him to dig into his past and see if he could find any dirt on him. Then he gave Marcus all the information he could remember about Emerton from their time at Harvard together.

He also told Marcus to drop everything else he had to do as this was now the priority for him. He should look into his financial situation, his personal life, family life, and pretty much everything he could think of. He told Marcus that cost was not an issue and he was prepared to pay as much as it took to get this information.

Jason wanted to be fully prepared for Emerton just in case this did go to trial, and it had now become a personal matter for him. He was going to make sure he did whatever he had to do to beat Emerton and win this case if it went that far. A part of Jason actually wanted him to take this case to court, just to try and wipe the floor with Emerton, but he did not want to put Alexia through that for his own personal agenda.

Marcus said he would start immediately and let Jason know as soon as he found anything out about him, but it would probably take him a few days.

Jason carried on with the work he had at hand, trying to get Emerton out of his mind during the afternoon, and pretty soon, it was time for him to get ready and go home. Just as he was about to leave the office, his cell rang, and he answered it.

Before he could even say hello, the voice on the other end said, "Hello, Jason. Did you think I had forgotten about you?"

"Good afternoon, Miss Summers. No, I did not think that at all," he replied anxiously.

"**Mistress**, I am calling you as your **mistress** now, not as your client. Remember this, Jason, if I call your cell, I am calling as your mistress; if I need to call you as a client, I will call your work phone," Alexia snapped firmly.

"Yes, of course, Mistress. I'm sorry," Jason replied excitedly.

"That's ok, Jason. As I said, I will teach you the rules as we go along. So did you do anything last night, Jason?" she continued in a very soft-spoken voice.

"No, Mistress, I did not, but it was not easy," he replied, hoping she would be pleased.

"No, I can imagine it wasn't. So, do you have Skype, Jason?"

"Yes, I do, Mistress. Why do you ask?" he said, immediately realizing he was not supposed to question her on anything.

"I asked because I wanted to know. And remember, it is not for you to question anything I say or do," she replied in a now very stern voice.

"Yes, I'm sorry, Mistress. I did not mean to question you: I was just wondering, that's all."

"Ok. Well, I am going to send you my Skype details, and I want you to log on and invite me as a contact," Alexia said in a firm voice.

"Ok, Mistress, I will," he replied in anticipation of what would happen next.

Alexia put the phone down, then sent Jason a text with her details, and he did as ordered. A short while later, Alexia made a video call to Jason, which he accepted, so they were now able to see each other while they spoke.

"This is one of the ways we will speak to each other from now on, Jason. Sometimes you will see me via the camera, and sometimes you won't. It will depend on how I feel and what I decide at the time, but I will always expect to see you."

"Yes, Mistress, whatever you want," he replied excitedly.

"You are learning, Jason; well done. It *is* whatever I want, and right now, I want to reward you," she said as she stood up, taking her dress off. Alexia then sat back down on the chair so that Jason could see the top half of her body, showing the black lace bra she was wearing.

"Do you like what you see, Jason?" she asked him.

"Yes, Mistress, very much so," he replied, unable to take his gaze away from her breasts.

"Very well, Jason. Before I show you more, I want you to stand up, unzip your pants and take out your cock for me to look at," Alexia said in a very seductive voice.

Jason was just about to question what she asked when he remembered that he was not allowed to. However, he was also worried about doing this in case his boss would simply walk in without knocking, as was his tendency to do. But he did not want to say no to Alexia and thought that he could quite easily sit down if he heard anyone at the door.

Jason did as he was asked and was already beginning to get stiff by the time he had taken his cock out for Alexia to see.

"My, my Jason. You are a very excitable man, aren't you?" she said in a kind of giggly way.

"I'm sorry, Mistress," he replied, embarrassed.

"Oh, don't be sorry, Jason. I would have been offended if you did not get excited. Now I will keep my end of the bargain," she said as she took off her bra, revealing her fairly large, firm breasts. She then took her nipples between her thumb and index finger and gave them a little squeeze so that they were now hard. "And what about now? Do you like them even more?" she asked.

"Oh, yes, Mistress, they are wonderful," he replied, constantly staring at them while his cock was now very stiff.

"Ok, Jason, now I have given you your reward, you are going to do something for me. You are going to wank yourself, and you are going to make yourself come for me. I want to watch you while you do it, and I want to see how much cream comes out. Off you go," she said in a very teasing way.

Jason, shocked at what she had just told him to do, began stroking his cock while staring at her breasts. He imagined that she was actually standing in front of him and that he could see them, touch them, and, if lucky enough, even be allowed to suck them. Oh, what he would have given for that to be the case right now. Just then, Alexia raised her hands and began to squeeze her breasts in a very erotic way for Jason to see, watching his every reaction and his hand now moving faster and faster.

She could tell he was getting close as his breathing began to get heavier and faster, when suddenly she said to him, "Come on, Jason. Let it out for me. Let me see your cum all over the screen."

Within a few more seconds, Jason began to shoot his load all over his laptop, and he kept going until every last drop was out, moaning a little as he did so.

"Mmmm, I enjoyed watching you do that, Jason, and it seems that a fair bit came out, so I do believe that you did not do anything last night. Maybe next time, I will reward you even more, but that will do for now as I have a regular client coming to see me soon, who I'm actually going to fuck. You got to come, and now it's going to be my turn. Goodbye for now, Jason, and unless there is any news regarding my case, I will speak to you when I decide to call you," she said as she logged out of her Skype.

"Goodbye, Mistress," Jason said, wishing that it was him that she was going to be fucking.

'Oh well, perhaps next time,' he thought to himself as he cleaned himself and his laptop up, before getting ready to go home for the evening.

Chapter Seventeen

Jason woke up the next morning, had a shower, got dressed, then went to work. He was still thinking about what had happened in his office the day before and wondered what, if anything, Alexia had in store for him today. But, alas, there was no contact from her at all.

In fact, three days had now passed by without any contact from Alexia, and Jason so wanted to telephone her but knew that he was not allowed to unless it had something to do with the case.

Later that afternoon, Marcus called Jason at work and told him that he could not find anything on Roy Emerton. He lived a normal life with his wife and children, had no gambling debts, was just a social drinker, so, no problems there, and he pretty much went from home to work and back again. He lived a rather dull life, in fact, and there was nothing even remotely close to any dirt on him.

Jason was not happy about this news and told Marcus to keep following him.

'Everyone must have at least one skeleton in their closet,' he thought to himself, 'including Mr. Goody-Two-Shoes, Emerton.'

Jason so badly wanted to have something on him and was prepared to use all his resources to find it if necessary.

A few more days had now passed, and it was now the weekend. Jason was at home relaxing when Marcus telephoned him and asked if he fancied meeting up for a drink. Jason agreed as he did not have anything else to do and he told Lydia that he had arranged to meet a friend of his but forgot to mention it to her, and he was just going out to have a couple of beers with him. The less she knew about how close he and Marcus were the better.

After they met up, they ordered a couple of drinks and before too long Jason brought up the subject of Emerton. Marcus told him that he could still not find anything on Emerton. He was sending a colleague of his to LA, where Emerton had worked before, to see if he could unearth anything there. In the meantime, Marcus assured Jason that he would stay on the case for as long as he wanted him to and would continue to have Emerton followed at all times.

Jason was happy that his friend was dealing with this matter because it was important to him that someone he trusted was in charge, and he knew only too well that Marcus would give it 100% at all times. After all, if it wasn't for Jason helping him out when he needed it most, Marcus could very well be in prison right now.

After a while, they finished their drinks, and both headed off home. Jason was feeling very confident something would come up regarding Emerton and that he would have the upper hand.

Jason arrived home, then went into the garden where his wife was sunning herself on a lounger, reading a magazine, and said, "Hi, Lyd, I'm back."

"Hey, honey, did you have a nice time?" She asked him as she took off her sunglasses and put them on the top of her head.

"Yes, it was good, thanks. We had a good catch-up. Fancy a drink?" Jason asked as he leaned over and gave her a kiss on the cheek.

"Sure, a glass of wine would be nice," Lydia replied, wondering why Jason was in such a good mood.

"Do you fancy having a barbeque today?" he asked Lydia a few minutes later as he handed her the glass of wine.

"Now, that sounds like a great idea," Lydia replied, still wondering exactly what was going on in Jason's mind, which was slightly unnerving for her. Jason had been quite lost in thought lately, and it was not like him to want to do anything, so she began to wonder why he was being so different now.

"Is everything ok, Jason?" she asked.

"Yes, everything is great; why do you ask?" he said as he took a sip of his drink.

"You just seem different today, that's all."

"Well, the sun is out, I had a good laugh at the bar, and I feel happy at the moment. Should I not be?" he asked jokingly.

"No, not at all; I am glad you are feeling happy. Are you ok to go and get the meat for the barbeque, honey, or shall I go?" Lydia asked.

"No, that's fine, Lyd. You stay where you are, and I will be back shortly," he replied as he made his way back inside the house.

Jason drove to the store to get the things he needed for the barbeque and was surprised at just how happy he was right now. He had a strange feeling that things would now start to fall into place and that his life was beginning to get to where he wanted it to be. Not only was he getting more involved with Alexia and the domination she offered, but if things fell into place where Emerton was concerned, then everything would be perfect. Oh, how he hoped that Marcus would uncover something that he could use to have a hold over Emerton.

After returning home, he poured himself and Lydia another drink and lit the barbeque. Lydia kept looking at Jason on and off for the next thirty minutes and wondered exactly what it was that made him feel this way. 'Did something happen that he's not telling me?' she thought to herself, 'or is there something else going on that I'm not aware of?'

She knew he could not have found out about her affair as he would not be happy if that was the case, and she even wondered if he had met someone. Lydia was not happy that Jason was being like this, and it was driving her mad trying to guess the reason.

"So, who did you have a drink with today, honey?" Lydia asked Jason, trying to see if she could pick anything up.

"You remember Marcus, don't you?" he replied as he went into the kitchen to get the meat so he could begin to cook it.

"Yes, I do, vaguely," Lydia said as Jason came back out into the garden with the meat.

"Well, I met up with him for a catch-up."

"Oh, I see, but you don't really see him that often, do you?"

"No, not as much as I would like, really, but it's not always that easy with work and everything," Jason said as he began to put the meat on the barbecue.

"And what does he do for a living again?" Lydia asked curiously.

"He works in security," Jason replied, wondering why he was getting all these questions from Lydia and not daring to say that Marcus was, in fact, a private investigator.

"Oh, ok, and how has your work been, honey?" She now asked, figuring that whatever was making Jason feel this way was probably nothing to do with his friend Marcus.

"Oh, I have a self-defense case that may not even go to trial, so nothing too major at the moment. So when am I going to meet this new friend of yours? What was her name again? Valerie, was it?" Jason quickly asked to change the subject.

"Oh, she is a model and is always traveling for photoshoots. I never really know when she is going to call me to meet up, so it's really hard to arrange anything with her, to be honest, honey, but hopefully one day soon," Lydia replied as she picked up her magazine again as if she was going to read it some more.

'Ok, enough with the questions,' Lydia thought to herself, fearing that if she continued to ask more questions, then Jason could also start asking her things. Perhaps it was better to let dogs lie rather than risk anything. 'Maybe it's nothing,' she thought to herself. 'Perhaps Jason is just having a good day, and that's why he's so happy.'

The afternoon passed by quickly and they both enjoyed the barbeque, chatting away about nothing really, just having a few drinks and doing what they would normally do.

Jason had spent the rest of the weekend just lazing around at home, wondering what information Marcus would have for him and, more importantly, how he could use it for his own gains. His thoughts then turned to Alexia, wondering when she would contact him again and exactly what she would have in mind when she did. Eventually, he went to bed, still imagining what lay in store for him on Monday.

CHAPTER EIGHTEEN

Jason arrived at work on Monday morning and was busy as usual when he received a Skype message from Alexia that simply said Jason was not allowed to have any sex until after she had been to see him. Jason's heart thumped like crazy in his chest, and he quickly sent a message back saying that he wouldn't. He knew that a meeting with Alexia was coming, but of course, he did not know when that would be.

Jason continued with his work for the rest of the day, trying not to think about when Alexia would be visiting him.

The next few days seemed to pass very slowly for him as he anxiously waited for the day when Alexia would visit him. In fact, he began to get quite impatient and was not happy that he had no control over anything where she was concerned.

Little did he know that this was the way Alexia trained her slaves so they could learn patience and self-control: making them wait for as long as she thought necessary. Jason was no exception to the rule, and he would have to learn just like all her other slaves did. This was a good way for her to find out if any new potential slaves had what it takes to submit to her totally, without question, and Jason was certainly heading in the right direction.

During the course of the week, Jason had called Marcus on a couple of occasions to get an update, but there was no new information regarding Emerton at all. In fact, this whole week had passed extremely slowly for Jason, what with waiting for information that did not come and also waiting for Alexia to contact him, which also never happened.

However, it was now Friday afternoon, and Jason was getting ready for another weekend at home when Alexia decided to pay him a visit at work.

"Good afternoon, I'm Alexia Summers, and I would like to see Mr. Carini, please," she said to Jason's secretary.

"Do you have an appointment, Miss Summers?" Martha asked as she looked up at Alexia.

"No, I do not, but please tell Mr. Carini I am here as I am sure he will want to see me."

"I'm sorry, but Mr. Carini does not see anyone without an appointment," Martha replied.

"Well, I can assure you that he *will* see me, and I can also assure you that he will not be pleased if you do not inform him that I am here. I suggest you tell him I am waiting, or I shall just go in anyway. Now, what is it going to be?" Alexia asked in a very stern, almost angry voice.

Martha paused for a brief moment and then buzzed through to Jason. "Miss Summers is here to see you, Mr. Carini."

"Miss Summers?" he asked. "Please show her in, Martha."

"Mr. Carini will see you now," Martha said as she got up from her seat, walked over to the door, opened it to let Alexia go inside, and then closed it behind her. 'What a bitch,' Martha thought to herself.

"Good afternoon, Miss Summers. Please, sit down," Jason said as he pointed to the chair.

"It's Mistress, today, Jason, and I am here to continue with your training. Now, tell your secretary you are not to be disturbed, lock your door and then come here and stand in front of me."

Jason did as he was told, then went to the front of his desk as ordered, and stood in front of Alexia.

"In the future, when I come to see you, Jason, I expect your secretary to show me through. I do not expect to be told you will not see me without an appointment, and I do not expect to be kept waiting either. Of course, if you are with another client, then that is understandable, but I will **not** be kept waiting if you are alone in your office. Do I make myself clear?"

"Yes, Mistress. I will tell Martha that if you come round even without an appointment, she should let me know," he replied in an almost nervous tone of voice.

"Very well, now get down on your knees, slave!" Alexia demanded.

Jason did as commanded and got onto his knees in front of Alexia. She then slowly moved her hands up her thighs, lifting her dress up as she did so until it was around her waist, revealing her lacy white thong and black stockings.

"Now, take my thong off," she said, again in a very demanding way.

Jason obeyed her by reaching out and taking hold of it at her waist, pulling it past her thighs, before leaning down and slipping it first over one foot and then the other.

"Now, smell and lick my thong," she said, looking down at him.

Jason again did as he was told by putting the thong to his nose, first smelling and then licking it.

"Does it smell and taste nice, Jason?" Alexia asked him.

"Yes, Mistress," Jason replied in a soft voice as he continued what he was doing.

"Well, it's time for the real thing," Alexia said as she slowly sat in the chair behind her, positioning her bottom on the edge of the seat and spreading her legs as far as they would go so that Jason had easy access to her.

"Now, lick my pussy, slave," she told him in a firm voice.

Jason got down a little lower and slowly began to lick Alexia's clit as he gently moved his hands up and down her stockinged legs.

"Mmmm, that's it, Jason. Make me nice and wet," she said, but this time in a soft voice.

Jason continued to lick her clit, moving his tongue a little faster, and Alexia was now beginning to get quite wet when she said, "Now, stick your tongue inside my pussy."

Jason did exactly what he was told and began to push his tongue inside her now very wet hole. As he pushed in deeper and faster, Alexia began to move her hips so that she was moving at the same pace as Jason's tongue. A few minutes later, she began to moan, her hips now jerking suddenly rather than the constant movement they were making earlier and then she gave out a longer moan as she reached her orgasm.

"Not bad, Jason, but I expect better next time. Now bend down and kiss my shoes."

Jason obeyed and got completely down so he could get to them, kissing her shoes for a couple of minutes.

"Now, lick my clit, but this time, put a finger inside me while you do so," Alexia said as she spread her legs once more.

Jason again began to lick Alexia's clit while pushing his middle finger inside her now very wet pussy, moving it in and out in a gentle way to begin with.

After a few minutes, Alexia had begun to moan a little. She told Jason to go faster and to now use two fingers inside her. As always, he did what he was told, and his tongue was now moving faster, as was his hand, pushing his fingers inside her deeper and quicker. Again Alexia began to move her hips in time with Jason, and after a short while, she began to feel that she was going to come again, but this time it was much more intense.

She then moaned to Jason, "That's a good slave, keep licking my clit, good."

Jason continued as Alexia began to get to the point of no return. Within a couple of minutes, she began to give out a long moan as she reached out her hands and placed them around Jason's head, pushing his face harder into her.

"Oh, yes, that's it, keep going," she said as she reached yet another orgasm which was indeed better than the last one.

When Alexia had finally finished, she told Jason to stand up, and as he did so, she could see he was hard by the bulge in his pants.

"Take your cock out," she said to him.

Jason unzipped his pants and pulled his stiff cock out as was commanded by her. Alexia then raised one of her legs and pressed the heel of her shoe against his hard cock, which caused Jason to give out a little ouch.

"Did that hurt?" she asked him as she pushed her heel in again.

"Yes, Mistress, a little bit," was the reply from Jason as her heel was now constantly pressed against his very stiff cock.

"Well, that's just tough," she replied as she now moved her heel away. She sat up in the chair and brought her hand down, slapping Jason's cock hard with it, resulting in another ouch from Jason, clearly feeling the pain.

"Oh, my poor Jason, is this better?" Alexia asked as she slowly and gently rubbed his pulsating manhood with her hand.

"Yes, Mistress, much better, thank you," was his reply to her.

She lifted her hand up and again brought it down on his already sore cock, but much harder this time round, making Jason move quite sharply, due to the pain.

"Well, Jason, you will have to learn that there will be pleasure as well as pain when you are with me, but you are never going to know what you will get until you get it. As I have said before, you are here strictly for my pleasure and amusement, and I will do whatever I want with you. I will reward you when you earn it and punish you when you deserve it. Today I had to tell you to make me come twice before I was satisfied, so next time you had better satisfy me the first time, do you understand?"

"Yes, Mistress, I am sorry, and I will do better next time."

"Oh, I know you will, Jason, I know you will," Alexia replied as she once again began to stroke his cock gently with her hand, moving it slowly, to begin with, but getting faster as she went on. Jason was now certainly enjoying this, and it wasn't too long before Alexia began to wank him quickly, which got Jason to the point of getting ready to come.

Alexia, sensing this, suddenly stopped and said to Jason, "Now, toss yourself off while I watch you."

Jason immediately took hold of his throbbing cock and began to play with it, looking at Alexia as he did so. Within a couple of minutes, he began to come, spurting jizz all over the floor until his balls were empty.

"Not bad, Jason, and again, quite a lot of cum. It seems you are obeying my commands about abstaining from sex when I ask you to," she said as she began to put her thong back on and straightened herself out.

"Yes, Mistress, I will always obey you," Jason said as he zipped up his pants then used his foot to rub the cum into the carpet.

They then said their goodbyes, walked over to the door, and Jason opened it for her to walk out.

'Oh my god, how great was that?' he thought to himself as he went back into his office and sat down. 'Even the painful part was good,' he thought, and he could not wait till the next meeting.

He wondered when he would actually get to have sex with this sexy lady, and he could not wait till that happened.

For a brief moment, his mind turned to Selene, but he realized that what he did with her was nowhere near as fulfilling as what had happened so far with Alexia. 'How good would it be if I could see her whenever I want, just like I did with Selene?' he thought, but he knew that was not going to be likely, at least not for the time being. All he could do was simply hope and pray that Alexia would grace him with her presence as much as possible.

It was now time for Jason to head off home, and so he left the office, saying goodbye to Martha as he did so, went to the garage, got into his car, and began to drive home.

Chapter Nineteen

A few more days had passed, and it was now a Wednesday morning when Jason received a telephone call from his friend Marcus to say that the DA's office had asked for the police to interview Alexia again. He also told him that Roy Emerton would be present as he wanted to hear what she would say regarding what happened that night before making a decision about the case.

This was not the news that Jason wanted to hear. As her lawyer, he would also have to be there, and he knew that Emerton, after finding out Jason would be representing Alexia, would then most certainly take this to trial. Jason now had to think long and hard about how to play this out.

By that afternoon, he received a call from Alexia saying that the police had asked her to go to the police precinct in the morning as they wanted to speak to her again. She asked if Jason could go with her.

Well, the shit had most certainly hit the fan now, as there was no way for him to keep it from Emerton that he would be representing her. So Jason arranged to meet Alexia at her house, where all this took place, the next morning, and they would go to the precinct from there.

Jason then called Marcus back and told him that he not only wanted Emerton followed but also his family, wanting to know everywhere they went and everything they did. He did not care how much this would cost in extra manpower, as Jason was not going to be taking any prisoners here. Helping Alexia to beat this was his number one priority, with getting one over on Emerton coming a very close second. Jason was now prepared to do whatever was necessary to make sure that happened because this was now a personal matter for him - not only because of Alexia but also because of his past history with Emerton.

The following morning, Jason arrived at Alexia's house. After prepping her about what she should and should not say, they headed to the precinct together. Once they had arrived there, an officer began to lead them to one of the interview rooms. Just then, as they turned the corner, Emerton and Jason saw each other for the first time in many years. You could hear a pin drop in the silent tension as they stared at each other for what seemed an eternity. Even the detective stared at them both in silence, wondering what the hell was going on.

"In here, please," said the detective eventually as he opened the door to the interview room and followed everyone inside.

Emerton had been unsure about what he was going to do with this case before arriving at the precinct. However, the fact that it was Jason who was representing Alexia made him decide in that instant that he would be taking it to trial.

Emerton began to ask Alexia a series of questions regarding what happened that night, and she answered them in the way that Jason had instructed her to. Still, all the while, Emerton's gaze rarely moved away from Jason for too long.

Once he had finished asking his questions, Emerton turned to the detective and said, "Charge her with murder."

"WHAT?" Jason shouted out, and even the detective seemed surprised at this decision, while Alexia put her hand to her mouth in disbelief.

Jason stood up, put his hands on the table, stared Emerton in the face with looks that could kill, and said to him, "What are we doing here, Roy? Don't play games with my client's life for your own personal reasons!"

"I have no idea what you are talking about," was the cold reply from Emerton before turning to the detective and again telling him to charge Alexia with murder.

Jason paused for a brief moment as the detective began to read Alexia her rights. Then, in an angry tone of voice, while still staring at Emerton, he said, "Fine, This isn't over, Roy."

He then turned to Alexia and said, "Don't worry, Miss Summers. Leave it with me, and I will have you out of here as soon as possible."

Alexia was then led away to a holding cell where she was told she would stay until her arraignment, and Jason left the precinct. He called Marcus as he did so, telling him what had happened and asking him to talk to his contacts to see if he could get any help.

Jason went back to his office, gathered his thoughts, and then went to speak to Mr. Langley. He told him what had happened and also explained the situation between himself and Emerton.

"I see, so this Roy Emerton is using the justice system for personal gain, is he? Leave it with me, and I will call the DA and deal with this myself," Langley replied.

Jason went back to his office while his boss telephoned and had a long chat with the DA, Clive Montague, who he had known professionally for a great many years.

Langley told Montague that Emerton was using this case for some sort of revenge, and he would not sit back and let this happen to one of their clients. The district attorney then told Langley that he would talk to Emerton about it to find out what was happening and get back to him as soon as possible.

After a short while, the district attorney telephoned Langley back, informing him that the murder charge was now being changed to a manslaughter one instead. They had arranged for the arraignment to be in the morning. Langley then called Jason to tell him the news, and Jason then spent the rest of the day and evening going over what he was going to say at the hearing.

Jason woke up the next morning feeling confident that he would be walking out of the courtroom with Alexia in tow. After getting ready, he left home, got in his car, and made his way to the courthouse.

Jason arrived for the hearing, and as expected, he got a cold, glaring look from his adversary, but his main concern was getting Alexia out of there.

The hearing began with the charges being read out, and when asked about the plea, Alexia replied in a soft, well-mannered voice with the obvious not guilty. Emerton then asked for Alexia to be remanded due to the death of an upstanding citizen. As the accused was an escort with no ties to the community, she was, therefore, an obvious flight risk, he stated.

Jason then responded by having his say. "Miss Summers is not a mere escort, your Honor, as the prosecution would have you believe, but is, in fact, a mistress. This may sound to you that it is the same thing, but it is not, and the defense will show this during the trial. The death of Mr. Morley, as unfortunate as it was, was, in fact, caused due to my client having to defend herself against him. We should not even be here today as this is a clear case of self-defense. He attacked Miss Summers, and she had no choice but to defend herself."

"Save that argument for the trial, Mr. Carini, the judge replied.

"Yes, your Honor, my apologies. However, I would like to add that due to the fact this was indeed self-defense shows that my client is not a dangerous person and, actually, she is a victim herself. My client is also a well-established author, who has properties in New York, and she also runs a business here. She would be happy to surrender her passport and abide by whatever order the court pleases to give her, but please do not punish my client even more than she has been already. Remember your Honor, Miss Summers is also the victim here, and she should be treated as such. The prosecution has no evidence whatsoever that she is guilty of anything other than defending herself, and I would beg the court to afford my client the benefit of the doubt until the trial is at hand."

"Indeed, Mr. Carini. I have to admit that I see no reason to remand the defendant, so bail is set at $500,000 cash or bond. Additionally, she must surrender her passport and not leave New York," the judge replied after carefully listening to both parties' statements.

"Understood, and thank you, your Honor," said Jason in a relieved and happy voice.

Alexia stood up and thanked Jason, putting her arms around him and giving him a hug.

"That's what I am here for, Miss Summers," Jason replied as he slowly turned to look at Emerton with a wry smile on his own face … 'Oh, if looks could kill,' he thought to himself.

As they left the building, Jason could not help but feel overjoyed at this victory, a small one, but a victory nonetheless, but he knew that the real battle was still to come.

"Would you like me to take you home, Miss Summers?" Jason asked.

"Yes, thank you, Jason. But can you take me to my actual home, please, rather than the one you picked me up from yesterday?"

"By all means, Miss Summers," he replied, still feeling happy with himself.

"Please, Jason, when we are alone, and I am your client, it is ok for you to call me Alexia rather than Miss Summers, but never, ever, call me that when I am your mistress."

"Yes, Alexia, I understand," he replied with a little smile on his face.

Jason and Alexia chatted away during the journey until they reached her house on Long Island and Jason drove up the long driveway leading up to her front door.

"Thank you again, Jason, for getting me out of there," she said as she turned her body to face him and then put her hand on his lap.

Alexia then slowly moved her hand up his thigh and onto the front of his pants until she could feel his cock. She then gave it a little squeeze, and Jason took no time in getting a hard on as Alexia then unzipped his pants and put her hand inside, playing with his now very stiff cock while it was still in his briefs.

She began wanking him faster while squeezing it harder, and Jason was now beginning to breathe heavily, moving his hips ever so slightly. Alexia could tell that he was getting close and began moving her hand as fast as she could, still on the outside of his briefs. Jason suddenly arched his body upwards and exploded with an ecstatic moan as his hips were now thrusting with each shot of spunk into his briefs, which were by now very wet with his cum.

Alexia removed her hand from his pants, sat back in her seat, and said, "Thank you again, Jason, for helping me today, and that was a little reward for you."

Jason was speechless and simply looked at Alexia as she got out of the car, walked to her front door, opened it, walked inside, and turned to give Jason a small smile before closing the door. Jason just sat there for a few moments before zipping up his pants. He drove away from Alexia's house with a broad grin, thinking how wonderful it felt, having her do that to him. All the way home, he had a smile on his face as if to say he was the luckiest man alive.

Chapter Twenty

Over the following week, Jason read through everything he had regarding Alexia's case, and he also saw her in his office on two occasions to discuss those events. He told her to be as exact as she could be regarding each aspect of what had happened that night and to try and remember every single last detail.

This was not an easy week for Jason because he wanted so much to talk about what happened when he dropped her off at home. However, he knew better than to bring up any mention of that or indeed any talk of domination. Only Alexia could bring up that subject, and he had to wait until she was ready to do so, but it seemed that this was not going to be any time soon as she made no effort at all in the two times he saw her this week.

However, she did say one thing to Jason, which was to let him know that if he was able to defend her successfully, she would not only be extremely grateful but would also consider making him one of her personal slaves and reward him accordingly. This made Jason even more determined to win this case and to do whatever had to be done to achieve that victory.

To make things worse, the preliminary hearing this morning did not go as planned, and the judge had set the trial date for the middle of July, which gave Jason just over two months to get Alexia prepped and ready for it. He knew that during these next couple of months, he completely had to forget about anything else other than the trial itself.

This was a difficult case because there were no witnesses for either side to question, apart from, of course, Alexia herself, the police officers involved with the case, the paramedics who attended the incident and the forensics team. It was simply going to be a case of whether the members of the jury believed her or not, and it was certainly not going to be a long trial. This would be a matter of which lawyer could convince the jury to agree with them.

Jason had never had a case like this before. He knew that Alexia's future was in his own hands and that it was up to him to convince the jury that she was telling the truth. Jason spent the next few days reading the reports made by the police, paramedics, and forensics team to see what he was up against and to decide which way to go about defending Alexia.

During the next five weeks, Jason and Alexia saw each other quite a few times. For the most part, it remained professional between them, except for a few occasions when Alexia told Jason to make her come by licking her pussy. She, in turn, would sometimes tease him, by playing with his cock, bringing him close to cumming, but would then stop. She loved teasing her slaves with orgasm control and denial.

Jason began to understand what it meant to be under the control of someone else, a concept he had never known before, but he got used to being patient. He was always more than happy to pleasure Alexia when she wanted it. He also knew that she was not a selfish mistress, and indeed, he would get a little reward from her here and there.

In the meantime, Jason was also in constant touch with Marcus. There still was nothing to report regarding Emerton, although he kept hoping that something would turn up. Over the next couple of weeks, Jason had read all the reports from any witnesses who would be called to give evidence against Alexia. For him, it all seemed a clear case of self-defense, but he knew only too well that the jurors might not see things the same way, especially given Alexia's profession. 'Sure, she may get the men's vote, but what about the women?' he wondered.

Nothing was certain, and Jason knew that anything could happen in a case like this. He wished there was something more he could do to ensure a win. The trial was now just over three weeks away, and there was nothing else for Jason to do except wait. He was all ready for it, as was Alexia, but he was still frustrated that he had nothing on Emerton he could use.

Jason thought long and hard during that day, then called Marcus and arranged to meet him in a bar for a drink that evening. They met after work, found a quiet table, ordered some drinks, chatted for a while, and then Jason began to speak about the case.

"Just before the trial starts, when I know who they are, I will give you a list which will be the names of the jurors. I want you to look into their lives and see what you can dig up."

"Are you serious?" Marcus asked, shocked at what he had just heard.

"Yes, I'm very serious, my friend," Jason replied, taking a sip of his drink.

"Look, Jason, you are my friend, and I want to help you, but what the hell is going on with you and this escort?"

"She is **not** an escort, Marcus; she is much more than that. I can't explain it, but I need to help her at all costs," Jason snapped.

"You know if we do this, we could both end up in prison, don't you?" Marcus asked him.

"Yes, I do, my friend, but I need to do this. If you want no part of it, I will understand, but give me the name of someone who can help me."

Marcus looked into Jason's eyes for a brief moment and said to his long-time friend, "After what you did for me, do you really think I am going to walk away from you now, Jason?

No, I am in this all the way, buddy, and I will do whatever I can to help you."

"Thank you, Marcus. You are a good friend, and I really appreciate this," Jason said sincerely.

"Anytime, buddy, anytime, but we are going to have to buy our souls back from the devil with this one," Marcus replied, shaking his head as he spoke.

"Indeed we are, Marcus; indeed we are," Jason said as he laughed out loud.

They stayed there for a while longer, finished their drinks, had a bite to eat together and chatted away about normal everyday things. Then they said their goodbyes and went their separate ways.

Jason got home about nine that evening, not realizing how late it was.

Lydia asked, "Where have you been, Jason?"

"Oh, sorry, Lyd. I met with Marcus for a drink and a bite to eat, and I totally forgot to call you," Jason replied, not really meaning his apology.

"And so you should be. I did not know what had happened to you," Lydia replied.

"As I said, I'm sorry; I forgot."

"Well, I'm going out now with Valerie, and I'm not sure what time I will be back."

"Ok, have a nice time," Jason replied, thinking to himself, 'Don't bother to come back.'

He did not even ask her where she was going as he really did not care at this moment in time. The only thing on his mind was Alexia and this case. Besides, Jason was beginning to get fed up with the way things were at home now. She always wanted to know everything he was going to do, where he was going, who he was with, but would never afford him that same courtesy.

Jason knew she only wanted to know in case he was going to be anywhere near where she may have been with her lover, but it got to the stage now that he did not care about them anymore. He had Alexia in his life now. If he could successfully defend her with this manslaughter charge, his life would be so different and happier, especially as Alexia had told him she would make him one of her personal slaves. He actually felt both nervous and excited at the prospect of being one of her personal slaves without really knowing what that meant exactly.

He could only hope that she would allow him to see her regularly, like her other personal slaves she had told him about previously. Then he would have his life back the way it was before meeting Lydia. 'Oh, how wonderful that would be,' Jason thought as he went over to the drinks cabinet and poured himself a large whiskey.

He spent the rest of the evening dreaming about just how different his life could be with Alexia. He also began to think if there was any way that he could actually end his marriage with Lydia without her causing too many problems.

Lydia had a very spiteful streak to her. She was the sort of person who would turn up at Jason's work, a fundraiser, or any one of the many events Jason would be invited to and cause a scene, just for the sake of it. This would almost certainly cause problems where his position at Langley & Foster was concerned, and he could not afford to have that happen.

Jason so wanted to have his life the way it was before, with the inclusion of Alexia, but Emerton and Lydia stood in his way. Emerton would not be so much of an issue once he had won this case, but Lydia would be a much bigger problem to solve. He even thought of resigning and starting out on his own again just so he could be rid of Lydia and have Alexia in his life. However, at this moment in time, he did not even know exactly what part of Alexia's life he would be included in, and perhaps he was making far too much of all this.

'Oh, well, one thing at a time,' he thought to himself, then finished his drink, watched some television, went for a shower, and then off to bed.

Chapter Twenty-One

It was now Friday, and Jason woke up at 6.30 am. He got up as quietly as possible so as to not wake Lydia as he was not in the mood to talk to her. He showered, got dressed, and then went downstairs to make himself some coffee and toast for breakfast. As he sipped his coffee, he began to think back to when he first met Lydia and how she would always get up and make him breakfast before he went to work. That seemed almost a lifetime ago - when he believed that Lydia loved him rather than loving his money and status, which had become obvious to him over the last year.

After finishing his breakfast and reading the daily newspaper, he left home to drive to his office, arriving at 8.45 am. He had a quick chat with Martha, who had been with Jason from the first day of his working at Foster & Langley and had proved to be an invaluable secretary for him. Martha reminded Jason of a couple of telephone calls he had to make and then told him that Mr. Langley wished to see him at 10 am in his office.

Jason then went into his office and made those telephone calls. When it was time, he went to see his boss precisely at 10 am as his boss was not the type of person who would tolerate tardiness. Mr. Langley's secretary told him that Jason was here to see him, and he asked her to show him into his office.

"Good morning, Mr. Langley," Jason said as he entered the room.

"Good morning, Jason. Please take a seat," was the reply from Langley.

"Thank you. You wished to see me, Mr. Langley?"

"Yes, Jason. Where are we with the Summer's case?" he asked.

"Everything is in hand, Mr. Langley, and I am very hopeful that we will win this case," Jason replied in a confident way.

Langley looked at Jason for a very brief moment and then asked him, "Can you be more specific, please, Jason? I need to know exactly where we are. I do not normally get involved with your cases as I have every confidence in your abilities. However, if you remember when I first gave you this case, I mentioned that a very influential client of ours has asked me personally to deal with this, and he is now asking how the case is progressing."

"Well, the prosecutor, as you know, is doing this as a personal vendetta against me, which is why the original charge was going to be murder before you arranged to have it changed to manslaughter, but they have no evidence of foul play. The only reason this case is even going to trial is because of her profession, and we both know that."

"Yes, indeed," Langley said as he drummed his fingers on his desk.

"Without any real evidence to the contrary, it will be very hard for the prosecution to get any kind of conviction against her self-defense plea. I shall be meeting with Miss Summers to prep her for trial, and she will know exactly what to say and how to behave in the courtroom. All the facts and forensics go to show that Miss Summers is telling the truth, and I see no reason why the members of the jury would not see that. The only thing that concerns me is her profession, which could sway some of the jurors. Of course, as always, my job will be to make the jurors believe what I want them to believe, and as you are well aware, I have a very good track record of doing that," Jason said, again very confidently.

"Indeed you have, Jason, which is precisely the reason I have entrusted this case to you."

"And I shall not let you down, Mr. Langley. Will there be anything else?"

"No, that will be all; thank you, Jason. But please keep me informed of any further developments," Langley replied, feeling confident that Jason was the right man for the job.

"I will do," replied Jason as he arose from his chair and headed for the door.

The two men then said their goodbyes, and Jason made his way back to his office, where he poured himself a whiskey and took a large swig of it. 'That was intense,' he thought to himself, as it was not normal for Langley to question him about his cases or that Langley himself had to answer to anyone else. Jason then wondered just who this influential client could be that was putting so much pressure on his boss and to what extent his involvement was with Alexia.

Now that Alexia had popped into his mind, he realized that just the thought of her stirred feelings in him that he had not experienced in the past. It was so strange for him to feel this way for someone he had known for such a very short period of time. He could not explain it, and this was an alien feeling for him as he was normally in strict control of his emotions and life in general. He then wondered when they would next see each other and wished that he could see her again this weekend because he felt he needed to.

After all, he was going to take such a big risk with what he was planning to do for her, and it could, if it backfired, see him end up in prison. He felt that he deserved to see her more often due to the risks he was taking for her. However, of course, she had no knowledge of the sacrifices he was prepared to make in his decision to break the law to ensure success with the trial.

'Still, all in good time,' he thought to himself and could only hope that one day he would be able to spend a lot of time being in her company.

Jason was now not in the mood to do any work and decided to take the rest of the day off. He told Martha that he had a couple of leads he wanted to follow up on regarding Miss Summer's case, just in case Langley enquired where he was. He telephoned Marcus on his way to his car and asked if he wanted to meet him for a couple of drinks.

"But I don't have any more information for you yet," Marcus told him.

"Oh no, that's fine. I just fancy having a drink with a friend," Jason replied.

"Ok, yeah, great," said Marcus, and they arranged to meet at Maxwell's bar, which was a regular meeting place for them for after-work drinks.

They began the afternoon with some general chit-chat as was intended, but before long, the conversation changed to Alexia's case. Jason sought reassurance concerning what was being done regarding getting any dirt on Emerton and his family.

"What is it with you and this woman, buddy?" Marcus asked. He had known Jason for such a long time and

knew that this was so uncharacteristic of him to get so personally involved.

Jason picked up his glass of whiskey and drank the whole lot down in one go. He put his arm up to call the waitress over, asking for another two doubles for him and Marcus, before turning to his friend and replying, "Where should I begin, my friend? We go back a long way, and I know I can trust you with this. I have become involved personally with Alexia and her lifestyle. Before you say anything, yes, I know what I'm doing as she is a very special lady, and she makes me feel like I have never felt in the past."

"But she is just a hooker," Marcus said, unable to understand the hold Alexia had on him.

Jason gave Marcus a steely gaze and, in a stern voice, replied, "No, Marcus, I have told you before that she is *not* just a hooker. She is so much more, and she is very important to me."

Marcus was taken aback by Jason's tone of voice and attitude. He wondered what was happening to his friend before asking, "What exactly is going on, buddy? I have never seen you like this before, and it is so unlike you to be like this with someone you hardly know, especially a client."

"It's a long story, Marcus. I apologize for talking to you like that, but you have no idea of how I feel about her or my relationship with her, and I have no wish to go into it at this moment in time. Just know that she means the world to me, and her freedom is the only thing that matters for me right now."

Marcus took a very deep breath and then asked his friend, "Ok, how can I help?" Deep down inside, he knew that this was not the time to push Jason for any more details.

Jason thought for a minute and wondered if Marcus would understand this whole mistress and slave situation. But he was also embarrassed to let his friend know that he had become this submissive person in the presence of Alexia. After all, how could he expect his friend to understand when he himself did not fully understand these submissive feelings he had while around her. No, he could not bring himself to tell him everything, and perhaps it was better for Marcus to continue to think that he was seeing her as an escort instead.

"She just makes me feel so very young and alive again, my friend, which is a feeling I have not experienced in such a very long time. Plus, with Lydia being a cheating bitch, why shouldn't I have my fun, even if it is with a client of mine? Let's face it, Marcus, we have both done much worse things in the past."

"Yeah, I hear you, buddy, I really do, and I get where you are coming from, but I am just a little concerned as this is not like you at all. Just know that I will have your back, as always."

"I know you will, Marcus, and I appreciate that more than you will ever know. We both have our skeletons, and that's why we can both trust each other the way we do. Ok, let's forget about this for now and just enjoy a few drinks together, as we have not done that for a long time."

"Amen to that, brother," Marcus replied as he signaled the waitress over for another round of drinks.

Before they had realized it, they had spent all night in the bar and had a lot more to drink than they had planned. There was no way either of them was capable of driving, so they both left their cars there and got a cab.

By the time Jason got home, it was the early hours of the morning, and he just sat on the couch and fell asleep.

CHAPTER TWENTY-TWO

Jason woke up the next morning on the couch with a massive hangover. He was regretting the amount he and Marcus had to drink the night before when he heard Lydia, who was standing over him saying in a very sarcastic manner, "Have a nice evening, did you?"

"Oh, Lyd, I feel like crap. What time is it?" Jason said, putting his hands up to his head.

"Never mind what time it is. Where the hell were you till the early hours of the morning?"

"I was having a drink with Marcus, and please don't shout as I have a terrible headache."

"Fuck your headache! I did not know where you were all night. Do you not think you should have called and told me you were going out for a drink?" she shouted at him.

"Don't pretend you give a damn, Lyd. Besides, you were going to be out last night anyway, so what difference does it make? I never really know where you are most of the time," he replied angrily.

"Well, for your information, Valerie canceled on me last night, and I was home all evening. Perhaps if you bothered to answer your cell, you would have known that."

Jason reached into his jacket pocket to get his cell and realized that the battery had died at some stage during the night. His first thought was, 'What if Alexia had tried to call?' He then turned to his wife and said, "Damn, my cell died."

"Don't use that as an excuse. You could have used the phone there and should still have called me," she shouted back.

"Yeah, ok," he replied as he could not be bothered to argue with her. After all, she did not afford him the same courtesy. Who the hell did she think she was anyway, sneaking around behind his back with that bastard? He was almost tempted to tell her as much, but he wanted to keep what he knew to himself for now. If he told her that he knew about her affair, he would then lose any leverage he could use in the future.

This was a very difficult thing for him to do as it was not in his nature to take this attitude from anyone. However, he had to keep that information until it could be used for something more important than just shutting his wife up, such as using it to help Alexia if the need arose. 'How ironic that my own wife may have provided me with the ammunition I need to help out Alexia. I could always try to blackmail the politician she is having an affair with for some leverage in Alexia's case,' he thought to himself.

Before Lydia could say much more, Jason got up and put his phone on charge, then went to take a shower. He was not in the mood for Lydia's tantrums right now, and he was still concerned that Alexia may have tried to contact him last night.

Angry at Jason, Lydia decided to do what she did best, which was to go out and spend his money. She got dressed and shouted out to Jason, "I'm going out shopping." And then she simply left the house.

Jason was only too relieved not to have to face any more of her complaining and was happy to spend the rest of the day on his own. He then realized that he had to go back to the bar to pick up his car as he got a cab home.

So, after he had his shower, he powered up his cell and checked to see if Alexia had indeed left a message, but he was disappointed that there were none. His cell still only had a partial charge, so he waited until it was fully charged before going to pick up his car, just in case Alexia decided to call him that morning. But the call he so wanted to get did not come.

It was now nearly a week since he had last seen her, and he could not stand it any longer. He decided that it was time he called, and he could use the excuse that he needed to arrange for them to meet on Friday so he could prepare her for the trial as it was getting closer.

After arriving back home from picking up his car, he gave Alexia a call.

"Hello, Jason, how are you?" she said, answering her cell.

"I am very well, Miss Summers. How are you?"

"I am well, thank you, Jason. So this is a professional call, is it?"

"Well, yes, it is. I am calling to arrange for you to come and see me at my office so that I can get you ready for trial and go over what is likely to happen."

"Oh, I see, and do you generally call your clients yourself on a Saturday to make such arrangements, or does your secretary normally deal with that during the week?" she asked.

Jason paused for a few seconds, realizing that she was no fool and was perfectly aware that this was not the reason for calling her.

"Yes, you are right, and I am sorry. I do need to arrange a meeting with you, but I guess I have used that as an excuse to speak to you today. Please forgive me, as I know I am not meant to contact you, but it has been a while since I last saw you, and I just wanted to make sure that everything was ok," he replied, afraid that she was going to be angry.

"I see, and did you really think that I would fall for that?" she replied sarcastically.

"No, I guess not, but I just wanted to speak to you, and again, I apologize," he said, putting one hand on his head as he still had a bad headache.

Alexia purposely did not reply for a few seconds, then said, "That's ok, Jason. This was simply another test, which I am happy to say you have passed."

"What do you mean, Alexia?" he asked.

"Do **not** forget your place, Jason. Is it not obvious that if I am talking about you passing a test, then I am talking to you as your mistress? As such, you should address me in the correct manner," she snapped in a very stern voice.

"Of course, please forgive me, Mistress." he quickly replied.

"The test I refer to, Jason, is that I purposely did not contact you as your mistress for the last week so I could see how long it would have taken you to contact me even though I told you that I would always be the one to contact you. Had you done so too soon, then you would have been far too eager for my liking, and it would have shown me that you had no self-control. However, if you had left it for too long, that would have told me that you were not too bothered if you had contact with me or indeed if you really wanted me as your mistress. The perfect time for you to have contacted me would have been around one week, and that is exactly how long you left it. This is a very big bonus for you, Jason, and as a reward, I expect you to visit me at my home this afternoon at 4 pm."

"Yes, Mistress, it would be my pleasure," Jason said with his heart racing in anticipation of not only seeing her again but also of what the reward would be.

"Very well, then, I shall see you this afternoon, Jason. Goodbye for now," she said as she ended the call.

"Goodbye, Mistress, and thank you very much," he replied as he put the phone down.

The next few hours seemed to drag on forever, but eventually, it was time for him to leave. He left Lydia a note saying that he was going out and unsure of exactly what time he would be back so that she would not start moaning again once he did return home. Then he got himself ready and jumped in his car to drive to Alexia's house on Long Island.

Chapter Twenty-Three

Jason arrived at Alexia's home ten minutes early and decided to wait in the car before pulling up into her driveway as he did not want to seem too eager. Once it was precisely 4 pm, he pulled in, parked his car, then got out and rang the doorbell.

A completely naked man opened the door to him and said, "Good afternoon sir, my name is Henry. Please follow me. The mistress is waiting for you in the garden."

"Thank you," replied Jason, who felt very uncomfortable about the fact that a naked man was answering the door to him. He was also a little jealous of this man who must live with Alexia when Jason himself would have loved to have been the one living with her.

He was led to the garden, which was surrounded by a high fence which made it very secluded. Alexia was sunning herself in a lounger, totally naked as well, and Jason could not take his gaze away from her beautiful body as he approached her.

"Hello, Mistress," Jason said, taking his gaze away from her body and looking into her eyes.

"Hello, Jason, one minute. Henry, can you bring us a very chilled bottle of champagne and two glasses, please?"

"Yes, Mistress," he replied as he walked off.

"So, how are you, Jason? Please, take a seat on the sun lounger next to me."

"I am very well, Mistress, thank you," replied Jason as he sat down on the edge of the sun lounger.

Alexia could see that Jason was having a hard time taking his eyes away from her naked body and asked,

"Do you like what you see, Jason?"

"Yes, I do, Mistress, very much so," he replied in a very excited voice.

"Well, you have me at a disadvantage, so you should undress for me now," she said in a commanding voice.

Jason began to take his clothes off, wondering what was about to happen next. He suddenly stopped when Henry returned with the bottle of champagne and continued to open it, then poured out two glasses, setting them down on the little table that was in between the two loungers.

"Thank you, Henry," Alexia said in a soft voice as she stretched out her hand and stroked Henry's cock for a few seconds, staring at Jason while she was doing so. "That will be all for now, Henry," she said as she pulled her hand away.

Jason continued to undress but found it very weird for another man to be naked there, let alone Alexia touching him. Yet it was also extremely difficult to keep himself from becoming hard as he looked at Alexia's naked body until he too was totally naked and sat back down on the sun lounger.

"Have a drink, Jason," said Alexia as she picked up her glass and took a sip from it.

"Thank you, Mistress," Jason replied as he did the same and then put the glass back down on the table, still wondering if this was his reward or if there was more to follow.

"Now, it's time you massaged my feet, Jason," Alexia said as she took yet another sip of her champagne.

Without hesitation, Jason got up and made his way to the end of her sun lounger, where Alexia had bent her knees and lifted up her right leg for Jason to massage her right foot. He was now in direct view of Alexia's pussy, and without being able to help it, he found himself becoming aroused very quickly. Alexia, who then changed her legs over, putting her right leg back down and lifting her left leg so that Jason could now massage her left foot, noticed that Jason's cock was now very stiff.

After a short while of him massaging her foot, she said, "Now, kiss my foot." Then she stretched out her right leg and began to rub Jason's hard cock with it while he kissed her left foot. He was in heaven at this very moment and let out a little groan of pleasure as she pushed her foot harder against his stiff cock.

"Suck my toes," she then commanded.

This was not something that Jason had done before, and he did not like the thought of sucking anyone's toes, but this was not just anyone. He knew that he could not say no to her, and so, as much as he disliked the idea, he began to suck on them gently.

A very short while later, Alexia changed legs again so that Jason was now kissing her right foot before sucking her toes. While doing this, she, in turn, was using her left foot on his very hard cock. 'So far, so good,' she thought to herself as she watched Jason doing exactly what was commanded of him while she stroked his now throbbing cock with her foot.

Alexia could see that Jason was enjoying this immensely and lowered her right leg so that now both of her feet were around his firm shaft. She moved them up and down while looking directly at him as he looked deep into her eyes.

"Don't you dare come until I give you permission, or there will be consequences," she said to him in a stern voice.

"Yes, Mistress, I will try not to," he replied, knowing full well that because he was so excited he would not be able to last a long time before wanting to come.

"Try is not good enough," Alexia replied as she increased the speed of her feet.

"Yes, I am sorry, Mistress," he said as he tried everything he could think of to hold off from shooting his load.

He knew that it would be only a very short matter of time at this pace before he would have no choice.

When only a few more minutes had passed, he said to Alexia, "I can't hold it any longer, Mistress, I really can't."

"Do not disappoint me, Jason, as I do not want you to come yet, and as I have already stated, there will be consequences if you do," she said in a firm manner.

She had barely even finished her sentence when Jason could not hold off any longer and exploded, jizzing all over her feet, apologizing to her as he did so, shot after shot of his cum covering her feet.

"What did I say, Jason? I am very disappointed in you. Look at the mess you have made on my feet. Now you must pay the price, so clean it up."

Jason reached over to grab a towel that was on the chair, but before he could do so, Alexia shouted at him, "What are you doing?"

"I'm getting the towel so that I can clean it up, Mistress," he replied.

"Oh no, you are not going to dirty my towel with your mess," she laughed.

"Well, how shall I clean it up then, Mistress?" Jason enquired.

Alexia really wanted to see what Jason was made of and whether he was true slave material or not, as well as wanting to push his boundaries. She decided to see just how far he would actually go and if she really did have his obedience, so she needed him to do something that she knew he would cringe at.

"With your mouth, of course!" Alexia commanded in an almost evil tone of voice, knowing too well that only a true obedient slave would actually do something like that.

Jason looked at her in utter shock, but before he could even say anything, she continued.

"Now, get on your knees and lick my feet clean."

Jason looked at her and then looked at her feet, covered in his spunk.

But again, before he could say or do anything, she shouted very loudly at him, "NOW, SLAVE!"

"But Mistress-" Jason began to protest.

However, before he could finish his sentence, Alexia said in a very stern, almost angry voice, "Do it now, or you can get dressed, leave my house, and never return."

Jason was horrified at what he was being told to do. However, he suddenly remembered what she had told him before - that he would sometimes have to do some things he did not enjoy or even want to do. He got down on his knees and felt physically sick at the prospect of what he now had to do. But he also knew that if he refused, it would be over as far as his relationship with Alexia was concerned.

However, as sick as he felt, he hesitantly began to lick his cum from her feet, feeling sick as he did so, until Alexia was satisfied that her feet were clean before telling Jason to stop. She then spread her legs wide apart, and while pointing with her finger to her clit, she said to Jason in a demanding voice, "Now, lick me as I need to come."

Jason did as was commanded, but of course, this time, it was a pleasure for him to do so, as this was something he enjoyed very much, and he spent the next five minutes licking her clit and along the length of her slit every so often.

Once Alexia had come and was satisfied, she told him to stand up.

"There will always be consequences when you disobey me, Jason, and this was a little lesson for you to learn from. The more often you disobey me, the worse the consequences will be. Is that clear?" she asked in a very firm manner.

"Yes, Mistress, I am sorry that I could not hold out any longer, but I was just far too excited."

"Oh, I know you were, Jason and I will always be pushing your boundaries in one way or another, and this was simply yet another little test. But at least you got your reward by having me make you come."

"Thank you, Mistress, it was very good of you to do so," Jason replied.

"You have shown a lot of promise since we began, Jason, and I am confident that, in time, you will have a long and happy future as one of my slaves. But again, I must warn you about doing exactly what you are told immediately or else."

"Thank you again, Mistress; it would be my pleasure to serve you."

"Very well, Jason, the time has now come for you to leave, so get dressed, and I shall speak to you soon."

"Yes, Mistress," he replied as he began to dress.

When he was ready, he said goodbye, left her home, made his way back to his car, and drove to his house, arriving home before Lydia returned from her shopping spree. He dreaded to think just how much she would have spent today to punish him for last night, but right now, his mind was replaying the events of this afternoon and just how far he could go with Alexia.

Eventually, Lydia did return with a big smile and lots of shopping bags. 'Yeah, ok,' Jason thought to himself, 'she is in a much better mood now after her shopping spree.' He wondered if he would have a heart attack when his credit card statement arrived. Still, at least there was peace in the household tonight.

CHAPTER TWENTY-FOUR

The following week went by without much incident, and it was now Friday morning, the 10th of July, which was also the day for the jury selection to begin. The morning began with the possible jury members being spoken to and asked questions by the judge as well as both lawyers. After having gone through the process of voir dire, the 12 members of the jury were selected. The judge then instructed the jurors on what they were not allowed to do, such as to discuss the case with anyone, and by the time he had finished, he said that the court would reconvene on Monday morning for the opening arguments.

Jason then left the courtroom and made his way to his car. Once he was inside it, he telephoned Marcus asking to meet him for a chat, which, of course, Marcus agreed to. They never spoke over the phone about anything connected to work, as someone could be listening in to their conversation. If anyone was ever to get a hint of what they were doing here, they would both be in very deep water indeed.

Around an hour later, they met up, and after talking for a short while, Jason handed Marcus a folded piece of paper.

"In here, you will find all the names of the jurors that will be in Alexia's trial, and I want you to find me something I can use," Jason said to him.

"Are you really sure you want to do this, buddy?" Marcus asked him, concerned that he was getting far too involved with Alexia and was biting off more than he could chew.

"Yes, my old friend, I do. So I'll say it again - if you want out, then tell me now."

"No, Jason. I told you before that I will go all the way with you, but just know that if we are caught, we are going to be knee-high in it, and we will both spend a long time in prison."

"Yeah, I know, pal, and I really do appreciate you doing this for me," Jason replied.

"Ok then, buddy. I have some of my people waiting for these names, so I will have them get to work straight away. They will work through the whole weekend to see if anything can be found. Let's keep our fingers crossed we don't end up in the same courtroom as your escort, but for the wrong reasons," Marcus said jokingly as he got up to leave.

After Marcus had left, Jason sat there for a short while and pondered what he had gotten himself into, but he could not help how he felt about Alexia. He was as confused as he was excited about these thoughts and feelings he had for this woman, even though he had never, ever felt like this before about anyone else, not even Selene.

He stayed there and had another drink before leaving to go back to the office, where his first job was to report to Langley to give him an update about how the jury selection went. Jason was shown into Langley's office.

As he sat down, he was asked by his boss, "So, how did it go, Jason?"

"As well as we could have hoped for, Mr. Langley," he replied confidently.

"Very good, Jason. I knew you would not let me down. Now give me all the details, will you please?" Langley asked.

Jason went on to tell him everything that happened and what was said. When he had finished, he went back to his own office and again wondered exactly why his boss was being so inquisitive about this case. Once more, he began to wonder just who this influential client was, that was putting pressure on his boss and if he would ever find out his identity.

It was now 5 pm, but the afternoon had passed by very slowly for him, and Jason was still lost in thought while he got himself ready to go home for the weekend. The evening also went by quite slowly for him, and he was very quiet throughout the whole night, which was unusual for Jason. Even Lydia noticed the difference, and asked him what the matter was, but Jason just told her he was thinking about the trial that was due to start on Monday.

She gave him a cuddle, telling him that everything would be ok as he was a great lawyer and should not doubt himself. He thanked her for those kind words, and they stayed up chatting while sharing a bottle of wine together for the next couple of hours before going to bed.

Saturday morning came, and Jason, who did not get much sleep, got out of bed, had a shower, and told Lydia he was going to have some breakfast then go for a walk to clear his head, which is something he did before a trial began. He asked if she wanted anything to eat or drink, but she said no, so he went downstairs, had his breakfast then left the house.

He walked around for about an hour before returning home and going into the garden to lay down in the sun for a while. He had only been there for a very short time when Marcus called, saying that he needed to see him urgently and could they meet.

He then told Lydia he had to go out later to meet someone regarding the trial, and when the time came, he left home. They met at lunchtime as arranged, and Marcus told Jason that his people had not only worked through all of yesterday afternoon and evening but also the whole night.

He said that they spoke to many people in person and did online searches as well. Marcus even used his very close friends and contacts he still had in the police force. His people also visited and spoke to all the known bookies and loan sharks, which eventually paid off. They had found out that one of the jurors, Tony Samuels, had a gambling habit and was in quite a bit of debt.

Jason thought long and hard for a minute, then told Marcus to approach this man to see if he could be used to their advantage.

"How far do you want to take this?" Marcus asked him.

Jason paused briefly, then said, "Do whatever is necessary."

By this, of course, Jason meant that if they could pay Samuels off, then well and good, but if not, then perhaps force would need to be used. However, Jason did not need to say as much because Marcus knew exactly what he meant.

Now Marcus, having been a police officer in the past, knew a lot of people who he could use for such a job. He picked out two brothers, Abe and Carl Jackson, who had spent most of their lives on the wrong side of the law. As Marcus had done them a favor in the past when he was on the force, he knew that they would help him now that he needed it.

After leaving Jason, Marcus called and arranged to meet the brothers, where he told them what he wanted them to do, and they indeed said they would help him out. He told them to approach Samuels and offer him the money to clear his debts if he were to be sympathetic to Alexia's cause, so to speak. If he refused, they should resort to whatever means necessary to get his cooperation, and they knew exactly what that meant. These brothers were hard-core criminals who would not hesitate to put the pressure on if it needed to be done and, as such, they were the perfect candidates for such a task.

Marcus could never do this himself as he did not want to get his hands dirty, and of course, it would not have been wise anyway due to his connection to Jason. And Jason could never have been seen to be doing anything illegal either, so this is where Marcus's contacts came into such good use. Jason and Marcus trusted each other due to their past. Anyone Marcus would ever use for anything of questionable legality would have been someone who Marcus himself would have a hold over and could get them in trouble at any time.

Things were now looking up for Jason. If he could get Samuels to vote not guilty and convince a few of the other jurors to do the same, it would lead to a mistrial. If this were indeed to happen, it would be doubtful that the DA's office would retry such a case. So Jason knew that he did not need to win the case, just avoid losing it. Even though he would have loved nothing better than wiping the floor with Emerton, Alexia's freedom would have to come first and certainly before any personal reasons.

Later that afternoon, Marcus called and arranged to meet Jason again. He then told him that the two brothers would be going to see Samuels today. His debt would cost $15k to clear if, indeed, he agreed to do as was asked of him.

"And if he doesn't play ball?" Jason asked.

"Don't worry about that; they know what to do," Marcus replied.

"But can you trust them?" Jason asked anxiously.

"They owe me, and they will pay that debt to me, or certain information I have will find its way to one of my friends at the precinct," Marcus replied, assuring Jason that everything was under control and that there was nothing for him to worry about.

"Ok then," Jason said, thinking that $15k was a lot of money, but he could afford it, and it would be worth every cent if it would help clear Alexia. However, he was still very annoyed that nothing could be found on squeaky-clean Emerton himself.

After they had finished talking, Jason went back home and began to watch some television when his cell phone rang.

As he picked it up, he saw that it was Alexia and quickly answered it with a "Hello, Mistress."

He remembered what she had told him about her calling his cell, and he was also thankful that Lydia was in the garden soaking in the swimming pool and not in the same room as him.

"Very good, Jason, you remembered," Alexia replied.

"Yes, Mistress, I did," Jason said, feeling very happy with himself.

"Tomorrow morning at nine, I want you to come to my home, not my house in Manhattan, but my actual home on Long Island as before. I want to go over a few things regarding the trial, but I also have a little surprise for you," Alexia said, without giving anything away.

"Yes, Mistress, whatever you want," Jason replied excitedly.

"That's correct, Jason; it is whatever I want," Alexia replied before saying goodbye and putting the phone down, leaving Jason to ponder what the surprise could be.

Jason was now very excited at the prospect of seeing Alexia in her own home again and was fairly certain that she did, in fact, plan to make him her personal slave if he could indeed win this case. He went out into the garden, staring at the clear blue sky.

He began to daydream about what lay ahead the following day when he heard his wife's voice call out, "Can I have a drink, Jason?"

Jason turned to see Lydia coming out of the pool, then going to sit on the deck chair, and he thought, 'Get it yourself, you lazy bitch,' but instead, he replied, "Sure thing, Lyd. What would you like?"

"Oh, a glass of cold white wine would be nice," she said.

Jason poured her wine and took it over to her. "Are you doing anything tonight?"

"No, but I'm playing golf tomorrow with some friends," she replied.

"Oh, that will be nice; unfortunately, I have to go to work tomorrow," he said.

Lydia sat up in her deckchair and asked, "Work on Sunday?"

"Yes, I know, but this self-defense case beginning on Monday is going to be a bit trickier than I initially thought, and I need to prep my client as she is very nervous," he replied.

"Oh, is she?" Lydia asked suspiciously.

'What a fucking nerve,' Jason thought to himself about the way Lydia asked that last question before replying in a semi-sarcastic manner.

"Yes, she is, Lyd. Wouldn't you be, if you were being charged with manslaughter?"

"Yes, I guess I would, but then I have a great lawyer as a husband," she chuckled.

Jason was taken aback for a brief moment and wondered whether she really just complimented him. 'Wow, it has been a long time since that has happened,' he thought.

"Anyway, I'm going for a shower," he told Lydia as he finished his drink and headed off upstairs.

Jason had his shower, put on his dressing-gown, and went back downstairs, pouring both himself and Lydia another drink.

He sat down in a deckchair next to her and asked, "So what's for dinner tonight?"

"Oh, do you mind if we just get a take-out tonight? I have just had my nails done this afternoon, and I don't want to ruin them," Lydia replied.

"Yes, sure thing," Jason said and thought, 'Hmm, nails just done and playing golf tomorrow, yeah, right!'

A short while later, Jason ordered some Chinese food, and after they had eaten, they had a couple more drinks. Jason then said he was going to bed to get some sleep as he had a busy week coming up, starting with tomorrow. He kissed Lydia on the cheek, said goodnight, and off he went.

Chapter Twenty-Five

In the meantime, Abe and Carl went to Samuels's home that Saturday, then just waited and watched to see who was home and who wasn't. Through their search, they had found out that he goes to his bookie every Saturday to either gamble or pay back the money he owed. So they waited in their car for the opportune moment to speak to him, as they did not want to arouse suspicion by knocking on his door just in case his wife answered.

They did not have to wait for long as Samuels left his house as usual, got into his car, then began to drive. The two brothers knew that this was the perfect time for them to speak to him as he was on his own, and they obviously did not want any other witnesses. They followed him to where his bookie was, and after he went inside, they decided to wait for him to come back out before approaching him.

After around an hour, they saw Samuels come out from his bookie and make his way to his car, so the two brothers got out of theirs and walked up to him.

"Can we have a little chat?" Abe asked him.

"What do you want?" Samuels asked in a terrified voice, fearing it was the people he had borrowed the money from to pay his gambling debt to his bookie.

"We just want to talk to you, that's all. We are not here to squeeze you for the money you owe, but we are here to offer you a solution regarding your debts," Carl said calmly.

"What debts? What do you mean? Who are you?" Samuels asked, appearing frightened.

"Relax, we are not going to hurt you unless you give us no other choice; we just want to talk to you," Abe said, tapping Samuels on his arm.

"I don't have time now; I have to go," Samuels replied as he tried to push past them to get into his car.

Carl grabbed Samuels by the shoulder, spun him around, and punched him in the abdomen as hard as he could.

"Ouch," Samuels screamed as he bent over from the pain.

"Perhaps you misunderstood. We are not asking you; we are telling you. We are going to have a chat either here or go for a little ride in our car. Now, we can do that the easy way or the painful way; the choice is yours," Carl said as he patted Samuels on the back.

However, before Samuels could even answer, Abe said to him, "You have a very pretty young wife, and it would be such a shame if something terrible were to happen to her, wouldn't it?"

"No, please. Leave my wife alone, don't hurt her," Samuels begged.

"And we won't. We just want a little chat with you, that's all. Now, is it going to be the easy or the painful way?" Carl said with a massive grin on his face.

"The easy way, just please leave my wife alone," Samuels said in a quiet voice.

The brothers continued their chat with Samuels, explaining the situation with the trial he had coming up as a juror. They told him that they would be willing to pay off his $15k gambling debt if he were to help them with a little problem they had. Samuels asked what they wanted him to do, and they said that the defendant had to be found not guilty. Or, at the very least, the judge had to be forced to declare a mistrial due to a few of the jurors voting not guilty. They told him that if he was indeed able to convince other jurors to vote the same way as him and the defendant was either found not guilty or a mistrial was declared, his debt would be paid off, and he would never see them again.

"How am I supposed to do that?" Samuels asked, knowing that if he got caught, then he would end up in prison.

"Use your imagination, charm, or any means necessary to make sure that she is not found guilty," Abe said as he pointed his index finger straight at Samuels.

"And what if I can't do it?" he asked nervously.

"Well, let's see now. If you don't pay the people you borrowed the money from on time, including the very high interest, they will probably just break an arm or a leg, am I right? However, if you don't do what we say, then we shall have to pay you a visit at home one evening. As your wife is so pretty, maybe she will entertain us, if you know what I mean. But as for you, well, I hear that the beds at the general hospital are very comfortable, so it won't be too bad when you have to spend the next three months in there," Carl said with a big grin.

"And, of course, while you are in the hospital, we will make sure we pay your wife a visit from time to time just to make sure she is not lonely," Abe said as he winked at Samuels.

"No, please, leave my wife out of it. Please don't hurt her; I will do my best," he said.

"Your best is not good enough. We want your guarantee that at least three jurors will vote not guilty," Carl said as he prodded Samuels in the chest with his finger.

"Yes, yes, ok, I will do whatever is necessary to make sure. Just please, leave my wife alone," Samuels begged the two brothers.

"There you go. See what you can do when you put your mind to it? Now you can get back into your car, but remember one thing, someone will be watching you from time to time. You will never know when they are watching, and if you tell anyone about this little chat or even think about going to the police, your wife will get a visit real soon, got it?"

"Yes, I got it. I won't say anything to anyone, I promise."

"Good. Now get into your car and fuck off back home," Carl said as he and Abe moved back a little, allowing Samuels to go past them.

Later that evening, Abe called Marcus, giving him the good news, saying that this makes them all square now and that the debt they owed him has now been paid in full. Marcus agreed, and as it was late, he decided to wait till the morning before calling Jason with the positive update.

Marcus was worried about what he was getting himself into or, more to the point, what Jason was getting him into, but he felt he had no option but to help his old friend, who had been there for him in the past when he needed it. He still felt guilty about the death he had caused, and there was a part of him that thought he deserved to get caught, but of course, he did not want to go to prison. He knew only too well what would await him there as an ex-police officer. There were bound to be people he had arrested in the past in any prison he would end up in, and that being the case, his life would surely be over if he were indeed to go to jail.

No, he knew only too well that he could never do the right thing, no matter how guilty he felt. Not only would he go to prison, but his friend Jason would be right there alongside him for lying to the police and giving Marcus a false alibi for that fateful evening. As guilty as he felt, there was no way he could do anything that would see his close friend of so many years pay the price for his mistake caused by his excessive drinking.

Marcus knew that he would have to take that guilt to his grave, and at times over the last few years, death seemed like a good option for him. So much so that he thought about putting his gun inside his mouth and blowing his brains out on many occasions. However, he never could bring himself to do it even though he was almost tempted a number of times. Deep down inside, he knew that doing so would be him taking the easy or cowardly way out, and he felt that he had not suffered enough yet to warrant doing that.

'One day soon,' he thought to himself.

Chapter Twenty-Six

Jason woke up earlier than usual on Sunday morning, feeling refreshed and very excited about going to see Alexia later. He got up, showered, had breakfast, and then wondered what the situation would be with Samuels once the brothers had paid him a visit. His thoughts then turned back to Alexia and exactly what the surprise was going to be, which he looked forward to very much, without even knowing what she had in store for him.

Before too long, Marcus had called Jason and simply told him that it was in the bag. Jason knew this meant that the brothers were successful in their attempt to convince Samuels to help, and at least that was a big weight off his shoulders. He knew that if the judge were to call a mistrial, it would be unlikely that the district attorney would charge Alexia a second time. Langley would use his influence to try and make sure that the DA's office would decline Emerton's request for a retrial, although nothing was certain. Jason was pretty sure that he would win the case anyway, but he was not prepared to take any chances where Alexia was concerned, hence the extra insurance with Samuels.

Jason was feeling quite pleased with the way things were progressing. However, he also knew that there was no guarantee his boss could stop a retrial or that Samuels would be able to pull it off if it came down to it, but he was hopeful. He still wished that he had some kind of leverage over Emerton to use if the need arose, but for now, there was nothing more he could do about it.

Time was passing quickly, and before long, it was time for Jason to go and meet Alexia at her home on Long Island, so he got in the car and drove there, making sure he was not late.

Upon arriving, Jason got out of the car and walked up to the door, but before he could ring the bell, the door opened. Alexia stood there in a silk dressing gown purposely left open so that Jason could see the sexy see-through panties and matching bra she was wearing, the seamed black hold-ups, and the very high-heeled shoes. 'Wow,' thought Jason to himself as he said hello to his mistress, who moved to one side so that Jason could enter.

"Welcome, Jason. How are you?" she asked him.

"I am well, thank you, Mistress," was the reply from Jason, unsure if he should indeed call her mistress or Alexia, but he chose mistress just to be on the safe side.

"Please take a seat, Jason, and tell me if there is any news regarding the trial."

"Thank you," Jason replied as he sat down on the couch opposite Alexia and told her he was very hopeful that things would go smoothly from now on.

"So I do not have anything to worry about then?" she asked him with a smile on her face.

"I am as certain as I can be that all will go well, but even if it doesn't all go according to plan, I have a trick or two up my sleeve, so I do not want you to worry," he replied confidently.

Alexia breathed a huge sigh of relief as she heard that comment and asked Jason if he wanted a coffee, to which he said he did.

"Henry, come here," shouted out Alexia and waited as her middle-aged slave came from another room with nothing on but a very small apron covering his blushes.

"Bring us some coffee please, will you, Henry?" commanded Alexia, and of course, he went off to do exactly as he was told.

"You remember Henry, don't you, Jason? He is one of my most loyal slaves who has been with me for many years. He lives here on the grounds for whenever I need him to do various chores."

"Yes, I do, Mistress," Jason replied, trying not to look at him.

"Now, I bet you are wondering what surprise I have in store for you, are you not?" she asked with a smile.

"Yes, Mistress, I am," he excitedly replied.

At that moment, Henry came back with the coffee, placing the cups on the table. Alexia told him to kneel down before her and give her feet a massage, and as always, he did as was told without question or hesitation.

"Sandy, come here," Alexia commanded, and a blonde-haired young beauty came into the room wearing an above-the-knee purple dress and high heels.

"This is Sandy, and she sometimes helps me with the domination of my slaves when the need arises, but she is also a loyal slave and companion whenever the mood takes me. Do you like her, Jason?"

"Yes, she is very pretty, Mistress," Jason replied, taking a good look at her.

"Yes, she is, and if you could, would you want to fuck her, Jason?" Alexia asked, taking Jason by surprise.

He paused for a moment, unsure of how he was supposed to answer that question, as he did not want to say the wrong thing, but then Alexia snapped impatiently.

"It's a straightforward question, Jason. Do you find her attractive enough to want to have sex with her?"

"Yes, I do, Mistress; I'm sorry."

"Oh, there is no need to be sorry. After all, **she** is your surprise. Go and help Jason to relax, will you Sandy?" Alexia said as she turned and looked at her.

Without hesitation, Sandy went over and sat next to Jason. She put one of her hands on his thigh, then slowly began to move it up towards his crotch, rubbing Jason there for a while until he became aroused. She then unzipped Jason's pants, putting her hand inside and pulling out his now very hard cock. Sandy then lowered her head and took him in her mouth.

"Just relax and enjoy it, Jason," Alexia said as she watched Sandy go down on him.

Jason leaned back on the couch and enjoyed the head that Sandy was giving for the next few minutes.

"Kneel on the couch, Sandy," commanded Alexia, and as she knelt down, Alexia tossed Jason a rubber. "Now, put this on and fuck her, Jason. I want to see how you fuck a woman."

Without needing to be asked twice, Jason stood up and put on the rubber. He pulled up Sandy's dress, pulled her panties to the side, pushing his hard cock inside her, and began to fuck her.

"Henry, come here and lick my clit, nice and slowly, while I watch them," Alexia said.

Henry went over to where she was sitting, knelt down, and did exactly as she demanded.

In the meantime, Alexia's gaze was fixed on Jason, as he now began to fuck Sandy faster and harder as though he was trying to impress his mistress.

After around five minutes, Alexia told Henry to stop. She played with his cock until it was nice and hard, then she lay down on the couch so that she could still see Jason and Sandy fucking and told Henry to get on top of her. Again, Henry did as was told, getting on top of Alexia, entering her, and then beginning to fuck her while she watched what was happening on the other couch.

Jason could not help but turn to look at them, unsure about how he felt watching her have sex with another man. Yes, he knew that she was a mistress and that she did this sort of thing all the time, but he felt a kind of jealousy actually watching her do it.

"Don't look at me, Jason; look at Sandy. After all, she is the one you are fucking, not me," Alexia shouted out at him.

Jason turned around quickly and looked once again at Sandy. However, in his mind, he was still thinking that it was Alexia he was having sex with and still had a strange feeling about her doing it with Henry.

Within a few more minutes, Jason began to breathe heavier as he was getting ready to come and Alexia, realizing this, turned to Henry and said, "fuck me harder." As he did so, she began to moan, moving her hips and, within moments, began to come, giving out long moans of ecstasy, as her juices began to flow, which, in turn, led to Jason reaching a climax, shooting his cum inside the rubber he was wearing.

After they had both finished, Alexia told Henry and Sandy to leave the room, then looked at Jason and asked, "Did you enjoy your little surprise?"

"Yes, Mistress, very much so, thank you," he replied, quite breathless.

"Good, and who knows, perhaps one day soon I may decide to make use of your cock for my pleasure," Alexia said with a broad grin.

"Thank you, Mistress. I shall look forward to that very much," Jason replied as his face lit up with the thought that he would get to have sex with her, while he rearranged his clothing.

"Now, Jason, let us talk about the trial. You previously said that you would need to prep me the day before the trial in order to get me ready to face what was to come."

"Yes, Mistress, oops, I mean Alexia, or do I?" he asked, unsure exactly what he was meant to call her at that precise moment.

"Yes, Jason, it is Alexia now. But before we start, I want to make us something to eat. I will not be long. Please make yourself comfortable," she said as she got up and left the room.

Chapter Twenty-Seven

Jason waited patiently as he sat on the couch for a short while before deciding to take a look around the very large room he was in. There were plenty of ornaments on the shelves, some of which looked like valuable antiques, a good range of paintings, and a large bookcase that must have held at least a hundred books on various subjects. He did notice that there were a lot of books on psychology and, of course, many of the books that Alexia had written on the domination lifestyle.

He picked up a couple of those books, read a few short passages from them, and flicked through the pages of a few of the others. He realized that Alexia was not only a very sexy, beautiful lady but that she also had a good head on her shoulders. She certainly had talent, good taste, and an eye for the arts, but above all, she seemed to be a very sophisticated lady as well.

Jason was just putting one of the books he was holding back on the shelf when Alexia returned fully dressed in a sexy way and with a tray of canapés. He walked back to the couch, as she put the tray on the small coffee table in front of them before sitting down on the couch opposite where Jason had just sat. He took a quick glance at the way she was sitting and saw that the split on the side of her dress was rising up onto the outside of her thigh, going all the way to her hip, clearly showing the top of the stockings she was wearing.

A little smile came over Jason's face, which did not go unnoticed by Alexia as she asked with a wry smile of her own, "Is everything ok, Jason?"

"Yes, Alexia, everything is just fine," he replied, thinking to himself, 'Even after everything that just happened, she dresses like this ... what a woman!'

They then looked into each other's eyes for a few seconds before Jason began to speak.

"So tell me, just how many books have you written on the subject of domination, and what is the fascination with psychology?" he asked her.

"Oh, I see you have been looking at my collection of books. Well, I have written many books, Jason, and not all of them are about domination, although most of them are. Some of the books are simply educational about how to get the best out of each other's bodies in bed ... or anywhere else the readers decide to have fun. As for psychology, it certainly helps when writing my books, dominating my slaves, and I am actually a fully qualified psychologist too," she replied as she pointed to the canapés on the table and told Jason to help himself.

Jason just sat there and looked on in amazement for a brief moment before asking, "You are a qualified psychologist? This will be very helpful to the case. Why did you not mention this before?" he queried as he reached over and took one of the canapés.

"That is because I do not actually practice it and never have. Although I am qualified, I have never seen a client as a psychologist. I simply use it to help me understand my slaves better when they come to me for their sessions."

"Oh, I see, but never mind, because the jury will be told that you are a psychologist. Even if you do not see clients in that way, it will help with how they see you. After all, they won't know that you are not a practicing psychologist, as I will omit that little fact." he replied with a smile.

They spoke in a little more detail about her being a psychologist before Jason began to tell her what he expected from her at the trial.

"Ok, Alexia, I now need to tell you how to act and behave during the course of the trial and also tell you about the way the prosecution will treat you."

"What exactly do you mean by that?" she asked.

"Well, Alexia, you will have to behave in a very specific way and also dress accordingly during the trial. Meanwhile, the prosecutor is going to try and make you look like something you are not and to make the jury believe what he says. It will be my job to make them believe otherwise."

"What do you mean when you say behave in a specific way and what is wrong with the way I normally dress? Do you not like it, Jason?" she asked, unsure what her clothes would have to do with the trial.

"Oh, Alexia, you have no idea of how much I do indeed like how you dress, but you cannot dress like this in court," he replied, looking her up and down.

"Perhaps not this particular dress, but I shall dress how I choose, and if anyone does not like it, then they can look away," she replied angrily.

"Alexia, please listen carefully to what I am saying and try to understand what I am about to tell you. The prosecution is going to portray you to the jury as just a cheap escort who killed her client. That is exactly what the jury will see unless I can convince them otherwise. But I can only do that with your help. You need to act, and dress as I tell you, and say what I tell you to say; otherwise, the members of the jury may not believe what I tell them. If you dress in a sexy way, then they may very well see you as the prosecution describes you, which will be a cheap escort," Jason said, trying to make her understand.

"*I* have to do what *you* tell me, Jason?" she asked in a very stern, almost angry way.

"Yes, I know this is hard for you, Alexia, but this is not about dominance. It is about doing what must be done to ensure your acquittal. You **are** and always **will** be the mistress, but we have to do things my way for the trial, and you will have to do as I say. Have faith in me during the trial, and believe me when I say that I will be your most obedient slave once you are free. But for now, you must do as I say," he pleaded with Alexia.

Alexia paused for a moment before saying anything, staring Jason in the eyes, and then replied in a very commanding way. "Be very careful, Jason. I understand what you are saying, and I will allow you the power to do what you must. However, if I feel that you are enjoying that power too much, then you **will** pay the price afterward."

"Thank you, Alexia. I assure you that whatever I do or however I act will be in your best interests. I have no wish to be the dominant one where you are concerned, but I will do what I must to help you, and you must do exactly as I say if we are to be successful."

"Pour me a glass of orange juice, will you, Jason? And you may have one as well," Alexia said, interrupting him assertively, showing him that she was still in charge. Jason got up, walked over to the bar in the corner of the room, poured out two glasses of juice, and placed them on the table before sitting back down.

Alexia thanked him, then took a sip from her glass and asked, "So, how would you like me to act and dress, Jason?"

Jason took a sip from his glass, put it back down, and then replied. "I want you to dress elegantly, but not in a very sexy way. I want the men on the jury to find you attractive, but not to see you as a sex symbol or as an escort, which is how the prosecutor will try and portray you. And I want the women to see you as the sweet girl next door. I do not want you to wear too much makeup, and please do not wear very high heels. Do not wear anything that is too short or has a split in it, like you have on today, and please do not show too much cleavage either."

"So, basically, you want me to be the total opposite of how I am today. Does that sound about right, Jason?" she asked quite sarcastically.

"Yes, I guess it does, Alexia. I need the members of the jury to see you as a lady that would not hurt a fly, and perhaps someone who is a little weak. I do not, in any way, want you to come across as being strong. If the jury sees you as too strong, they may believe what the prosecutor is telling them, which would be very bad for us. The members of the jury must like you if they are going to believe what I tell them, and for that to happen, they need to see a little weakness and even a little fear. If they see you as they see themselves, then they will like you." he replied.

"I see," Alexia replied, unsure if she was happy with portraying herself like that, but agreed that she would do as Jason had told her.

They both took another sip of their juice and a couple of canapés before Jason continued.

"When you look at the jury, you must look at both the men and women equally. The men will feel flattered that you are looking at them, while the women will see that you are showing them respect by looking at them also. If you spend too long looking at the men, the women may feel that you are coming onto them, and they will not like that. Never gaze at any person for more than a few seconds, and please try to make eye contact when you do look at them. Do not, however, smile at any of them, as this may seem a little flirtatious or even arrogant."

"I understand, Jason," Alexia replied, not really happy, but she understood that she had to listen to her lawyer.

"Now, when the prosecution asks you a question, do not be hesitant with the answer and always keep your answers short. Never over-answer any question and never, ever get angry, regardless of what he says. He will try to get to you; he will try and accuse you of things that are not true, and he will try to get the jury to hate you. You cannot let this happen, so just let him say what he wants. You just need to stay calm, and if you ever feel you are becoming angry, look at me and take a few deep breaths," he explained.

"Ok, Jason, but it will take more than that to get me angry," she replied confidently.

"Oh, believe me, Alexia, he will say whatever he needs to so that he can get to you, but you must never let him. When I question you, I will allow you to tell your side of the story, but again, you must tell it the way I tell you to. Remember, this is not about what is right and wrong, not about the truth, and not about how anything happened. This is all about whom the members of the jury believe, him or me; it is as simple as that. My job is to make the jury believe me, and your job is to help me by doing exactly what I say, the way I say it," he emphasized.

"I will put my trust in you, Jason, and I pray that you will not let me down."

"I won't, Alexia. Just trust me when I say everything is in hand, and all will be fine."

"And what exactly does that mean: everything is in hand?" Alexia asked in a very inquisitive manner.

"Oh nothing, Alexia. I just mean I am very confident that this will all be over soon," he replied, realizing that he had to be very careful with what he said. Alexia was no fool, and he could see the suspicious look in her eyes. He wished he could tell her about Samuels but thought it best not to mention anything. He was still concerned about who this influential client Langley spoke of was, and if she would tell him something like that or not.

Jason and Alexia spent the next two hours going over what she was going to say and, just as importantly, how she was going to say it. Eventually, when Alexia knew everything she needed to, the time came for them to say their goodbyes. Jason then left, got into his car, and began to think that their meeting had gone well apart from what could have been a small slip at the end there. Jason was sure that even if he had told Alexia what his plan was with Samuels, she would not have said anything. However, he was not prepared to take that chance just yet, especially as it was not just his life he would be playing with but also Marcus's.

Chapter Twenty-Eight

Jason was driving home after leaving Alexia when he got a telephone call from Marcus telling him that they had to meet as it was really important and he did not want to say anything over the telephone. Not understanding what this was all about, Jason agreed to meet Marcus for a coffee and a chat. He drove straight to the cafe where they had arranged to meet, rather than going home first.

All the while, as he was driving to meet Marcus, he wondered what could have been so important. Suddenly it dawned on him that it could only be about Samuels and that he was now either refusing to play along or he had perhaps gone to the police and told them everything. If this was indeed the case, then they were in deep trouble and would certainly both be facing charges for witness tampering.

Meanwhile, Marcus arrived at the cafe first, sat at a table, ordered a coffee, and waited for Jason, who came along fifteen minutes later. He sat down then ordered a couple of coffees for them, and they waited until they were brought to them before beginning to talk about why they were there.

"Ok, so what is so important, Marcus? Is it Samuels? Are we in trouble? Did he talk?" Jason asked him anxiously.

"No, it has nothing to do with Samuels. I told you that he was in the bag, but I did find something out about your old nemesis, Roy Emerton," Marcus said with a smile on his face.

"What? Did you really? Well, come on, tell me," Jason said in a very excited tone of voice, thankful that not only did this meeting have nothing to do with Samuels but also that Marcus may have finally found some dirt on Emerton.

"Well, last night after he finished work, instead of going home, he went to an Italian restaurant called The Treviana. You'll never guess who he met and had dinner with there."

"Just tell me, Marcus," Jason said frustratedly as he was in no mood for guessing games.

"Steven Conrad," Marcus replied, then sat back in his chair and took a sip of his coffee.

Suddenly there was an eerie silence for a brief moment before Jason asked, "Steven Conrad, are you sure?"

"Yes, Jason, I am certain."

"Hmm, let me think for a minute," Jason said as he took a sip from his coffee.

Steven Conrad was the married politician his wife was having an affair with, and it seems that he and Emerton knew each other, but he was not sure just how well.

After a few moments, Jason turned to Marcus and said, "I want you to find out just how well these two know each other. Was this a professional meeting, or are they good friends? If it was a professional meeting, then find out what it was about, but if it turns out they are friends, then just how good friends are they? I want to know everything that connects them, and I want to know today."

"Today?" Marcus asked.

"Yes, today, or have you forgotten the trial starts tomorrow?" Jason replied.

"Sure thing, buddy. I will get my people to start right away and let you know as soon as I have something."

They stayed for a while longer chatting about this, among other things, then they left after finishing their coffees.

All the way back home, Jason wondered how this news could be used, not only to get one over on Emerton, but perhaps he could also use it in some way regarding his wife and her lover. Of course, he was not going to say anything at this time and would see what Marcus would discover before making any kind of decision, but there was a part of him that was quite hopeful about this news.

By late afternoon, Marcus again called Jason and said he wanted to meet with him, which Jason agreed to in anticipation of what news Marcus managed to uncover. They arranged to meet in a park near where Jason lived.

As soon as they met, Jason asked, "So, what did you find out?"

"Ok, here goes, buddy. Steven Conrad is, in fact, Roy Emerton's uncle on his mother's side, and Conrad used his connections to get Emerton started on his career. Emerton then went to LA to practice law but was not too successful, so again, his uncle used his connections to get him the job at the DA's office here in New York. What's more, Conrad's wife is the cousin of the wife of the DA, Clive Montague, and naturally, I presume they are also very good friends." Marcus replied, feeling very pleased with himself.

"Wow, ok, let me think about this information," Jason replied, becoming deep in thought.

So now Jason knew that the man who was having an affair with his wife was Emerton's uncle, but just as importantly, he was also a friend of the DA.

'So that's how Emerton landed the job at the DA's office,' he thought to himself.

"Well, this is very good news indeed, my friend. I want you to continue with your investigation in the hope that you can discover even more things about them all. I want to know everything there is to know," he replied, feeling very happy, before saying goodbye to Marcus and parting company with him.

On the way home, Jason began to get a few ideas about how to deal with this information if the trial did not go according to plan. However, for now, he would do nothing to rock the boat and would simply see how these events unfolded. If possible, he would rather keep this information for when he needed it most, but he would not hesitate to use it if he needed to in order to help Alexia.

Yes, things were certainly looking up for Jason right now. He could not help but have a big smile on his face as the thought of having these people in the palm of his hand was too much for him to resist. He was now as happy as he could possibly have been and knew that, should the need arise, he could certainly have these people of power over a barrel. Just as importantly for Jason was the fact that he may be able to use this information where his wife was concerned, which brought an even bigger smile to his face, and he eventually began to laugh out loud.

All the way home, Jason thought about this great news and just how he could best use this to his advantage.

When he finally reached home, he opened the door, took off his jacket, and put the keys on the stand as Lydia called out.

"I'm in the kitchen, honey."

He walked through the house to where his wife was, and as he walked into the kitchen, he saw her by the stove, cooking.

"Hey, Lyd. What's for dinner?" he asked.

"Slow-cooked rib of beef," she replied.

"Very nice. I will go and find a nice bottle of Rioja to go with that," he said while thinking to himself, 'I got you now, you bitch.'

Jason spent the rest of the afternoon deep in thought and was like that even through dinner, which brought the attention of his wife.

"Is everything ok? Did you not like the food?" Lydia asked him.

"Oh no, the food was very nice, and everything is just fine. I have this self-defense case beginning tomorrow, and I'm just going over my opening statement through my mind; that's all, Lyd," he replied with a big smile on his face, knowing that was not really the reason.

"I'm sure you will do great, and everything will be fine," she said as she got up.

They both began to clear the table, having finished their dinner.

'Yes, everything will indeed be fine,' Jason thought.

He finally had information he could perhaps use against his wife and her lover; his friend was gathering more information on Emerton he could use to his advantage, and, of course, he had Samuels to help him get an acquittal for Alexia.

'Could life get any better?' he wondered.

Chapter Twenty-Nine

Jason got out of bed at 4 am on the morning of the trial, as he did not get much sleep during the night. He had a shower, got dressed, ate breakfast, and gathered his thoughts for today's opening statement that he was going to make. He now had a little under three hours left before he had to leave home and make his way to the courthouse for what was now becoming a very emotional trial for him. This was no normal client or normal trial, and what he was doing regarding the whole Samuels situation was going too far, even for his standards.

Even though he did not have to leave home yet, as he still had quite a bit of time, he decided to leave anyway. He telephoned Marcus and asked to meet him at a cafe near the courthouse for a chat, and of course, Marcus agreed, even though it was still very early in the morning. They met a short while later, which gave them just under a couple of hours to chat as the courthouse was only a ten-minute walk away from the cafe. They ordered their coffees, and once they got them, they began to speak.

"So, what's going on, buddy? What did you want to see me about?" Marcus asked him.

"Oh, I don't know, Marcus. I just wanted a chat, I guess, as the trial starts this morning," Jason replied, feeling unusually nervous today.

"Yeah, I wondered if that was what this was all about. Are you worried, Jason?"

"I'm not so much worried about the trial itself, just a little concerned in general, that's all. Are you sure Samuels is still in the bag?" Jason asked, looking for reassurance.

"Don't worry about Samuels, buddy. Have I ever let you down before?" Marcus asked, trying hard to reassure Jason.

"No, you haven't, my friend," he replied.

"And I won't now," Marcus said as he reached over and patted Jason's shoulder.

"Ok, Marcus, thank you. You are such a great friend and I'm really grateful for what you are doing for me," he said with a small smile just breaking out on his lips.

Marcus took a little sip of his coffee and then replied, "I would not be here if you had not helped me out of that jam I was in all those years ago, and I am more than happy to repay that debt to you, buddy."

"I don't see it as a debt, my friend, but I really appreciate you putting yourself on the line for me like this," Jason said as he picked up his coffee cup and took a long sip from it.

He then paused for a brief moment before asking, "So, any more news about our little friends, and have you found any skeletons?"

"Sadly no, there's nothing new on that front," Marcus replied, wishing he had more news for him.

"Well, keep looking, Marcus. Check other members of their family as well. Someone from their family must have something we can use to our advantage, if not for this case, then in the future. I need to have something more if I am going to divorce Lydia at some stage."

"Divorce Lydia? Is this to do with Alexia?" Marcus replied, somewhat in shock. "Your wife is a hothead and will certainly cause you problems; you know that, don't you?"

"Yes, Marcus, I know, and yes, it does have something to do with Alexia. As I have said before, there is something special about this lady, and I have never felt happier than when I am with her. Besides, Lydia does not love me and is cheating on me, for fuck's sake. Why shouldn't I divorce her? This is why I need something more on her or that bastard, Conrad, to be able to use against them to help my position when the time comes," Jason replied, very frustrated.

"I understand, buddy, and I have people checking as we speak. I will not stop looking until I have found something you can use ... if it exists, that is," Marcus replied, unsure if he would even find any more information.

Jason had another sip of his coffee before thanking Marcus for all the hard work he was doing on his behalf. He then asked him, "Hey, you fancy some breakfast?"

"Sure, why not? If you have enough time, that is," Marcus replied, rubbing his stomach to indicate that he was rather peckish.

They called the waitress over to order something to eat.

While they waited, Jason asked his friend, "And what about you, Marcus? What is going on in your life? Any new lovers yet?"

Marcus looked at Jason and laughed out loud before replying in a joking way. "And when do I have time when I am working all hours for you, Jason?"

Jason began to laugh as well, and they were both still laughing when the food they had ordered was brought over by the waitress.

"I know, Marcus, and I am sorry for taking all your time up," Jason replied as they both tucked into their breakfast before he called the waitress over for some more coffee.

"Whatever happened to that blonde you were dating a while back?" Jason asked him.

"Oh, that was just a thing for a short time, to be honest, buddy, and nothing was ever going to come of it. Besides, you know me, I am not the settling down kind anymore, at least not yet," he replied, looking down into his plate of food, losing himself in thought for a moment.

"Do you still miss her?" Jason asked sympathetically.

"Yeah, I do," Marcus replied, looking up at Jason and then back down with his eyes watering up.

Jason knew that his friend was in pain now due to remembering what had happened to him in the past.

Marcus married his childhood sweetheart a long time ago, but one night, fifteen years ago, while they were on the way back to their car after a night out, a drive-by shooting that was meant to kill Marcus killed his wife instead. Marcus had been undercover on a drugs sting when he was found out, hence the drive-by shooting. Marcus was also shot but made a full recovery; however, sadly, his wife died instantly. The only consolation for Marcus was that his wife never suffered, if indeed she even knew what happened, as she did not have time due to the bullets hitting her in the head, amongst other places.

"But life goes on," Marcus suddenly replied as he looked up at Jason again.

"Yes, it does, my friend, and at least those animals that killed her are rotting in prison. It's a small consolation, I know, but at least it's something for you," Jason replied as he reached out his hand and put it on Marcus's hand for support before continuing. "You know I am here for you, and anytime you need anything, even if it's just a chat, then call me. We go back a long way, Marcus, so just remember that I am always here for you, just as you have been here for me lately."

"Thank you, buddy, and it is very much appreciated," Marcus replied, managing a little smile.

Time was now upon Jason as he had to get to the courthouse, so they both finished their coffees and said their goodbyes.

As they were leaving, Marcus said to Jason, "Call me later, buddy, and let me know how it all went."

"I will do, my friend," Jason replied as he left the cafe and began to make his way to the courthouse, ready to take on Alexia's trial, but just as importantly, taking on Emerton. Jason certainly relished both challenges, but to him, Alexia's freedom would always be the number one priority and beating Emerton a very distant number two. A little smile came on his face as he thought about the phrase, killing two birds with one stone. That is exactly what he was hoping for with this trial ... Alexia's freedom and Emerton's defeat.

Chapter Thirty

Jason made his way into the courthouse, chatting to a few people he knew along the way, and a few minutes later, Alexia arrived, joining him. They had a quick catch-up with Jason asking her if she was ok and if she wanted to go over anything quickly, but Alexia said she was fine. Indeed she seemed to be and had certainly listened to Jason about what she should wear.

Jason looked at her outfit and said, "Very good; you look exactly the way I wanted you to look."

"Thank you, Jason, but I hate how I am dressed," she replied unhappily.

"I know you do, but it is for the best," he said, reassuring her she was doing the right thing.

They then just chatted for the next ten minutes before being called into the courtroom, and Jason again tried to reassure her that everything would be ok. Alexia got the feeling that Jason was not telling her everything, as she thought he was being a bit overconfident. She asked him if everything was ok, to which he simply replied that everything was going to be fine. They then sat down and waited.

"All rise. The honorable Judge Daniel Johnson is presiding."

The announcement was made as everyone rose from their seats when the judge entered the room. The judge then sat down, and everyone else followed suit. This was it; the trial was now in process, and it was the prosecution's turn to begin with his opening statement.

Emerton stood up, walked over to the jurors, and began to speak.

"Members of the jury, we are here to prosecute Miss Summers on the charge of manslaughter because she killed one of her clients. This is not in dispute, as the accused herself will admit that she did, in fact, kill Mr. Morley. She shot him dead without mercy after taking his money to have sex with him. Yes, you heard correctly, she took money to have sex with Mr. Morley because that is what she does. She is a prostitute, and she gets paid to have sex with her clients, plain and simple. However, it is not quite as plain and simple as that, because on the night in question, after inviting Mr. Morley into her home to have sex with him, she shot and killed him instead. Take a good look at her," he said as he quietly walked up and down the length of the stand where the jurors were seated.

All the jurors turned and looked at Alexia before turning their gaze back at the prosecutor as he began to speak again.

"That is the face of a killer who, without reason, decided to take the life of another human being. Why did she do this? We will never know for certain, but according to Miss Summers, Mr. Morley tried to rape her. Yes, that's right, the accused says he tried to rape her. Now, ladies and gentlemen, are we seriously going to believe that an upstanding man of the community was going to rape a prostitute that he had already arranged and paid to have sex with? Why would he need to rape her if he had already paid her for sex? Why would he need to rape her if having sex with men is what she does for a living? Why would he need to rape her at all, is the question we should all be asking ourselves. Why, indeed?" Emerton paused for a few seconds to look into the eyes of the jurors before he continued to speak.

"It makes no sense at all that Miss Summers should kill Mr. Morley as she certainly had no reason to, but kill him she did. Perhaps she did not need a reason, perhaps she just felt like doing it, perhaps she was in a bad mood, or perhaps Miss Summers is simply just an evil person who wanted to know what it felt like to kill someone. Who knows? Only Miss Summers knows the answer to that, but it certainly was **not** because Mr. Morley was going to rape her. After all, she is just a prostitute that was there to have sex with him, and this is why, when the time comes, you must find her guilty. Thank you, ladies and gentlemen, and I am certain that you will make the correct decision."

Emerton then went back to his table and sat back down while still looking at the jurors, feeling good about how his opening statement went. He then looked over at Jason with a little smirk on his face.

It was now Jason's turn to make his opening statement, so he rose from his seat, walked over to the jurors, and began to speak.

"Good morning, ladies and gentlemen of the jury. That was quite an opening statement by the prosecution, but he is very much mistaken as to the why. Yes, we must ask ourselves why. Why did Miss Summers kill Mr. Morley? What could possibly be the reason? Well, the prosecution is wrong on so many things and the defense will show this during the course of the trial. Miss Summers is *not* a prostitute, as the prosecution is leading you to believe, but she is, in fact, a mistress. What is the difference, you may ask? Well, I can assure you that there is one, and the defense will explain this to you during the trial. Miss Summers does *not* get paid to have sex with her clients, as again, the prosecution will lead you to believe, but instead gets paid to dominate her clients, and again I say, there *is* a big difference. Please do take a very good look at Miss Summers. Does she strike you as the sort of person who would simply just shoot and kill someone for no reason at all?"

Jason paused for a bit while the jurors looked over at Alexia, and she, in turn, looked at them before he continued.

"So yes, the prosecution is correct when he asks the question why. Why would Miss Summers kill a client if, in fact, she **was** a prostitute? Why would she kill a client who has paid her for sex if, indeed, she **was** a prostitute? Why would she kill a client who would be supporting her lifestyle and putting food on the table if she **was** indeed a prostitute? The answer is simple ... she would **not** because she is **not** a prostitute, she does **not** get paid to have sex with her clients, and she did **not** have a reason to kill this client. Unless, of course, he really did try to rape her! This is what the defense is going to prove to you, that Miss Summers is **not** just a prostitute as the prosecution would have you believe, and she does **not** get paid to have sex with her clients. Once we have explained and proved to you that these are the facts, then you will realize that Mr. Morley did, in fact, try to rape her, which is why Miss Summers shot him in self-defense as she feared for her life. The evidence will show that Mr. Morley not only ripped Miss Summer's dress but also that he hit her. She, in turn, scratched his face, trying to get away. Only as a last resort did she shoot Mr. Morley in self-defense."

Once again, Jason paused for a brief moment as he walked the length of the juror's stand before continuing.

"There is one more thing for you to please remember. The prosecution has no proof that it was **not** self-defense, no proof that the defendant shot Mr. Morley just because she felt like it, as was suggested by him, and, in fact, no proof at all that it was anything other than self-defense. And please also remember, ladies and gentlemen, that our legal justice system is based on the fact that we judge everyone as innocent until proven guilty. So unless the prosecution offers you any evidence of Miss Summer's guilt beyond any shadow of a doubt, then you must find the defendant not guilty. Thank you, ladies and gentlemen, and I am certain that by the end of the trial, you will, in fact, see that the prosecution indeed has no evidence, no proof, and their whole case is based on assumptions and nothing else. I am equally certain that by the end of the trial, you will see the truth clearly and will have no alternative but to return a verdict of not guilty."

Jason turned and walked back to his table, looking first at Alexia, then Emerton, and lastly, at the members of the jury as he sat down.

The judge then spoke to the jury, reminding them that they should not discuss anything they had heard or would hear during the course of the trial with anyone. He also explained to them that after hearing all the evidence from both parties, if necessary, they should ask to speak to the court official if they are unsure about anything they have heard, or would simply like to ask any questions. He went on to say that at the end of the trial, when they had weighed everything up, should they have any doubt as to the guilt of the defendant, then they must find her not guilty. The jurors listened to what the judge had told them, and they seemed to understand everything that was said. All that was left now was for the trial to continue.

CHAPTER THIRTY-ONE

"Are you ready to begin, Mr. Emerton?" The judge asked.

"Yes, your Honor," he replied.

"Very well, you may call your first witness, Counselor," the judge then said.

"The prosecution calls Samantha Morley," Emerton said as he stood up.

Mrs. Morley entered the courtroom and made her way to the stand, where she was asked to put her hand on the bible. She was then asked, "Do you, Samantha Morley, swear to tell the truth, the whole truth, so help you God?"

"I do," she replied.

"You may be seated," she was then told.

Emerton walked over to the witness stand, and asked, "Can you please tell the court who you are, Mrs. Morley?"

"I am the mother of Simon Morley," she replied as she brought her hand up to her nose, holding a handkerchief.

"I know this must be a difficult time for you, Mrs. Morley, and I am sorry for your loss, but please could you tell the court a little about your son, Simon?" Emerton asked.

"He was a very hardworking man, caring, thoughtful, and loving. He was kind and would always help anyone who asked him for a favor. He would come over for dinner every Sunday and always bring me flowers. He would never hurt a fly, let alone try and rape someone," Samantha replied tearfully.

"And was your son married, Mrs. Morley?" Emerton enquired.

"He was, but his wife cheated on him and ran off with a work colleague. My son got divorced about a year ago." She replied, again bringing her hand up to her face, still holding her handkerchief.

"I won't keep you much longer, Mrs. Morley, as this is obviously too painful for you, but I do have one last question. What do you think about the accusation that has been made about your son trying to rape the accused?" Emerton said as he pointed to Alexia.

"That is a lie; he would never do that. My son was a good man, and she murdered him," Samantha replied in a raised voice.

"Objection, your Honor," Jason shouted out.

"Sustained. Please refrain from making any such remarks, Mrs. Morley and Mr. Emerton; please instruct your witnesses to only say the facts of the case from now on."

"Yes, your Honor, my apologies," Emerton replied. "That is all from me, Mrs. Morley," Emerton said as he walked back to his seat.

"Cross-examination, Mr. Carini?" the judge asked.

"Indeed, your Honor," Jason replied.

Jason stood up and walked over to the stand, looking at the jurors, and as he did so, he said, "I am very sorry for your loss, Mrs. Morley, and I will be very brief with my questions."

Samantha just looked at him without saying a word.

"After his divorce, did your son have a new girlfriend or partner?"

"No, he didn't," was the reply from Samantha.

"And you would have known if he did, would you?" Jason asked.

"Well, yes, I knew my son very well, and he would have told me if he was seeing anyone," she replied confidently.

"I see, and how often did your son visit with ladies of pleasure, shall we say?" Jason quickly asked her.

"My son did not visit those sorts of women!" Samantha screamed out in anger.

Jason paused for a minute, looked at the jury, then looked back at Mrs. Morley before saying, "I am sorry if I offended you, Mrs. Morley, but my client is accused of being a prostitute and of killing your son. If your son did not visit those sorts of women, as you put it, then why was he in the defendant's house?

Or could it be that the defendant is, in fact, ***not*** a prostitute? What do you think, Mrs. Morley?"

"I don't know what she is, but my son did not sleep with prostitutes; he was a good man," she replied in a much calmer voice.

"No one is saying anything at the moment, Mrs. Morley, but the facts remain that either your son ***did*** visit certain ladies of pleasure, or you did not know your son as well as you thought you did. Which is it, Mrs. Morley?"

"Objection, your Honor, Mrs. Morley is not on trial here," Emerton said as he stood up.

"Your Honor, I am just trying to show that people, even mothers, do not always know what kind of a person someone is, even if they are their own son. We have Mr. Morley's own mother saying he did not visit ladies of pleasure and that he was a good man, but as the prosecution would have us believe, he was killed by my client, who is accused of being a prostitute. Both facts cannot be true, your Honor, and as such, I have the right to try and find out which fact is indeed true. If Mr. Morley did, in fact, do things that even his own mother did not know about, then perhaps she did not know him as well as she thought. If that is indeed the case, then what else did his mother not know about Mr. Morley? It is possible that he was not the kind, caring, upstanding citizen that we are led to believe he was."

The judge paused for a few seconds before saying, "Overruled."

"Your Honor-" Emerton began to say.

However, before he could finish, the judge said, "Your objection has been noted and overruled, Mr. Emerton."

"Yes, your Honor," Emerton replied as he sat back down in his chair.

Jason then looked at the jurors before turning back to face Mrs. Morley and said, "I am sorry about that, Mrs. Morley. I am not suggesting that your son was not a good man, but simply exploring the possibility that he was not exactly the way you thought of him. And perhaps, just perhaps, there was a part of him that you did not know as well as you thought you did. Please accept my apologies for this discomfort, Mrs. Morley, but again I ask, which is it?"

"I don't know. My son was not a bad person; I just don't know what to say anymore," she replied, crying into her handkerchief as she did so.

"That's ok, Mrs. Morley; I will not be asking you any more questions," he said as he turned once again to look at the juror's faces. Jason then walked back to his chair while the judge told Samantha she was free to leave the stand. She rose up and held her handkerchief to her face as she walked out of the courtroom, still crying.

"The prosecution would like to call David Morley to the stand," Emerton said, and a minute later, Mr. Morley walked into the courtroom, stood on the stand, and was sworn in.

"Can you please tell the court who you are, Mr. Morley?" Emerton asked him.

"I am Simon's father," David replied quickly.

"And can you tell us a little about your son, please, Mr. Morley?" Emerton said.

However, before David could answer, Jason stood up and said, "Your Honor, is it the prosecution's intention to call all of the deceased's family and friends to tell the court just how kind, caring, and an upstanding citizen he was? If this is the case, then the defense is prepared to accept that all of his family and friends will say the same thing and perhaps even believe it. They would also all probably say that they cannot believe this man would visit prostitutes and pay for sex either. We will then find ourselves in the exact same position we just found ourselves in with the deceased's mother. Maybe he was all the good things they would say about him, but it seems that he was perhaps also a man that paid for sex. After all, is that not the reason we are all here? Because, your Honor, my client is accused of killing Mr. Morley after he supposedly paid her to have sex with him.

"So, in order to save the court a lot of time and money, can we all simply accept that his family and friends would say he was a kind, caring, hardworking man. However, at the same time, they did not really know him as well as they thought they did because he apparently paid women for sex. Just one last thought, if Simon Morley did not pay women for sex, then why was he in my client's house? The defense is prepared to accept that Simon Morley was indeed a kind, caring man and a pillar of the community if the prosecution is prepared to accept that perhaps his family and friends may not have known the truth about his personal life. After all, he was in my client's house, who is accused of being a prostitute, so again I ask the question, why was he there if he did not pay women to have sex with him? Or perhaps it could be true that he did not pay for sex, and if that is the case, then why is my client being labeled an escort? The prosecution cannot have it both ways, your Honor."

The judge pondered Jason's statement for a brief moment, then looking up, he said, "I would like to see both of you in my chambers to discuss this further before making my decision."

The court was adjourned for lunch, and the three of them went into the judge's chambers to discuss in length what Jason had just said. They spent well over an hour discussing this, and then the judge took another couple of hours pondering his decision and having some lunch himself.

Once he was ready, the judge entered the courtroom, and the court was now back in session. The judge then issued a statement to the jurors.

"Ladies and gentlemen of the jury, in cases like these where the character of a deceased is to be determined by the people that know him, such as family and friends, it can sometimes turn the facts away from the case in hand. It has been agreed upon by the people, the defense, and by me that we can perhaps dispense with unnecessary proceedings. I am certain you will understand that all of the deceased's family members and friends would have said that Mr. Simon Morley was a kind, caring, hardworking man who loved his family. He was a pillar of his community and would help people if he was able to. He was thought of very highly by the people who loved him, and none of them can believe that he tried to rape the defendant."

The judge paused for a brief moment to look over the faces of the jurors before continuing.

"Having said that, it is also likely to be true that none of his friends or family members would have believed him to be the type of man who would pay to have sex with a woman. However, he *was* in Miss Summers's house apparently for that reason, and as such, it is safe to suggest that his family and friends did not know everything about him as they thought they did. I am therefore instructing you to take into account that Mr. Morley was indeed a kind, caring, hardworking man, but that he was also a man who, at least on this occasion, was prepared to pay to have sex with a woman. I want you to remember one other thing as well: just because Mr. Morley was prepared to pay to have sex with a woman, it does ***not*** make him a bad person. However, just because he was a kind, caring, and hardworking man, it does not mean that he could ***not*** have done what he has been accused of by the defendant."

The judge then turned back to face the rest of the courtroom, looked at his watch, and said, "We will continue with the trial tomorrow morning at 10 am. Court is adjourned."

Jason turned to Alexia, put his hand on top of hers, then gave her a smile and said, "Today was a very good day for us."

"What do you mean?" Alexia asked.

"Well, the jury now know that he was not an angel and that he was prepared to pay to have sex with you," Jason said, looking into her eyes.

"But Jason, I told you that was not the case," Alexia replied in an almost angry way.

"I know, but the jury doesn't know that yet. They will come to learn the difference between you and an escort as the trial goes on. But for now, to them, perhaps he is not as good a man as his family are saying he is. Do you understand now?" Jason asked her.

"Yes, I see, you are attacking his character, and that's why you said what you did regarding his family's statements," Alexia said, nodding her head and beginning to understand what Jason meant.

"Yes, exactly. The last thing we needed was for a lot of his family to say how nice a man he was over and over again, to the stage where the jurors would have believed it."

"You are a very cunning man, Jason," Alexia said as they both stood up to leave the courtroom.

CHAPTER THIRTY-TWO

Jason left feeling quite pleased with the way things had gone today, but he still had doubts regarding Samuels and whether or not he was up for the task he had been given. He was pretty sure he would not need him, but just in case things did not go according to plan in the courtroom, Jason wanted him in his pocket anyway.

He called Marcus and arranged to meet him before going home as he wanted to make sure everything would go smoothly.

They met up at the pre-arranged place and ordered their coffees before Jason quickly asked him again, "Are you sure about Samuels?"

"For fuck's sake, Jason, how many times? Yes, don't worry about him. I told you that Carl and Abe can be very persuasive when they need to be," Marcus said, frustrated by the question.

"I just want to be sure, my friend, because I was watching him today, and I am a little concerned, that's all," Jason replied.

"I can assure you Samuels will comply," Marcus said, trying yet again to reassure him.

Jason paused for a moment, looked at Marcus in the eyes, and then said, "Send them to see him again as a reminder."

"Jesus, Jason! Have I ever let you down?" Marcus asked in disbelief.

"No, Marcus, you have never let me down, but please do this for me as I want to be sure."

"Ok. I will call them as soon as we are done here and tell them to go and pay him another visit, but I can assure you that Samuels is in the bag."

"Thank you, my friend. I would never have had any doubts if it was you who was dealing with it, but I do not know these brothers. I guess I am just a little concerned as to whether they can be trusted," Jason said in a very apologetic way.

"Yes, they can, Jason, but I will send them again just to put your mind at ease."

"Thank you, Marcus; you are a good friend."

"As are you, buddy," Marcus replied, again remembering the time when Jason saved him from going to prison.

The two friends then chatted away for a short while longer, and after ordering and finishing a couple more coffees, they said their goodbyes and then parted company.

Jason went home while Marcus got on the phone and called Carl and Abe, asking them to pay Samuels another visit just to remind him of what was at stake. They said they would go and see him that very evening and, indeed, they did just that.

Carl telephoned Samuels and told him to come outside as he wanted to speak to him. Samuels tried to make excuses that he was under orders from the judge not to speak to anyone, but Carl insisted, despite his attempted avoidance. Suddenly Carl, who was fed up with the excuses, told Samuels that he either came out or they would go in. Eventually, Samuels agreed to come outside to where the two brothers were waiting for him by their car across the road.

As he neared the car and the brothers, Abe opened up his jacket and pulled out a gun, saying, "This is for you if you don't get the decision we want."

Before Samuels could even say a word, Carl said calmly, "We just want a chat, that's all. Put the gun away, Abe, as you are frightening Mr. Samuels."

Abe put the gun away and told Samuels to get into the car, or he would be forced into it. Samuels, who was clearly afraid, did as was told and got into the back seat of the car, asking what they wanted.

"We are just going to go for a little drive," Carl replied as he pulled away.

"Where are we going?" Samuels asked in a very frightened voice.

"Don't worry; this won't take long. Now let's put this hood over your face." Abe said as he reached his arm beside the seat, pulled out a hood, and put it over Samuels's head.

"Wait, what are you doing?" he asked fearfully.

"Just be quiet and keep the hood on," Abe replied in a threatening tone of voice.

Samuels just did as was told and did not put up any more resistance. Carl drove around for fifteen minutes, and all the while, Samuels kept asking where they were going and what they were going to do.

Eventually, Carl pulled into an industrial area that had several derelict buildings, and then Abe pulled off the hood from over Samuels's head.

"These buildings are empty, and no one comes here other than drug addicts, hookers, and other unsavory sorts," Abe said as he turned and looked directly into Samuels's eyes with a big grin on his face.

"Why did you bring me here?" Samuels asked, trembling as he did so.

"You have not forgotten our little deal, have you?" Carl asked, looking over his shoulder at Samuels.

"No, I haven't," he replied nervously.

"That's good. Because we will be keeping a close watch on your wife during the trial, and if we feel that you are not doing your job, then we will have to pay her a little visit, won't we, Carl?" Abe said with a big smile on his face.

"Oh, indeed we will, Abe. She is a very pretty little thing, and it will be a pleasure to show her what two men can do to her," Carl said with a little laugh.

"No, please leave her out of this. I told you I would do it the last time," Samuels replied.

"Yes, we know you did, but we are just making sure you understand the consequences if you don't uphold your end of the bargain. You see, after we are finished showing your wife a good time, we will bring her here and leave her in the capable hands of the junkies. Now, I don't know what is going to happen, but I am pretty sure they will have a great time with her," Carl continued.

"No, please, I beg you, don't do this. I will do what you want, just please don't hurt my wife," Samuels begged them.

"Oh, we won't hurt your wife; we are just going to have some fun with her. It is the people here that may hurt her," Abe replied as he looked at Carl, giving him a little wink of his eye.

"No, please stop," Samuels said as he broke down and began to cry, putting his hands up to his face.

"It's ok, don't cry, we don't want to hurt you or your wife, and we won't, as long as you do your job. Just remember, the jury must find her not guilty, or at the very least, you have to convince enough people to vote that way so that it ends in a mistrial," Carl said to him.

"Yes, ok, I will try," Samuels replied as he began to stop the tears.

"There is that awful word again, try," Abe said as he stared at Samuels, then pulled out his gun, pointed it at him, and continued. "Have you taken a good look at this place, and do you want your wife to end up here?"

"No, of course I don't," Samuels begged once again.

"Then stop using that word - try."

"Yes, you are right; I'm sorry. I **will** do it, not try, will do it."

Carl turned to look at his brother and said, "You know what, Abe? I think he finally gets the message."

"I think he does, brother," Abe replied as he again turned to stare at Samuels.

Carl then turned around, started the engine, and began to drive Samuels back to his home. Carl reminded him that some of their associates would be keeping a close watch on him, and they would be watching his wife during the whole trial. The brothers assured him that this would be his final warning and, if they thought things were not going well, they would pay his wife a visit.

Carl eventually pulled up across the road from his house, told him to get out, and then drove away, knowing that they had put the fear of God into him and were pretty sure he would do what had to be done.

A little while later, Carl telephoned Marcus, assuring him that Samuels would do well and that he had nothing to worry about. Marcus, in turn, then called Jason to give him the good news.

When Jason answered the call, Marcus simply said one word ... "Sorted," and by that, he knew that Samuels would do what had to be done. Of course, Jason was no fool, and he knew there was a chance that Samuels may not be able to convince anyone else to vote not guilty. However, he felt confident that Samuels was frightened enough to pull out all the stops to get at least another couple of jurors to vote not guilty.

He also knew that if the need arose, he could use the information he had about Conrad having an affair with his wife to get him to convince the DA to drop the charges. Yet he did not want to go down that road unless it was necessary. For now, he would put his faith in his friend Marcus and hope that all would end well, but at least he had a backup plan if he needed one. He was now far more relieved than he had been earlier and had high hopes that everything was going to turn out perfectly for him and for Alexia. So much so that he actually felt really happy at this precise moment, happier than he had felt for a very long time.

CHAPTER THIRTY-THREE

The evening passed very quickly for Jason, but not so for Alexia, as she spent most of it thinking about the trial and which way it was going to go. For so long now, Alexia was used to being in control of everything she did, and now she suddenly found herself having to put her life in someone else's hands, which she found very hard to do. It was difficult for her not to be in control of things, and she did not like that one little bit, as this was a very strange feeling for her. She had become so used to being a dominant woman that anything else was simply not good enough.

It's not that she did not trust Jason, as she knew she had him eating out of her hand and that he would try his hardest for her. However, the fact that she had to trust another person, and a man, no less, was the most difficult part of it all.

Eventually, she fell asleep in the early hours of the morning and was still tired when she woke up. But of course, Alexia being Alexia, she was not going to let a little thing like tiredness stop her from looking anything but her best. She got up, showered, did her makeup, and got dressed. She made sure she looked perfect as usual, although not as sexily dressed as she would normally be, before leaving home to make her way to the courthouse.

Jason also made his way there, and he arrived only a few minutes before Alexia did.

"Good morning, Alexia. How are you today?" Jason asked in a soft, welcoming tone of voice.

"Very well, thank you, Jason, and yourself?" she replied, giving him a big smile.

"Yes, I am very well, thank you, and I'm eager to get going today," Jason said confidently and with a big smile of his own.

Alexia kept smiling as she looked into his eyes, and she almost knew that he was not telling her everything. It was a feeling that she had experienced on a number of occasions recently, but she could not quite put her finger on it. 'He must know what he is doing,' she told herself as they both walked into the courtroom and sat down.

Everyone had to rise a little while later as the judge walked in and finally sat back down after the judge did so.

"You may call your first witness of the day," the judge said, looking at Emerton.

"Yes, your Honor. The people call Derek Jordan," he replied.

After the formality of being sworn in was over, Emerton asked his witness, "Can you please tell the court who you are and what you do, Mr. Jordan?"

"I am the lead forensic investigator on this case," he replied.

"And can you please tell the court exactly how Mr. Morley died?"

"Mr. Morley was shot once in the chest and died instantly," Jordan replied.

"Can you also please tell the court if this is the gun that was used to shoot and kill Mr. Morley?" Emerton asked as he handed over the bagged gun, which he called exhibit one.

"Yes, it is," Jordan replied after he looked closely at the gun.

"And were there any fingerprints found on the gun?" Emerton then asked.

"Yes, they belonged to the defendant," Jordan said as he pointed to Alexia.

"And does this gun also belong to the defendant?" Emerton asked, looking over at the jurors for a brief moment.

"Yes, and she is licensed to own it," Jordan responded.

"Would you please tell the court if any gunshot residue was found on Miss Summers's hands?" Emerton continued.

"Yes, there was gunshot residue found on the defendant's hands," Jordan confirmed.

"And finally, can you please tell the court roughly how far away the defendant was standing from Mr. Morley when she shot him.?"

"No more than a couple of feet away, I would say," Jordan said confidently.

"I have no more questions for this witness, your Honor," Emerton said as he walked back to his seat.

"Do you wish to cross, Mr. Carini?" the judge asked.

"Yes, I do, your Honor," replied Jason as he stood up and walked over to the witness.

"Good morning, Mr. Jordan. I only have a few questions to ask you. Did you examine Miss Summers in any way?" he asked.

"Yes, of course I did," Jordan replied.

"Please tell the court what your findings were," Jason said as he turned to look at the jurors.

"Well, her dress was torn, and she had a swollen lip that also had a cut on it," Jordan said, pointing to his own lip as if to show where the swelling was.

"And did she have anything under her fingernails?" Jason continued.

"Yes, she did; it was DNA from Mr. Morley."

"I see, and did Mr. Morley have any marks on his face?" Jason asked as he turned to look at the jurors again.

"Yes, he had a few scratches on his left cheek," was the response from Jordan.

Jason walked over closer to the jurors, and while looking at each of them in turn, he said, "So, Miss Summers had been hit across the face and had her dress torn, while Mr. Morley had scratches across his face and his DNA was found under Miss Summers's fingernails. Based on your expertise as a forensic scientist, would you conclude that what could have happened is that Mr. Morley attacked Miss Summers, tearing her dress as he grabbed and hit her, causing the cut to her lip? And during this attack, Miss Summers scratched Mr. Morley on the cheek trying to escape?"

However, before Derek Jordan could even answer, Emerton stood up, saying, "Objection, your Honor. The witness was not there at the time and therefore cannot state what actually happened."

"Indeed," the judge replied.

However, before he could say anything else, Jason said, "Your Honor, I am not asking the witness to state what happened, but only if it is possible for the events to have happened that way. He is, after all, an expert forensic investigator that has dealt with evidence like this many times. The prosecution has not offered any explanation as to how the dress was torn, how Miss Summers suffered the injury to her lip, how Mr. Morley suffered the scratches to his face, or indeed, how his DNA came to be under the fingernails on the defendant. These are questions that need to be asked, and although Mr. Jordan cannot state exactly how these happened, he *can* state in his expert opinion whether it is possible for these things to have happened the way I have stated," Jason replied.

"For all we know, the defendant scratched Mr. Morley first, and his instinctive reaction was to grab and hit her, tearing her dress in the process," replied Emerton as he turned to look at Jason. "Or, it is even possible that she tore her own dress and hit herself before scratching Mr. Morley's face *after* she shot him."

"That's exactly my point, your Honor; anything is possible, including the way I have suggested. I am simply asking the witness in his expert opinion if the events of that evening could have happened the way I have described them."

"Ok, sit down, both of you. Mr. Jordan, can any of these events be confirmed as possible explanations of what happened on that night when Mr. Morley died?" the judge asked.

"Yes, they are all possible, but I cannot say which one actually happened," Jordan replied.

"There you have it, gentlemen; anything is possible. We may never know what actually happened that evening, and you cannot expect Mr. Jordan to tell you, Mr. Carini, as he was not present at the time of the shooting. So, can we move on now, please?" the judge asked.

"Yes, your Honor," was the reply from both of them.

Jason was angry with himself for walking right into that one and did not expect Emerton to say anything. Perhaps his old nemesis was a little better at his job than he gave him credit for, or perhaps Jason himself was far too cocky for his own good. He was hoping the jury would hear the forensic investigator confirm his account of events, but it had the reverse effect after the judge's comment.

"Call your next witness, Mr. Emerton," the judge said.

"The people call Detective Nick Colby, your Honor."

After Colby entered the courtroom and had been sworn in, Emerton asked, "Are you the detective in charge of this case, Mr. Colby?"

"Yes, sir. Well, both me and my partner are," he replied.

"Can you tell us in your own words what you witnessed when you arrived at the crime scene, please?" Emerton asked.

"We got the call that a shooting was reported at Miss Summer's residence, to which we responded. We arrived only a minute or so before the paramedics, and upon entering the premises, after Miss Summers had let us in, we found Mr. Morley on the floor. There was a gun on the small table, which I secured while the paramedics attended to the deceased and then I asked Miss Summers what happened," Colby replied.

"I see, and how was Miss Summers dressed?" Emerton asked as he turned to look at and pointed to the defendant.

"She was dressed in a very sexy way, with a short red dress that showed her stockings, and she wore high heels," Colby replied, also looking at Alexia.

"And Mr. Morley, how was he dressed?"

"He was dressed in a suit, but his jacket was on the couch, and his shirt was unbuttoned," the detective said.

"I see, and did it look like to you that the two of them were perhaps in the process of having sex?" Emerton asked.

"Objection, your Honor," Jason interjected. "How could the detective know what was happening prior to him being there?"

"Sustained. Rephrase your question, Counselor," the judge said.

"Yes, your Honor. My apologies. Was an explanation offered by Miss Summers as to why they were both dressed in that way or indeed what had happened?" he asked the detective.

"Yes, the defendant told me that he was there for an appointment with her as she was a mistress, but he was not happy with the service she provided and had demanded sex. When she refused, he became angry, and that is when he attacked her. She managed to break free, and that is when she took the gun out of the drawer and shot Mr. Morley as he went for her again," Colby replied.

Emerton slowly walked over to the jurors and asked Colby as he turned to look at him, "An escort refusing a client sex after taking him back to her house. Have you ever heard of anything like that before, Detective?"

"No, I have not," Colby said.

"And what was your initial thought about that comment?" Emerton asked as he turned to look at the jurors.

"I must admit I found it quite surprising, if I am being honest," he replied.

"Yes, I can understand why. An escort refusing to have the sex she was apparently paid to have with Mr. Morley, or so the defense would have you believe. No more questions, your Honor."

The judge looked over at Jason, waiting for the cross-examination that was almost certain to follow.

"Detective Colby, do you understand the difference between an escort and a mistress?" Jason asked as he got up from his seat and walked over to the witness stand.

"Yes, one deals with everyday sexual acts while the other does domination role-plays. But either way, they both get paid by the client for sex, or at the very least, some form of sexual acts," Colby replied confidently.

"I see. Well, it is clear that you have no idea what the difference is because Miss Summers never gets paid to have sex with her clients. An escort gets paid to have sex, but a true mistress gets paid to dominate her clients, and that is exactly what Miss Summers is, Detective ... a mistress, not an escort."

"Objection, your Honor, is council trying to defend his client or teach us about the sexual acts an escort offers?" Emerton asked, almost laughing.

"Quite. Save it for summation, Mr. Carini, and only ask questions for now rather than make statements," the judge said, sustaining Emerton's objection.

"Yes, your Honor. The court has my apologies. No more questions for this witness," Jason said as he walked back to his seat, knowing that he had allowed his emotions to take over for a moment.

This was so uncharacteristic of Jason, who normally had a very cool and clear head when in the courtroom. However, for some reason, which was beyond him, he was unable to perform the way he would normally do. He was not thinking straight, asking the wrong questions, and he felt lost for the first time in his career as an attorney. Jason was really struggling and had no idea why, or indeed, how to get back to his best, but he needed to, for Alexia's sake.

"You may call your next witness, Mr. Emerton," the judge said.

"Yes, your Honor. The people call Detective Turolla."

Detective Turolla spent the time on the stand, pretty much giving the same answers as his partner did to the same questions. Jason did not even bother to cross-examine this witness as he felt it would not have done any good. Again, Alexia was painted as just another escort, and, as the judge had already told Jason to save his opinions regarding the difference between an escort and a mistress, he did not see the point.

After Turolla had finished giving his evidence, the judge asked Emerton to call his next witness, but Emerton told the judge that he had no other witnesses and that the people rest.

This was never going to be a long trial as there were no more witnesses to be called. The jury had heard from Morley's family and friends, or at least what they would have said, and also from the detectives in charge and the forensic investigator. There really wasn't anyone else to call, and this was always going to be a case of which lawyer the jurors believed. Jason knew this was going to be the case, as he had hardly any witnesses to call except for Alexia's best friend and Alexia herself. At least he would now have the opportunity to explain to the jurors the difference between what an escort does and what Alexia does.

"Ok, we will break for lunch and be back here at 2 pm. Court adjourned," said the judge as he rose from his seat and went to his chambers.

Jason and Alexia left the courtroom and found a restaurant to have lunch in, so they could chat about what would happen that afternoon.

Chapter Thirty-Four

Jason and Alexia sat at a quaint little restaurant and ordered their food.

While they waited for it to be brought to them, Alexia asked, "That last bit did not seem to go as well as you had hoped, am I wrong?"

"Don't worry about that, as the real case begins now. I always knew that Emerton was going to make you seem like just another escort, but we know better. When I put you on the stand, the jurors will learn the difference between you and an escort," Jason replied, trying to reassure her with a smile, even though he was still not sure how things would go or how he felt.

"I hope so, Jason, as I am putting my life in your hands, and I do not expect you to let me down," Alexia said in a stern voice.

"Trust me, Alexia, I will not let you down. Now, do you remember what you need to say and, just as importantly, how you need to say it, just as I explained it to you before?"

"Yes, Jason, I do," she replied confidently enough, although there was still this nagging doubt in her mind that she could not quite put her finger on.

"Good, now leave the rest to me and let's enjoy our lunch. This will all be over soon," Jason said with another big smile on his face.

The food had now arrived at their table, and they began to enjoy their lunch together, but all through it, Jason seemed to be lost in thought. He kept telling himself that he had to snap out of the way he suddenly felt and start concentrating on the case in hand. The weird thing for him was that he had no idea of what had come over him and why he was so distracted, but he had to get his act together as Alexia's life was on the line.

This did not go unnoticed by Alexia, and again, she wondered what was going on. She had the same feeling, just like before, that there was something wrong or that perhaps Jason was not telling her everything. She did not want to say anything to him right now, as he would obviously be thinking about the trial after lunch, but she was certainly concerned.

They finished their lunch and headed back to the courtroom for the afternoon session, which Alexia hoped would be the last one. The judge then entered the room, and everyone stood up before sitting back down again after the judge had done so.

"You may call your first witness now, Counsellor," The judge said to Jason.

"Yes, your Honor. The defense calls Olivia Tamsworth to the stand."

As Olivia entered the courtroom and headed to the stand, Jason looked at her, looked at Alexia, then Emerton, then Alexia again, and in that instant, he felt all his confidence come back to him. He suddenly realized what his problem was and why he had been feeling this way. Not only was he breaking all the rules to save Alexia, but he was also up against his old rival.

For a while, it all seemed like it was becoming two separate battles and that he was fighting on two fronts, but they were, in fact, the same one. He realized that he only had one battle to fight and that an acquittal for Alexia would also be a victory for him against Emerton. He also recognized that coming face to face with him brought back all the old conflict and was made worse by the fact that Emerton now stood between him and Alexia.

Jason knew exactly what he needed to do, and that was what he did best: questioning witnesses on the stand while oozing confidence for the jurors to see, and to totally forget about Emerton.

Olivia, who had been Alexia's best friend for many years, took the stand, swearing under oath to tell the truth, and then sat down.

Jason, who had suddenly regained his composure and confidence, stood up and then walked over to Olivia.

"Can you tell us who you are and how long you have known Miss Summers, please?" Jason asked her, pointing to Alexia in the process.

"Alexia, oops, sorry, Miss Summers, I mean, is my best friend and has been for a very long time," Olivia replied.

"And do you know what Miss Summers does for a living?" he asked.

"Yes, she is an author and also a mistress," Olivia said, looking over at the jurors.

"And does it not bother you what Miss Summers does for a living?"

"No, why should it? She is the nicest person you could ever hope to meet, and the fact that she is a mistress does not change that in any way. She has been nothing but kind to me and has been the best friend anyone could ever have. I do not let something like the fact she is a mistress change the way I think of her, and do not forget that she is also a great author as well," Olivia answered, feeling good about herself.

"Yes indeed, we should not forget that," Jason said as he turned and looked at the jurors.

"So, tell me, knowing Miss Summers as well as you do, what do you think about the accusations brought against her?"

"They are ridiculous. Alexia is no killer, and if she did shoot that man, then she must have thought her life was in danger," she replied angrily.

"Indeed, and after hearing what she has been accused of, do you still trust Miss Summers?" Jason asked, again looking over to the jurors.

"With my life," she replied, now looking at the jurors herself.

"Thank you, Miss Tamsworth," Jason replied, feeling much better with himself.

"Cross, Mr. Emerton?" the judge asked.

"Yes, thank you, your Honor," Emerton said as he rose from his seat.

"So, Miss Tamsworth, how much do you know about what Miss Summers does?"

"Only the little she has told me about her work, as she does not like to talk about her clients and what I have read from her books," she replied.

"I see, so you don't really know much then, do you, considering she is your best friend? Have you ever witnessed any of these domination sessions?"

"Well, no, never," replied Olivia, sounding slightly worried.

"I see, so you don't really know much about her work at all, and for all you know, she could simply be just another escort.

After all, you only know what she has told you and nothing more; is that not correct?" Emerton asked, staring at Olivia, waiting for an answer.

"I have no reason to doubt what she says," she replied confidently.

"But still, you don't really know for certain what she is capable of, do you? No more questions for this witness, your Honor," Emerton said as he looked at the jurors while walking back to his seat.

"You may step down, Miss Tamsworth, and you may call your next witness, Mr. Carini."

"Your Honor, I will not waste any of the court's time calling various friends of Miss Summers who will only echo what Miss Tamsworth has said. Therefore, I only have one more witness to call, and that is Miss Summers herself," Jason said.

Alexia stood up and elegantly walked to the stand where she was sworn in and then sat down. Jason walked over to her, quickly glancing at the jurors.

"Miss Summers, thank you for taking the stand. You know that you did not have to, so please tell the court why you chose to do so," he prompted.

"I am happy to, Mr. Carini, as I just want to tell the truth about what happened and clear my name," Alexia replied assuredly and confidently.

"And that is what we all want, Miss Summers, to get to the truth. So, please tell the court what you do for a living," Jason said as he turned to look at the jurors.

"I am an author as well as a mistress and *not* an escort as some would have you believe," she replied firmly.

"And please explain the difference between the two, would you?" Jason asked as he looked back at Alexia.

"Well, an escort gets paid to pretty much do whatever the clients want; a mistress does not. An escort will play out any fantasy the client asks for, but a mistress will not. An escort will have sex in any position a client wants or indeed do any sexual acts a client wants, but a mistress will not ... at least not a proper, professional mistress. Most escorts will offer a domination service, but that does not make them a mistress," she replied in a well-spoken, professional, but polite manner.

"I see, and what exactly will a mistress, in this case, you, offer and do?" Jason asked.

"I get paid to pretty much do what I want, not what I am asked or told because I do the telling, not my clients. You see, I am not with a client to indulge their every whim or sexual desire, but instead, they are there to indulge mine. There are many various fantasies or fetishes, and many men enjoy being dominated. Many of my clients are in very important, stressful jobs and, as such, have many decisions to make every single day of their lives. Sometimes, they want to get away from this life and not have to make any decisions at all; quite the opposite, in fact. They want to relinquish the decision-making and have their decisions made for them, at least sexually. They enjoy being told what to do, they enjoy not having control, and they enjoy giving me pleasure.

"This is the service I provide for them, and I make all the rules. I tell them what I want, and they do exactly that. They are there for my pleasure, plain and simple, because it is what they enjoy and is the fantasy they have; the fetish, if you like. They will give me sexual pleasure in any way I like, and they never expect anything in return. If they have been good and I feel they are worthy, I may have sex with them or give them some kind of sexual release, but I do it only if I choose to. As I said, I do not get paid to have sex with my clients, but if I decide I want sex, then it is my choice and not theirs."

"I see, so this is the difference between an escort and a professional mistress? With an escort, the clients expect to get what they want or at least what they pay for, but with a mistress like yourself, the client has no such right to expect anything except what you are prepared to give them. But please, tell the court why would one of your clients pay you if they know they may not get anything when they can pay an escort and get everything they want?" Jason asked.

"But who says they do not get anything? You are thinking like a client who wants sex, rather than like a slave who wants to be dominated," she replied assertively.

"And why do you use the term slave?" Jason asked as he turned and looked at the jurors.

"Because that is what they are, or at least that is what their fantasy is."

"Can you elaborate on that, please, Miss Summers?" he asked as he turned and looked at Alexia again.

"Yes, I will try and explain, but you must stop thinking of my clients as people who are just simply looking for sex because they are not. As I have said previously, there are many different fantasies or fetishes that so many people have, and my clients are no different. They are not looking for just sex, but instead are looking for something very different and unique. My clients enjoy sex just like most people, but they also enjoy other aspects as well. Some enjoy being bossed about and treated as my very own sex slaves, while others prefer being tied up and spanked. Some even prefer the heavier type of punishment, such as being whipped and beaten. Other clients want to be humiliated and made to dress up as a woman, yet others enjoy simply worshiping my body and wanting to pleasure me in any way I tell them to."

Alexia paused for a brief moment to look over at the jurors, which is one of the things Jason told her to do when prepping her, before looking back at him to continue what she was saying.

"I simply give them what they desire because it is what they come to me for and what they pay me for. This is why I refer to them as my slaves; because it is what they want to be. They pay me to dominate or humiliate them in the way that their fantasy of fetish is important to them, but they never pay me for sex like they would an escort. Of course, they would all like me to give them sexual pleasure or have sex with them, but they never expect it because they know I would never take money for sexual services as an escort does. But as I said before, if they have been a good, obedient slave and have given me lots of sexual pleasure, then I may, if I choose to, give them some pleasure back and maybe even have sex with them," Alexia replied in a very confident and assertive way.

"Well, that certainly explains a lot," Jason said as again he turned to look at the jury. "So, just to be clear, your clients, or slaves, as you call them, not only pay you to dominate, humiliate and punish them, but also for them to give you sexual pleasure in any way you want. Does that pretty much sum it up?" Jason asked while still looking at the jurors.

"Yes, that sums it up nicely," Alexia replied, turning to look at the jurors.

"Now you stated that you do not always have sex with your clients, or slaves as you refer to them, but you also say they give you pleasure. Can you be a bit more specific as to what kind of pleasure exactly we are talking about here if, as you say, you do not always have sex with them?" Jason asked as he now turned to look at Alexia once more.

"Pleasure is not always sexual, but more often than not, it is. They enjoy pleasing me by worshiping my body, and there are many ways in which they will do this. The obvious ones are, of course, having them give me an orgasm as often as I want, either with their hands or by giving me oral which they enjoy doing as well. But I also enjoy them doing other things that may not give me sexual pleasure, but pleasure, nonetheless. This could be massaging and kissing my feet, watching them lick my stiletto shoes, sucking my toes, and pretty much kissing or licking any part of my body I choose. They may not get any physical pleasure from doing these things, but they still enjoy the humiliation and being forced to do them, which, in turn, gives them a sort of psychological pleasure," Alexia replied, trying very hard not to smile while she said it.

"And you are a fully qualified psychologist, are you not, Miss Summers?" Jason asked to make sure the jurors knew she was a lot more than just an author or mistress.

"Yes, indeed I am, which ensures that I understand the psychological pleasure my slaves can get from whatever we do together," she replied, this time with a very slight smile.

"Please continue with what you were saying, Miss Summers," Jason said as he walked over to the jurors so that he was now standing next to where they were seated.

"Well, there are many forms of pleasure that a person can have, and remember, my clients do not come to me for the normal types of pleasure they can get at home or with an escort. They come to me to fulfill their fantasies and fetishes, which most people would not understand. For example, some of them enjoy being punished by me, doing things such as digging my high heels into their thighs or even their groin and also having me slap their erect penis or squeezing their testicles, to whip them, even scratch them with my nails, to name but a few things. As I have explained, sometimes I may decide to give them pleasure by making them have an orgasm, or even allow them to masturbate while I watch. I may even have sex with them, but as explained earlier, it is my choice, not theirs," Alexia continued.

Jason walked back to the witness stand so that he was now standing right in front of Alexia. He gave her an ever-so-slight wink of the eye to tell her she was doing well.

"And if you were to have sex with them, do you decide in which position you do so, or do your slaves have a say?" he asked her as he turned to look at the jurors.

"When I do decide to have sex with my clients, it is because I am either in the mood to, or I feel my slave has been obedient and is deserving of a reward, such as me having sex with them. However, I will always go on top so that I can control the speed and length of anything that happens. After all, they are there for *my* pleasure and not the other way around. As I have explained, this is what they want and enjoy, so I am simply fulfilling their fantasies and providing the service which they pay for."

Alexia paused for a brief moment and slowly looked at all the jurors, making sure she did not stare or indeed look at any of them for too long, as Jason instructed her, before continuing. "Please understand that not everyone has the same fantasies or fetishes, and my clients simply have the kind of tastes that perhaps most people do not. You would be very surprised to know just how many people there are out there that have secret desires, which I am happy to be able to fulfill. The things I have mentioned are just a few of a great many varied fantasies and fetishes that my clients have, which cannot be fulfilled at home for whatever reason. This is why they come to see me and become my slaves. I take the time to talk to them first and find out exactly what they are looking for, but more importantly, I tell them what services I offer. I understand their needs and know exactly how far to push the boundaries of their desires so that we both benefit from any time I spend with them."

"Thank you for the explanation, Miss Summers, and would you say that your training as a psychologist has been instrumental in your ability to read your clients so well? Also, please tell the court which field of psychology you trained in."

"I trained and qualified as a sexual therapy psychologist, so yes, it has absolutely helped me to understand my client's sexual problems as well as their fantasies. As such, I am able to analyze what my clients tell me about their desires or fetishes and can use my knowledge to push their boundaries just enough to enhance their satisfaction when I dominate them," Alexia replied in a relaxed yet very confident voice.

"As a psychologist, can you help us understand why your clients have these fantasies or fetishes, as you have called them, while most people do not?"

"Well, we all have fantasies if you think about it, such as winning the lottery, owning a sports car, having the vacation of a lifetime, or even owning a mansion. My client's fantasies are no different except for the fact that they fantasize about sexual acts, humiliation, and domination. Whether you fantasize about dining out at the best restaurants, drinking the best champagne, or about a sexily dressed mistress spanking you and forcing you to give her pleasure, it is all the same. They may be very different things, but they are all fantasies. So you see, we all fantasize about things in one way or another; it's just that some people's fantasies are sexual, while others are not. As for fetishes, well, what are fetishes really? Just because some people do not understand certain sexual preferences, they call them fetishes or even perversions. For some people, these so-called fetishes are just normal tastes that perhaps other people simply do not have."

Alexia could see, by the look on their faces as well as the way they looked at her, that a couple of the jurors seemed to understand what she was trying to say, but most of them still seemed a little confused by it all.

Taking a long deep breath, she again began to speak. "Allow me to give you an example. Some people prefer having sex in the missionary position, while others prefer doing it with the man being behind the woman. Some couples love to have sex outdoors because there is a risk of them getting caught, and that excites them. Some people love oral sex more than intercourse, while others do not. Some men prefer their partners to wear high heels and stockings, while other men are not too bothered. You see, everyone has different preferences, even though they are all sexual."

"But some people may argue that although those are different tastes, there is nothing that anyone can call kinky or perverted in what you have just mentioned," Jason said, looking at the jurors awaiting Alexia's response.

"You are correct, so let's try something different then. Some couples love to use sex toys during sex or even use food. And what about the people that enjoy having a threesome or even group sex, and perhaps even wife swapping? Also, let's not forget about homosexual and lesbian lovers who enjoy sex with people of the same gender as them. Some people may think all of these as kinky, fetishes, or even perversions? But they are not, because to the people that enjoy them, they are simply a natural way to enjoy sex. So you see, there is no difference whatsoever between these and the tastes my clients have. Just because a person does not understand or have the same tastes as another person, it does not make the act a fetish, kink or a perversion," Alexia said, and she could see that some of the jurors now seemed to understand what she was trying to say better.

"Yes, what you say makes sense, and thank you for helping all of us to understand that, Miss Summers. So in effect, due to your training as a psychologist, you are more than qualified to not only be able to understand your client's needs but also to be able to give them what they want. As well as that, you are also an author who has written a lot of books on the subject of domination, which have in turn made you a very wealthy lady, have they not?" he asked, looking at the jurors.

"Yes, that is correct, I have written a number of books on the subject, and it is also true that they have made me quite wealthy," she replied in a questionable manner.

"So to recap, you have a degree in psychology, earn money from your clients on a regular basis, and are a very successful author, which has made you wealthy. There is certainly no need for you to be an escort as was suggested by the prosecution," Jason said.

"Objection. Is there a question in there, your Honor?" Emerton called out.

"Sustained. Save the comments for summation, Mr. Carini." the judge said.

"My apologies, your Honor. Now, Miss Summers, let's move on to that awful night where you had to defend yourself. You say that you always take the time to talk to your clients to find out what they want and to tell them what services you offer. Did you do this with Mr. Morley?"

"Yes, I did. I asked him what he wanted, and his reply was that he was after some domination. I asked if he had tried any domination before and if he had any boundaries or anything specific he wanted to try out. He said he did not have anything specific in mind but just enjoyed being dominated. He also said that he had done this sort of thing a number of times with other escorts. I then explained that I was a mistress and not an escort and also explained the difference to him. He kept insisting that he knew and understood the difference, so he was happy and eager to continue," she replied, once again turning to face the jurors.

"So, can you please tell us what happened on that evening that led to you having to defend yourself, Miss Summers, and please be very specific with the details?"

Alexia paused for a moment, then turned to speak to the judge. "I am sorry, your Honor, but for me to describe what happened exactly would require me to be very frank because I will have to talk about sexual acts that happened. Would that be ok?"

"Yes, Miss Summers, but please only say what needs to be said," the judge replied.

"Thank you, your Honor," Alexia said before turning around and continuing.

"The session began just like any other session, and I told him to get on his knees and to call me mistress. I then used a crop to spank his ass with, to see what he could handle, and he took it all in his stride. I then told him to get up and massage my neck and shoulders, which he did. After a while, I told him to get down on his knees while I sat on the couch and ordered him to lick my shoes, and suck my stiletto heels and again, he did as was told. Then I told him to take my shoes off, massage my feet, then kiss them, once again obeying me, doing what he was told, as I would have expected any of my slaves to do. Then I told him to kiss up my legs until he reached my stocking tops. However, he did not listen this time and tried to kiss not only above my stocking tops but also tried to kiss between my legs. I put my hands on his shoulders and pushed him away, telling him to stop. To his credit, he did stop, and I said all in good time.

"Again, I explained to him that I was in charge and that he needed to listen or he would be punished. He then said that he would enjoy that, so I told him to unbutton his shirt. Once he did that, I took his nipples between my fingernails and squeezed them just enough for him to feel a little pain. After a few minutes of doing this, I stood up, took off my panties, and kneeled on the couch, lifting my dress up as I did so. I told him to get on his knees, and I then positioned myself so that my butt was right in front of his face and told him to lick it first before he could have the pleasure of giving me oral sex. Again, he did as was told, and after I was satisfied that he had taken his punishment, I turned around, sat back on the couch with my dress still around my waist, and told him to give me oral until I reached an orgasm, which of course he did."

Alexia paused and looked at the jurors before she heard Jason.

"Take your time, Miss Summers; there is no rush. It is important that we hear everything that happened, and I know it is not easy to relive that moment, so please just relax and tell us everything."

Alexia took a deep breath, gave a short smile to Jason, and then continued.

"After he had given me oral, he got up and tried to kiss me. I put my hands on his chest to push him back, telling him to stop as I did not want to kiss him and that he should remember who was in charge. He then said that as he had just given me some pleasure, it was now his turn. Again, I tried to explain to him this is not how this works and to remind him that at the beginning, he had said he understood that. However, he then said that's what all the other escorts did to start with, but they would have given him some pleasure by now. Again, I explained that I was a mistress and not an escort, but he would not listen and tried to kiss me once more. Once again, I told him to stop and to leave my house, but he then grabbed me by the hair and forced my lips onto his to kiss him. I managed to move my head out of the way and pushed him aside, but he just laughed and asked if I liked it rough.

"He said that one way or another, he was going to get the sex he paid for and again moved towards me, grabbing me by the shoulders, trying to kiss me. Once more, I told him to stop and managed to break the hold he had on me, but he grabbed my dress, pulling me back towards him, which resulted in my dress tearing. He then slapped me around the face, which hurt, before he grabbed hold of me again, but this time a lot tighter, and I could not break free. I then put one of my hands up to his face and scratched him on the cheek. As he put his hand to his face, I broke away from him and ran to the cabinet, opened the drawer where I kept my gun, took it out pointing it at him, and said I would call the police if he did not leave. He said that I did not have the guts to shoot him and that he was going to kill me, calling me a stupid bitch in the process. He then just surged towards me, and in fear for my life, I fired. He fell to the floor, and I telephoned the police. They arrived a little while later with the paramedics, and that is what happened."

"I am sorry you had to go through such an ordeal, Miss Summers, and I cannot even begin to guess at what you must have gone through that evening. Therefore, I will not be asking you any more questions," Jason said as he went back to his seat.

"Your witness, Mr. Emerton," the judge said.

"So, Miss Summers, you have a degree in sexual psychology, yet you did not read Mr. Morley very well. How do you explain that?" he asked.

"Well, when someone tells me they have done this before and say they understand what is involved, I have no reason not to believe them," Alexia replied.

"But as a psychologist, should you not have been able to tell if he was being honest with you?" Emerton asked in a patronizing voice.

"No, you can't always. Besides, I was not there as his psychologist but as his mistress," she replied, trying hard to keep her cool.

"I see, so moving on. Do you not think it harsh to punish a man simply because he kissed above your stocking tops? After all, he was there for sexual purposes, was he not?" Emerton asked, looking at the jurors.

"No, he was not there for sexual purposes, as you put it; he was there to be dominated, which means following the rules. He broke the rules and had to be punished to be taught a lesson," she replied sternly.

"So, Mr. Morley paid you his hard-earned money, and in return, you made him lick your shoes, kiss your feet and legs, you squeezed his nipples to hurt him, made him lick your butt and give you oral pleasure, but he gets punished because he kissed above your stocking tops and he did not even get any pleasure so far himself. Is it any wonder he perhaps became angry, Miss Summers?" Emerton said with a smile on his face.

"Objection, your Honor. Miss Summers has explained what she does and why Mr. Morley was there," Jason interjected.

"Withdrawn," was the reply from Emerton. "Moving on, Miss Summers, do you enjoy what you do?" he asked.

"Yes, I do, and so do my clients," she replied in a calm way.

"Except Mr. Morley, it seems," Emerton said, looking over at the jurors.

"Objection, your Honor," Jason shouted out again.

"Mr. Emerton, keep your remarks to yourself," the judge said.

"Yes, your Honor. My apologies to the court," Emerton said in an unconvincing voice. "So, Miss Summers, you said you enjoy your job, which says to me that you enjoy punishing men. Is that right?"

Jason stood up again to object.

However, before he could do so, Emerton said, "Your Honor, Miss Summers, by her own admission, has said that she punishes her clients by whipping them, digging her heels in their genitals, squeezing their testicles, and slapping their penises. I am simply trying to find out if she enjoys doing this. I am not stating anything that Miss Summers has not already said herself before."

"Yes, quite right. Please sit down, Mr. Carini," the judge replied.

"So, Miss Summers, do you enjoy punishing and hurting men?" Emerton asked again.

"This is what my clients want from me," she replied.

"That does not answer my question. Do you enjoy punishing and hurting your clients?" Emerton asked yet again.

"It is not a case of whether I enjoy it or not; I am simply doing what my clients want. Sometimes I am nice to them, and sometimes I am not. It depends on the situation and the mood of the moment," Alexia replied, becoming a little agitated.

"So is that a yes, Miss Summers?" Emerton asked.

"Objection, your Honor. Council is badgering the witness," Jason shouted out.

"I am simply seeking an answer to the question, your Honor. Does Miss Summers enjoy punishing and hurting men?"

Emerton said, knowing that her refusal to answer looked bad for her as far as the jurors were concerned.

"Will you answer the question, please, Miss Summers?" the judge said.

"Ok, yes, I enjoy all aspects of what I do, which includes the punishment as well as me giving my clients a reward," Alexia finally answered.

"So you are a sadist then Miss Summers."

"Objection your Honor" Jason shouted out.

"Your Honor, the definition of a sadist is someone who enjoys inflicting pain, and as Miss Summers has just stated that she enjoys punishing her clients, then by definition, she is a sadist, is she not?" Emerton said, looking at Jason.

"Overruled," the judge said.

"So, are you a sadist Miss Summers?" he asked as he turned around to look at Alexia.

"No, I do not think of myself as a sadist," she replied.

"But you enjoy inflicting pain, sounds sadistic to me," he said, knowing this was scoring points with the jurors for him.

"Careful Mr. Emerton," the judge said.

"Yes your Honor."

"Why do you own a gun, Miss Summers?" Emerton asked.

"For my protection," she replied.

"But if your clients all understand what you do and that you are in complete control, then from whom do you need protection?"

"Anything can happen, and it did with Mr. Morley. If I did not have my gun, it could have been me that was dead now," Alexia replied, becoming angrier.

"Or perhaps you are not in total control over your clients, and things are not so well understood by them, just like Mr. Morley did not perhaps fully understand."

"Objection, your Honor," Jason shouted.

"Withdrawn," was the quick reply by Emerton before the judge could say anything. "So, Miss Summers, how many ways have you punished a slave of yours so far?"

"I am not sure. I do not keep count," Alexia replied in frustration.

"Well, let's see. You have already stated that you hurt their genitals by slapping them and digging your heels in them. I wonder, do you also do that to a slave's back, torso, and legs?"

"Yes, I do, if the need arises."

"And how do you do this? Using your hands, or do you use a belt, a whip, or even some other tool or device?" Emerton asked, looking at the jury.

"I use a lot of different things, including the ones you mentioned."

"And I presume you mark their bodies during these punishments?"

"Well, yes, but they know this is likely to happen, and they all have a safe word to use if it becomes too much for them," she said defensively.

"I see, and have you ever broken any bones or cut anyone to the stage where they needed hospital treatment?" Emerton asked.

"No, of course not," Alexia responded, unsure why he was asking these questions.

"I see, so by your own admission, you enjoy hurting men, but it would seem that you are limited to what extent you can hurt them. This is either because they have a safe word or because they would need hospital treatment if you went too far, which would raise too many questions. Tell me, Miss Summers, did you shoot Mr. Morley on purpose just because you wanted to know what it felt like to not only really hurt a man, but maybe even kill one?"

"Objection, your Honor! This is a pure vendetta against my client by the prosecution!" Jason bellowed across the courtroom.

"Sustained, and Mr. Emerton, this is your last warning. Any more comments like that, and I will find you in contempt. Is that understood?"

"Yes, your Honor," Emerton replied.

"The members of the jury will disregard the latest comment made by the prosecution," the judge instructed.

Jason knew that even though the judge had ordered the jurors to disregard that comment, it is not always easy to do. A lot of damage could have been done by Emerton in these last couple of minutes.

"So, Miss Summers, can you please help us understand something with an answer? You claim to be a mistress rather than an escort, but we only have your word for this, as is the case of what happened that night. How can we be sure that you are telling us the truth about what you do, and how do we know you are not just a mere escort? Where are your clients to tell us what you do? Why are they not here to back you up, these so-called slaves of yours? Why should we believe you, Miss Summers, when you have given us no proof that you are a mistress and not just an escort? How do we know that you were not just walking the streets when you picked up Mr. Morley, or perhaps even in a bar when you met him? For all we know, it is possible that you are a prostitute who picked up Mr. Morley, took his money, then refused to give him what he wanted, or maybe he even changed his mind. You then refused to give him his money back, and when he tried to take it, you shot him. How do we know you are telling the truth, Miss Summers? You have no one here to confirm your story, after all, so please give us an answer, would you?" Emerton asked in an accusing way.

"Because I am telling you the truth, why would I lie to you?" she innocently answered.

"Because you killed a man in cold blood, Miss Summers," Emerton said sarcastically.

"Objection, your Honor," Jason shouted out.

"Sustained. The jury will disregard that last comment by council, and you are on very thin ice, Mr. Emerton."

"Yes, your Honor, my apologies. I have no further questions," he said as he walked back to his table.

"You may step down, Miss Summers," said the judge and waited until Alexia left the stand and sat back down next to Jason.

"Let's have a short recess, and then you may begin with your summations, councilors," the judge said, concluding the session.

CHAPTER THIRTY-FIVE

The judge came back into the courtroom, and once everyone was seated, he said, "Mr. Emerton, you may give your summation now."

"Thank you, your Honor," said Emerton as he got up from his seat and walked over to the jurors.

"Members of the jury, Miss Summers shot and killed Mr. Morley. This is not in dispute. The only thing in dispute is the reason. The defense claims it was self-defense, but can we be sure of this? Miss Summers claims that Mr. Morley went to see her and paid her for her time, as she put it. His family and friends say that this is not who Mr. Morley was and that he did not pay prostitutes to have sex with him. Who would know him best if not his family and friends? So what else could have happened on that fateful evening? The defense has shown no proof whatsoever regarding Miss Summers's testimony about what happened that evening, and we can hardly ask Mr. Morley now, can we? And she has only brought forward one witness to try and prove she is indeed a mistress, whatever exactly that is. None of her clients have come forward, not a single family member has been found, and only a single solitary best friend of hers has taken the stand and admitted that she only knows what little Miss Summers has told her."

Emerton paused, then walked up and down the juror's stand, looking at each and every one of them in turn, before he continued to speak yet again.

"Are we just to believe everything Miss Summers has said to be the truth, or should we look a little deeper into this crime? Let's take a closer look at what we have been told by the defendant, shall we? Miss Summers is a trained psychologist, yet she did not see through Mr. Morley's lies. She enjoys inflicting pain, abusing, and humiliating men and is by all definitions a sadist. She also enjoys treating men as her own personal sex slaves, ordering them to pleasure her sexually, and she punishes them if they do not oblige. If she is in the mood for sex, she has it with them, regardless of if they want to do it or not. And of course, let's not forget, she charges money for doing this. This has become a way of life for her, and she demands obedience from her slaves. Slaves: what a word. I thought slavery was abolished a long time ago. However, all this does not tell us exactly what happened that night."

Again he paused, then paced up and down the stand, looking each and every juror in the eye while doing so, before continuing.

"I will again refer back to what his mother said, as well as what his family and friends would have said, about Mr. Morley and that he was not the type of person to pay a prostitute for sex. Yet he was in Miss Summers's house when he was shot. What was he doing there? Who are we to believe, the woman that shot and killed him or his family and friends who knew him the best? And let's look at the evidence, shall we? Miss Summers scratched Mr. Morley on the cheek so hard that his skin and blood were found under her fingernails. She claims this was in self-defense, but how do we know this? For all we know, this was her way of punishing Mr. Morley because he did not please or obey her. She is, after all, a self-proclaimed mistress who commands obedience, so how dare a man say no to her. Perhaps Mr. Morley did go to see her but changed his mind after she began to punish him and tried to leave. Perhaps, in her anger or need to punish Mr. Morley for daring to say no to her, she scratched his face, and in reaction, Mr. Morley slapped her in order to try and get her to stop. And perhaps, it was in this moment that Miss Summers opened the drawer, took out the gun, and shot Mr. Morley dead. She then calmed herself down, thought up a story, and cried rape. The only thing we know for certain and will ever know is the fact that the defendant shot and killed Mr. Morley, plain and simple, and for this, she must be punished. Perhaps it is fitting that a woman who has spent her life punishing men should now herself be punished. Only you, the members of the jury, can now punish Miss Summers for killing Mr. Morley and get some justice for a man who cannot speak for himself."

He paused yet again while walking over to the witness stand before continuing once more.

"As I have stated before, there is no proof whatsoever that anything she has said is the truth, and although it is the prosecution's job to prove Miss Summers is guilty, there is no way we can do that without any witnesses. How convenient for Miss Summers. I now hope that you will see through these lies and give Mr. Morley and his family some peace and closure by finding Miss Summers guilty. Thank you."

Emerton walked over to his table and then gave Jason an evil look as he sat down.

"Mr. Carini, you may give your summation now," said the judge.

Jason got up from his seat and glared at Emerton as he walked past his table on his way to where the jurors were seated. He knew that his adversary had made an impact with his statement.

"Members of the jury, I am sorry you had to hear that fiction from the prosecutor as I thought we were here to deal with facts and not whatever assumptions are made. Facts, ladies and gentlemen, facts. Let's see what the facts are in this case, shall we? Fact: Miss Summers is a qualified psychologist and does not need to be an escort for an income. Fact: Miss Summers is a successful author, which has made her a wealthy woman, and she does not need to be an escort for an income. Fact: Miss Summers owns two homes that she does not owe any money on, so she does not need to be an escort for an income. Fact: Miss Summers has many clients who pay and obey her, so she does not need to be an escort for income or, indeed, sexual gratification. Facts, ladies and gentlemen, these are the facts. So the prosecution's theories of Miss Summers being an escort are just pure fiction."

Jason walked over to his table where Alexia was seated, drank a mouthful of water, then pointed to Alexia and continued with his statement to the jurors.

"Take a good look at Miss Summers. What do you see? Do you see an escort that would shoot a man because he refused to obey her or pay for sex? Or do you see an elegant, successful woman who could have any man she wanted. She is not only successful but also a very wealthy woman, so ask yourselves, why would she even think of taking money for sex? No, the truth is simple and is what Miss Summers told you from the witness stand. She is not an escort because she does not need to be one, but she *is* a mistress. The difference between an escort and a mistress is very clear indeed, and one cannot be mistaken for the other. Does Miss Summers enjoy punishing men? Yes, because her clients want her to. Does Miss Summers enjoy inflicting pain? Yes, because her clients want her to. Is Miss Summers demanding? Yes, because her clients want her to be. She is all these things and so much more because her clients want her to be, and it is what they pay her for. This does not make her a bad person or a killer. She has no need for any more money, and she has no need to be an escort because she is a mistress. As an escort, she would have to do whatever her clients wanted, regardless of how clean or filthy they may be, but as a mistress, she can do whatever she wants without any pressure to give her clients any more than she wants to. So why would she be an escort? She wouldn't."

Jason walked back over to where the jurors were sitting and said gently, "Mr. Morley may indeed have visited escorts in the past that offered domination role-plays. These are not the same as what Miss Summers offers, not even close. An escort may dominate her client, but at any time, if the client wants something different, the escort will be happy to oblige because an escort, by definition, is someone who gets paid to have sex. It is, after all, the oldest profession in the world. However, a professional mistress will never allow her client to change his mind about what he wants or have sex with him just because he wants it. A mistress has a job to do, which is to dominate her clients in the many varied ways that they want, but she never gets paid to have sex, unlike an escort whose clients mostly pay for exactly that – sex."

Jason walked up and down the juror stand looking at each one of them before continuing.

"Now, allow me to explain what happened. Mr. Morley, who quite possibly visited escorts in the past, may indeed have done domination role-plays with them, as I am sure many men have. During such role-plays, it is customary for these men to call the escorts 'Mistress' because they are taking on the persona of a dominant woman. When Mr. Morley made the appointment with Miss Summers, he must have assumed, wrongly, of course, that she was just another escort offering domination role-plays. This is understandable for someone who has never been with a professional mistress before, and when Miss Summers tried to explain what her services were, he just assumed she was going to tell him the same thing that all the other escorts had told him before. So, to not waste any time, he told her he knew what was on offer as he had done this many times before. Miss Summers had no reason not to believe him, so she began their session. It is perfectly clear that Mr. Morley had no idea what a professional mistress had to offer and became impatient, even angry, that he was not getting what he wanted. It was at this point that things turned ugly, and we all know what happened then. Miss Summers feared for her life and shot Mr. Morley in self-defense, as she stated under oath. You now have a decision to make, and, under the law, if there is a reasonable doubt as to the guilt of a person, then you must reach a verdict of not guilty.

The prosecution also has a job to do, which is to prove beyond a shadow of a doubt someone's guilt. Well, they have not met that burden, as no evidence has been shown that Miss Summers did not shoot in self-defense."

Jason once again walked over to his table, where Alexia was seated. He pointed to her while looking at the jurors and said, "Look at her. Miss Summers feared for her life, and the evidence says it all. Miss Summers's dress was torn. Her lip was swollen and cut. She was forced to scratch Mr. Morley's face in order to try and get away, the proof of which was under her fingernails. Finally, after all this, she was left with no choice but to shoot Mr. Morley. Please do not send an innocent victim to prison for defending herself. Yes, that's right, victim. Because Miss Summers *is* the victim here as she would have been raped and probably killed had she not shot Mr. Morley first in self-defense. Thank you, ladies and gentlemen, and I am sure you will come to the correct decision."

Jason went back to his table and sat down before the judge began to speak.

"Members of the jury, you have heard all the evidence and summations from both councilors. Your job now is a difficult one, and it is to weigh up everything you have heard. If you believe what the prosecution has said - that Miss Summers is an escort who picked up Mr. Morley, demanding money for sex, and you believe they have proved beyond a shadow of a doubt Miss Summers's guilt, then you must return a verdict of guilty.

If, on the other hand, you believe the defense - that Miss Summers is a professional mistress who simply accepted and trusted Mr. Morley as a client, who demanded sex from her and threatened to kill her, forcing her to shoot him in self-defense, then you must find her not guilty. You will now retire and talk amongst yourselves until you reach a verdict. You cannot talk to anyone else about this, regardless of the reason. Refreshments will be provided for your consumption, and please do not hesitate to ask if you require anything."

The trial was now over, barring the verdict, and the jurors were taken into a room to discuss the case and to try and reach a judgment. Meanwhile, Jason and Alexia had made it outside of the courthouse and went to get a bite to eat while they waited.

"So, how long will this take, Jason?" Alexia asked.

"It is hard to say, to be honest with you. They will first take a vote, and if everyone votes the same way, the verdict is reached. If not, then they will talk about it and see if they can get a unanimous decision. I don't think it will take more than a few hours, though, as I am sure a not guilty verdict will be coming your way very soon."

He replied confidently, but not necessarily due to his abilities in the courtroom, where he felt things did not go as well as he had hoped, but partly also due to Emerton doing a better job than he expected him to. He was, of course, thinking about Samuels doing what he was paid to do and helping bring in a favorable verdict.

Jason's fear from the very beginning was that the jurors would look at Alexia and see a prostitute, which could make their minds up as to her guilt, regardless of how good he was in the courtroom, and that's exactly what Emerton encouraged the jurors to think. If Alexia did anything else apart from being a mistress, he was sure he would not need Samuels for an acquittal, but a mistress she was, and that's why he did not feel as confident.

"I hope so, Jason, but whatever happens, I want to thank you for trying your best. Now, shall we order some food?" Alexia asked commandingly.

"Yes, Mistress," Jason replied jokingly, winking at Alexia as he did so and with a little smirk on his face.

CHAPTER THIRTY-SIX

By now, the jurors had been led into the room where they would try and reach a unanimous verdict. After they all sat down, the foreperson, Eddy Golding, stood up to speak to the rest of the jurors.

"Ok, let's all write our votes on a piece of paper and do a count," he said as he handed out sheets of paper and pens for all the jurors to write down their verdicts.

They all wrote down what they thought the verdict should be and folded the pieces of paper so that no one could see what each person wrote. Then all the papers were passed to Eddy, who unfolded each piece of paper in turn, reading the verdict out loud.

"Guilty, guilty, guilty, guilty, not guilty, guilty, guilty, guilty, not guilty, guilty, not guilty, guilty. Ok, so that's nine against three in favor of guilty," he said.

"Ok, so what do we do now, and who in their right mind thinks she is not guilty?" asked Danny Freeman, who was sitting to the right of the foreperson.

"Ok now, calm down. Everyone has the right to vote how they feel, so let's not get angry," Eddy said as he turned and looked at Danny.

"Ok, but if someone thinks that whore is innocent, then they need to tell us why. To me, it is clear as day that she is guilty. She shot him, didn't she?" Danny replied.

"Yes, she did, but before we condemn her, or start calling her names, let us hear the reason why three people voted not guilty. Would someone who voted not guilty like to respond?" Eddy asked, looking around the room at the jurors.

There was nothing but silence from the jurors as they all looked at each other, trying to guess who had voted not guilty.

"If the people who voted not guilty do not speak up, then we will get nowhere and stay here for a very long time. Everyone has the right to vote how they want, so please do not be afraid to speak up so we can get this done," Eddy said as again he looked around the room at the jurors.

There was another minute of silence and people looking around before someone spoke.

"I do not think she is a whore, as you put it, and please refrain from calling her that. Let us keep it respectful," Jackie Steward said as she looked at Danny.

"Quite right," Eddy said, looking at Jackie and giving her a nod of his head.

"Ok, fine, escort then, it's the same thing. So why do you not think she is an escort? After all, she advertises herself as such. Oh, sorry, she calls herself a mistress, but let's face it, it's the same thing," Danny said.

"No, it is not. Did you not hear the difference between an escort and a mistress? She does not sell her body to be used by her clients; she offers a different service instead. Besides, she is wealthy, so she doesn't need to sell her body for sex like an escort, does she?" Jackie asked as she stared at Danny.

"And if she is as wealthy as we are led to believe, then why offer **any** of these services at all? Would you?" Olivia Gibbs asked, looking at Jackie.

"Yes, exactly," Danny butted in.

Jackie looked at both Danny and Olivia, then thought for a minute before replying.

"Well, I don't know why, but no, I would never do anything like that. Maybe you are right, I don't know, but my instinct was to believe her and that it was in self-defense."

"And what about what was said about the victim Simon Morley? From what you heard, do you think he was the type of man to do what she said?" Danny asked.

"Well, he was there, wasn't he? Oh, I don't know. I'm confused now," Jackie replied.

"Would anyone else who voted not guilty like to speak?" Eddy asked.

There was a couple of minutes of silence before Sally Jordan began to speak and said, "I voted not guilty because I think she looks like an honest person and quite a strong character. I do believe that she is, in fact, a mistress and not an escort, as was explained the difference between the two, but I do not think we will ever know the truth. My gut feeling tells me she told the truth, but who knows, maybe she is guilty."

"Ok. There, two of the not guilty verdicts are going to change to guilty, so who is the last one?" Danny asked.

"Now wait just a minute. They have not said they are changing their verdicts, so stop putting words into their mouths," Eddy shouted out as Jackie and Sally looked at each other in an uncertain way.

"Well, they both said they were not sure," Danny replied as he looked at the two ladies.

"Maybe so, but that does not mean they are going to change their minds, so please stop trying to pressure anyone into doing what you want," Eddy said, looking straight at Danny.

There were a few minutes more of silence while everyone waited for the third person who voted not guilty to speak.

During all this time, Samuels, who said nothing but just listened, knew that he had a mountain to climb as it was quite clear that both Jackie and Sally could very easily be swayed to change their verdicts to guilty. He had to think quickly about what to say to try and get more people to believe Alexia was innocent, which was not easy considering he himself thought that she was guilty. However, he had to put that aside for now and think of a way to convince the others that she was innocent. Samuels was an avid reader and loved crime novels, which, of course, involved court cases in some of the books, and he began to think of something he may have read to help him.

"Well, come on, speak up," Danny said impatiently.

"I have asked you before to calm down, and we will all behave in an orderly manner. A person's life is at stake here, and we need to reach the right verdict, not just the quick or easy one because you may be in a rush," Eddy said in a firm voice.

"Yeah, ok, but if someone is going to vote not guilty, then they need to explain themselves," he replied in a frustrated way.

"Ok, it was me. I was the other person who voted not guilty," Samuels said as he got up from his chair and walked over to the window. He looked out of it for a brief moment, giving himself a few seconds longer before deciding on exactly what he wanted to say.

"Like Sally, my gut tells me that she is innocent. Oh, not of the shooting, as we know that she did, in fact, shoot him, but that it was in self-defense. I am not sure exactly why I feel this way, but something is telling me that Miss Summers was telling the truth. Bear with me, and I shall try and explain the reason why," he said as he turned and looked at the other jurors.

Samuels needed thinking time and was winging it for the moment, trying to think of what he could say that would help his cause. Half of his mind was thinking about his wife and what the two brothers would do to her, while the other half was thinking of what to say. What a mess he found himself in, and he knew that he would not be in this situation if it were not for his gambling habit. 'Oh, what to do?' he thought to himself.

"Ok, let's break down everything we have heard and see if we can make the right decision. Is there anyone here that does not understand the difference between a mistress and an escort?" Samuels asked, looking around the room.

"As I said, it's the same thing," Danny replied.

"No, it's not. There is a clear difference in the way it was explained in the courtroom, and you need to realize that," Rose Gardner said, speaking for the first time.

"Well, perhaps, you could explain it to me then," replied Danny angrily.

"Lose the attitude and the rudeness, or I will call the court official to take me before the judge and make a complaint against you," responded the foreperson sternly.

"Ok, ok, I'm sorry. Can you please explain the difference to me?" he replied in a much calmer voice.

"It is as we were told: an escort sells her body so the client can do pretty much whatever he wants, but a mistress does not. Instead, she gets paid to dominate her clients in whatever way **she** wants. Now, I am not saying she is innocent as I voted guilty, but at least I understand the difference between the two," Rose replied.

"But she admitted that she also has sex with her clients, so how is that any different from an escort, as they both have sex with their clients?" Danny asked.

"Ok, let me try and explain," Samuels said as he walked back to the table and sat down before continuing.

"With an escort, she will get paid to have sex, do a role-play, or pretty much whatever the client wants. After all, he is paying her for that reason, and an escort, by definition, is someone who is paid for sex. As a mistress, she gets paid to dominate her clients in the way that **she** wants and not **them** in a pre-arranged way of sorts. However, sex is never part of the agreement and is not what the client pays for. If the mistress, in this case, Miss Summers, wants to have sex with her clients, it is her choice, but she never **has** to have sex with them because that is not what she is paid for. Her clients go to her to be dominated in the way that they enjoy, and the mistress may, if she chooses to, reward her clients or, if she is in the mood, have sex with them. An escort does not have a choice on whether to have sex with her clients, as that is what she is paid for, but a mistress does have a choice, as it is **not** what she is paid for."

Samuels paused for a moment as he got up from his seat and walked to the window again before continuing.

"Another way to look at it is this, let us suppose you take your wife out for a meal because you want to treat her. Now you have two choices: you can order for her what you want her to eat, because after all, you are paying, or she can order whatever she wants because you want her to have that choice. Well, if you order what you want her to eat, it is like paying for an escort because you are giving her no choice on what happens. However, if you let her choose what she wants to order, it is like paying for a mistress because you are letting her make that decision. You have no control over what she is going to have, even though you are paying for it. Does that make sense, in a weird sort of way?"

"You explained that very well," Eddy said as the rest of the jurors agreed either verbally or by a nod of the head.

Danny looked at Samuels and at the other jurors, each realizing they seemed to agree.

"Ok, yes, I understand the difference between the two now, but that does not mean she is innocent," Danny said. "Even as a mistress, she could have had another reason for shooting him, and shoot him she did. So let's not forget the facts of this case, which are that she shot and killed a man. Even the defense admits that she did, but they are calling it self-defense. However, there has been no proof showing that it was, in fact, self-defense," he said, looking at Samuels.

"Yes, you are correct, but we cannot assume she had another reason because there is no evidence of that, and we must make our decision based on the facts. And the facts are that the prosecution has not shown any proof either that it was not self-defense," Samuels replied.

"Yes, I agree. The facts are that she did shoot and kill Mr. Morley," Jacob White said, also speaking for the first time since the deliberations began. "However, the reason she shot him remains a mystery. At first, I believed the prosecution when he referred to Miss Summers as an escort, and what he said about her shooting him was plausible. Yet now that I better understand the difference between an escort and a mistress, I have to ask myself why Miss Summers would shoot a client without a good reason. The only explanation I can think of is that Mr. Morley did not know the difference between the two, just like I didn't before this case, plus the defense's version of events seems more logical."

"Ok, I have not said anything so far, but here is what I think," Jack Marlow took his turn to speak. "If we go by the facts, then she is guilty of shooting and killing a man. It makes no difference if she is an escort or a mistress, but she did shoot and kill someone. Whether it was in self-defense or cold-blooded murder, we will never know, but she chose this line of work, and no one forced her into it. If someone is going to do this, then they have to accept that some clients will be more demanding. It does not give her the right to kill someone, and it's not like she has not had sex with probably hundreds of men before. I say she is guilty," he concluded, having no doubts.

There were murmurs of agreement by many of the jurors, and just as Samuels thought he was doing well, it suddenly all went backward due to Marlow.

"Ok, how about another vote so we can see if we all feel the same way after this discussion, shall we?" Eddy said.

Everyone agreed, and again, they all wrote down their vote on a folded piece of paper and handed it to the foreman. Once again, he read out each verdict in turn.

"Guilty, guilty, not guilty, guilty, guilty, guilty, guilty, guilty, guilty, guilty, guilty, and guilty. So that is now eleven against one in favor of a guilty verdict. That means two people have changed their vote from not guilty to guilty," he said.

"Not me," Samuels replied.

"One was me. It is true that no one forced her to do this job, and if she is going to do it, then she has to learn to expect things like this to happen," Jackie said as she put her hand up.

"I see, so what you are saying is that even if she does not sell her body for sex like an escort does, she should allow herself to get beaten and raped, should she?" Samuels asked.

"Oh no, that is not what I meant. Oh, I don't know, as this is so confusing without any real evidence to go on. I really have no idea, but no one deserves to be beaten or raped, regardless of what job they do, even if it is an escort or mistress," Jackie replied.

"And did the prosecution offer any proof that Miss Summers killed Mr. Morley in cold blood or that it wasn't self-defense?" Samuels asked.

"No, I guess not. Ok, I may change my vote back to my original one of not guilty. I just do not know right now," Jackie said, really uncertain of how to vote.

"Oh, come on. Seriously?" Danny asked.

"Everyone is allowed to change their vote if they want to. Remember, there is no proof of any wrongdoing, but there is also no evidence to show that Miss Summers is telling the truth," Eddy said.

"And there is the bottom line. As the judge said, if there is any doubt, then we must find her not guilty," Samuels said, feeling uneasy that things may not work out as he had hoped.

"But surely it is everyone's right to decide for themselves whether there is any doubt or not, and for me, there is no doubt that she is guilty of killing a man, regardless if she says it was self-defense or not," Jack said confidently.

"Ok, it looks like we are going to be here a while, so I will ask for some refreshments to be brought to us," Eddy said as he got up from his seat.

He then spoke to the court official and arranged for some food and drinks to be brought to them, and after a short while, the refreshments arrived.

"Let's take a little break to have something to eat and drink or to go to the bathroom if anyone needs to. We shall restart again with another vote in thirty minutes," Eddy said.

Chapter Thirty-Seven

Thirty minutes later, after they all had something to eat and drink, they were ready to resume.

"Ok, let us have another vote, shall we?" Eddy said as he passed out pieces of paper for everyone to write their verdict on. After a few minutes, he had received back all the pieces of paper and again began to read out the verdicts.

"Guilty, guilty, guilty, guilty, guilty, not guilty, guilty, guilty, guilty, guilty, guilty, not guilty."

"Oh, here we go again. It was you who changed their verdict again, wasn't it?" Danny said as he pointed his finger towards Jackie.

"No, it wasn't me," she replied.

"It was me. I changed my vote," Eddy said, looking at Danny.

"But why?" he asked.

"Because I am entitled to," Eddy replied.

"Ok, look, there are still ten people who think that she is guilty, so let's all just vote guilty so we can finish up here," Danny said.

"No, we must not do that. This is a person's life we are talking about, and we should never just agree to vote guilty simply because it is what the majority wants. I will never vote guilty as I believe it was self-defense," Samuels shouted out in frustration.

"Well, I will never change my vote because I feel she is guilty, and she deserves to be punished for shooting and killing a man," Danny said.

There were a few minutes of uncomfortable silence where they all looked at each other.

"Ok, let's think for a minute here," Samuels said as he got up and walked over to the window again, looking outward to the sky, trying to think of what to say before continuing.

"It seems that most people think she is guilty, but I wonder why that is. The prosecution has offered no proof at all that she killed Mr. Morley in cold blood, and from the statement that the judge gave us, it is clear that if we have any doubt at all, then we must acquit. So without any actual proof that it wasn't self-defense, how can anyone not have any doubts as to whether she is innocent? Please help me understand."

"Because she is a prostitute, oops, I mean mistress, and you should not believe what she says," Danny said coldly. "It is not like she is a normal hardworking woman, but instead chooses to work in the sex industry, regardless of what she calls herself. Whether or not she is a mistress, an escort, a prostitute, or a stripper, she is working in the sex industry, so I do not choose to believe her. Anyone who would sell their body or their time for any kind of sex act is not someone I would trust or believe. I see such women on the streets every day while I am driving home from work, and they look like they are either drug addicts or would rob you if given a chance. So I don't really care what she calls herself, as they are all the same. Does that help you to understand?" Danny said as he stood up.

Samuels looked at the other jurors, and most of them seemed to agree with what Danny had said. He then went back to his chair but stood behind it with his hands on the top of the backrest, facing the other jurors.

"Ok, so you are saying that every person who works in the sex industry is a drug addict and a thief, it seems. Well, what about if a single mother with a young child cannot get a normal job, as you put it, and has no choice but to become an escort or a stripper so she can feed her child? Would she also be a drug addict or a thief in your eyes? And what about if an actress does a sex scene in a film? Is she also a drug addict or a thief because she got paid to do a sex scene? Also, what about these models that appear in magazines? Are they also all drug addicts or thieves?" Samuels asked.

"Well, I don't know, but it is not the same thing," Danny replied.

"Oh, but it is. You are saying that anyone working in the sex industry is either a drug addict or a thief, perhaps even both. But you are simply categorizing these people when you know nothing about them. You cannot judge someone by what job they do or what they look like, but instead, you need to judge each person on their own merit," Samuels replied.

"Very well said," Eddy cried out as he looked at both Samuels and Danny.

Samuels walked up and down for a minute, thinking of what to say next when he had an idea. He looked at all the jury members and then decided to use Jackie as an example for his next statement. He chose her because, from the start, she had been unsure of how to vote and had already changed her mind before, so he thought she would be the best candidate to get to change her vote once again.

He then looked at Jackie and said, "Let me ask you something, and I know nothing about you, so please do not take offense at what I am going to ask you. Let us suppose you were in great financial difficulty, were a single parent with a young child, and no one around to help you. You had tried absolutely everything to put this right but were not able to do so. Let us also suppose you had a chance to make some money by having sex with someone, which would mean paying the rent and feeding your child, rather than ending up homeless on the streets. Would you do it?"

"What does that have to do with anything?" Danny stood up and asked.

"Just bear with me, please. Would you?" Samuels asked, again looking at Jackie.

"Well, I have never thought about anything like that, but I do, in fact, have a seven-year-old daughter who I would die for. If I ever found myself in that position, then I suppose I may have to consider it, but only as a last resort as I am not even sure if I could do that, to be honest," Jackie replied.

"But if it was a choice of selling your body for sex or ending up on the streets with your seven-year-old daughter, then would you do it?" Samuels asked.

"As a last resort, I guess I probably wouldn't have much choice," she replied.

"And under those circumstances, how would you feel if you were called a drug addict or a thief simply because you chose to sell your body for sex so you could house and feed your beloved daughter?" Samuels asked.

"I would be no such thing!" shouted out Jackie as she stood up and slammed her hand on the table while giving Danny a dirty look.

"So you see, to label everyone who may sell their body for sex, a drug addict or a thief is nonsense. People who work in the sex industry have many reasons for doing so, and it does not make them a bad person, a drug addict, or even a thief. We should not judge anyone for how they earn their living, but instead judge them on their own merit, despite how they may earn their living," Samuels said.

"Ok, yes, I may be wrong about that," Danny conceded, "but Miss Summers does not need the money yet still does it anyway. She is not forced into it due to having to pay the rent or having to feed a child but instead does it because she wants to. You have to ask why. Why would anyone want to do that?" he asked as he looked around the room.

"The why is not the question, nor should it matter what a person does. Just because she chooses to do that does not make her a bad person, a drug addict, or a thief, and it certainly does not make her a murderer. We should not judge her and find her guilty just because she earns her money as a mistress, but instead find her innocent due to any doubt that she is guilty," Samuels replied as he looked at the jurors before sitting back down.

"I agree with what you say that we should not judge Miss Summers by how she chooses to earn her money or even the why," Eddy said, nodding his head as he did so.

"Yes, I also agree, and I am changing my vote to not guilty, and it will be the last time I change," Jackie said, realizing that what Samuels said made a lot of sense.

"So that makes it nine to three then," Eddy said, making a note of it.

"Eight to four. I am also changing my vote back to how I originally voted," Sally said.

"Anyone else wish to change their vote?" Eddy asked.

There were a few minutes of silence as everyone looked at each other to see if anyone else would change their vote, but no one replied.

"Come on, folks, we need to try and reach a unanimous verdict here. Ok, look, let's take another vote just in case," Eddy said as he looked at everyone.

He passed out pieces of paper to all the jurors so they could vote again and, upon receiving them, began to count the verdicts out loud.

"So it stays at eight against four in favor of guilty. So, it would seem that we cannot reach a unanimous verdict. Does anyone have anything to say?" Eddy asked.

There was nothing but silence from the jurors, and all they did was look at each other. The discussion went on for another hour, without anyone changing their vote.

"Well, in that case, I have no choice but to notify the court official of this," Eddy said as he rose from his seat, then went to the door and opened it to call the official.

Samuels was overjoyed with this decision and hoped that the judge would call a mistrial. If that was the case, his job was done, and his wife would be left alone. His gambling debts would also be paid off as part of the agreement, and he vowed to himself to never gamble again. All he could do now was wait and hope.

The court official relayed the message to the judge, and the jurors was recalled to the courtroom, where the judge asked the foreperson to stand up and then asked him.

"I understand you cannot reach a unanimous verdict, is that correct?"

"Yes, your Honor," was the foreperson's reply.

"And if you had more time to deliberate, would you be likely to reach a unanimous verdict?" the judge asked.

"No, your Honor, I don't think we can," Eddy replied.

"Very well then," the judge said as he paused for a brief moment and told the court officials to let everyone know to return to the courtroom.

The information was relayed to all parties involved, and everyone made their way back to the courtroom. After the judge had entered and everyone had taken their seats, he began to speak.

"The jury has been unable to reach a unanimous verdict, so it falls upon me to make a decision regarding this case. The prosecution, in my mind, has failed to show proof that the shooting and subsequent death of Mr. Morley were intentional rather than in self-defense, as suggested by the defense. Also, due to the fact that there is in my mind a reasonable doubt as to the defendant's guilt, I hereby have no alternative but to declare a mistrial. Miss Summers, you are free to go, with the court's apologies."

Alexia and Jason looked at each other with big smiles on their faces and gave each other a hug before Jason looked over at Emerton with a big grin on his face as if to say I beat you. Needless to say, the look Emerton gave back to Jason was anything but a happy one. Jason was very pleased with the outcome, even though it was tainted, but that did not worry him. All he cared about was that Alexia was free, and he knew deep down that further charges would probably not be brought against her.

Chapter Thirty-Eight

Jason and Alexia left the courtroom elated and walked to Jason's car for the journey back to her house, as Alexia had asked Jason if he could take her home. During the journey, Jason reassured Alexia that it was all over and she would never have to go through that again. He knew that his boss would do everything in his power to stop the DA from prosecuting Alexia again, but he also knew that he now had the ammunition to ensure against it. If push came to shove, he could blackmail his wife's lover to make sure the DA did not bring any more charges against her, now that he knew they were connected.

Needless to say, they were both ecstatic over the victory. For Jason, not only was Alexia free, but he had also got one over on Emerton, which made the victory even sweeter for him.

Once they reached her house, Alexia asked Jason to come in, so he parked the car on the drive then they both walked up to the front door. Alexia opened the door and led Jason inside, where they sat on the couch next to each other.

"Thank you again, Jason, for all your hard work regarding the trial. I have a little surprise for you. You must now do exactly what I tell you, do you understand?" she said in a commanding way, which Jason took to mean she was now in charge again.

"Yes, Mistress," he replied, unsure if he should even call her that at this specific time or not, but thought it best to, just in case.

"Very good, my little slave; you are learning fast. Now take all your clothes off and then sit back down on the couch," she told him, and of course, Jason did as was demanded of him.

Alexia stood up, then put one foot on the couch just in front of Jason's crotch, and then gently pushed the tip of her shoe onto Jason's cock. Jason groaned quietly, almost immediately beginning to become aroused, and within a minute, he had become very hard.

"You seem to like that, Jason," Alexia said in a soft, gentle voice as she pushed her foot against his stiff cock even harder.

"Now, Jason, I am going to reward you for helping me with the trial and gaining my freedom, she said as she walked over to the cabinet and opened the drawer.

"Put this on," she said as she took out a condom from the open drawer and tossed it to Jason before she began to walk back toward him.

Without hesitation, Jason ripped open the packet, took out the condom, and quickly put it over his hard shaft. He was so excited by the thought that Alexia would finally allow him to have sex with her that he rose up from the couch.

However, before he could even take one step toward her, Alexia said to him in a very stern voice, "Sit down, Jason, and do not forget your place. I am still your Mistress, so do not presume anything. Is that understood?"

"Yes, Mistress, I am so sorry," Jason replied as he sat back down on the couch.

"That's better, Jason. You will get your reward, but I will decide how you are rewarded, not you. Now, you will just sit there and do nothing unless I tell you, is that understood?"

"Yes, Mistress, again, I am sorry," he replied as he looked up at her, practically standing over him now.

Alexia lifted up her dress, slowly pulled off her panties, and then knelt on the couch, straddling Jason in the process. She then slowly lowered herself onto him until his hard cock was fully inside her before beginning to move her body up and down very slowly, staring him directly in the eyes. After a few minutes, she began to increase the speed of her movements and dangled her long hair into Jason's face.

"Run your hands up and down along my legs and ass," Alexia said in a commanding tone, and Jason did exactly that, feeling her stocking tops before his hands could feel her naked skin along the back of her thighs and her buttocks, before moving them back down to her stocking tops.

Jason did this for the next few minutes then Alexia began to move her body even faster now, still staring into Jason's eyes. His breathing was now getting heavier, and his hips were beginning to move in time with hers, as was the speed of his hands moving along her legs.

"Squeeze my butt," she yelled out as she began to now move her body as fast as she could, and Jason put his hands on her butt, squeezing it hard while she pushed herself onto him faster.

"That's it, Jason," she said as she began to moan in pleasure. Jason, too, was now breathing heavier than ever before, while his own hips were now moving even faster, trying to push himself as deep as he could go inside Alexia with every thrust.

She could see that Jason was at the point where he could not last much longer, and she suddenly yelled out loud, "Come for me, Jason, come for your Mistress," in a very seductive tone of voice.

He suddenly gave out a massive groan as he began to shoot his load inside the condom.

"Oh, yes, that's it, Jason," she said as his hips continued to jerk as he shot more and more cum, his balls tightening with each spurt.

Alexia herself was now beginning to get to the point of where she was about to come and continued to ride Jason until she suddenly arched her body backward, moaning in ecstasy as she reached her own orgasm.

When she had finished, she leaned forward again, gave Jason a little kiss on the lips, and said, "I hope you enjoyed that, Jason, but do not for one minute think that this is going to be a regular thing for you. This was my treat for you as a thank you, but I am still and always will be your mistress, so you had better remember that. This is the kind of reward you may get from time to time if you deserve it, but you will always be my slave, and as such, my pleasure is what really matters."

"Yes, Mistress, I will remember that and thank you very much for your treat ... It was wonderful, Mistress."

"I am sure it was, Jason," Alexia said as she rose up, picked up her panties from the floor, and told Jason that it was now time for him to leave.

"I want you to come back tomorrow evening at seven, Jason. I have something very, very important I need to talk to you about, and I want to do it in person rather than over the phone."

"Yes, Mistress, I will be here," he replied.

"Do not be late!" Alexia demanded.

"I won't, Mistress," he replied as he began to get dressed.

When he was finally dressed, he said goodbye to Alexia and left thinking about the wonderful sex he had just had with her as he walked to his car. All the way home, he continued to relive what had just happened, but as he neared his house, he began to wonder what Alexia wanted to see him about the next evening. He could only hope that things were about to get even better, thinking that perhaps Alexia intended to make him one of her own personal slaves. However, if it was just that, then surely she could have told him there and then, rather than asking him to come back the following evening.

He parked his car, went inside his house, kissed, and spoke to Lydia for a short while before they had dinner together. After another normal evening, they both went to bed, said goodnight to each other, and rolled over as they usually did. Lydia fell asleep quite quickly, but Jason was still far too excited to sleep after what had just happened and continued to wonder what Alexia wanted to speak to him about. He was fairly sure it would be domination-related, but it still bothered him that he was told to go back the next evening. He tried hard to think of what she wanted to talk to him about, if not domination, but there was no way he could have imagined what was to follow the subsequent evening.

CHAPTER THIRTY-NINE

Jason woke up the next day and did his usual routine in the morning, then left for work just like any other day.

Once at work, he went to see Mr. Langley, who had asked to see him, and they discussed the trial. Langley congratulated Jason for a job well done and then gave him his next case.

He went back to his office and began to read through the file of his next client, but he could not get his mind off Alexia and what she had planned for him that evening. The day seemed to drag for Jason, and he was glad it was nearly over. He telephoned Lydia to tell her that he would be going to see a new client after work and that he may be home late that evening and then got himself ready to leave the office.

Alexia had told him to be there at seven, and as he was early, he decided to stop at a bar near her house and have a drink while he waited for the right time. When it was time, he left the bar and drove the short remaining distance to Alexia's house, arriving at the exact time she told him to be there. Jason got out of his car, walked up to the door, rang the bell, and waited for Alexia, who opened the door a few seconds later.

"Hello, Jason, I love a prompt man," she said as she opened the door.

"Hello, Mistress," was the reply from Jason.

"No, Jason, not Mistress right now," Alexia said as she opened the door fully and asked him to go inside.

"Oh, I see, so, is it Miss Summers tonight, then?" he asked.

"No, Jason, it is Alexia for now," she replied sadly as she showed him into the living room and then asked him to sit down.

Jason began to wonder why the sudden change and what could have happened for her to be like this. Did he do something wrong the previous night, he wondered to himself before asking, "Is everything alright, Alexia?"

"Yes and no, Jason. Please bear with me as I have something I need to speak to you about. Please do not interrupt me, and you must wait until I have finished before saying anything. Can you do that for me?" she asked.

"Yes, of course, I can," Jason replied, unsure of what was now happening and becoming quite concerned that perhaps his days of visiting Alexia would be suddenly over.

"I am not going to go into too much detail, but simply tell you what I feel you need to know. When I was young, my father left my mother and me, and she soon turned to drink.

Then she hooked up with another man who began to sexually abuse me when I was fifteen years old, and when I was sixteen, I was raped by a man in the park while I was walking home one evening. Soon after that, I left home to try and restart my life, but I ended up working as a prostitute so as not to end up on the streets."

She paused to regain her composure, then looked Jason in the eyes before she continued with the story she was telling him.

"Then, one day, my life changed when I met a woman called Veronica, who helped me to turn my life around, and it is because of her that I am the person I am today. I had put my horrific past behind me, but it all came flooding back when I met Simon Morley, and I, in fact, shot and killed him on purpose."

"WHAT?" shouted Jason.

But before he could say anymore, Alexia said, "Did I not say not to interrupt me until I was finished? Now please be quiet and listen."

Jason apologized and allowed Alexia to continue with her story.

Alexia paused for a moment, got up, went over to a cabinet, poured them both a drink and then set the drinks down on the table in front of them. After taking a sip, she continued.

"Simon did, in fact, attack me and tried to rape me because I would not have sex with him. He did not truly understand what a true mistress is all about, and I did fear for my life. That much is the truth, but when he had his hand around my neck and stared into my eyes, I suddenly found myself back in that park where I was raped, and then he suddenly said something that sent a chill down my spine. As he had his hand around my neck, he said - ***I always get what I want*** - which is exactly what the man who raped me all those years ago said to me.

"Hearing that voice and seeing his piercing eyes staring at me, I realized that he was, in fact, the same man who raped me when I was sixteen. There was no doubt about it in my mind. He had the same chilling voice, the same staring glare, and it was almost as though I was back in that park getting raped all over again," Alexia paused for another moment and took a large sip from her drink.

She put her hand on Jason's thigh and continued. "I knew it was him, and I was not going to be raped by him a second time, so I tried to calm him down by telling him that he did not need to do this and I would do whatever he wanted. It was obvious that he did not know who I was, and I would never have realized he was the same man that raped me if not for his stare or the words he said. I told him that I loved a masterful man and that we should go to the bedroom where we would be more comfortable. I said that I fancied a drink, asking if he wanted one, to which he replied yes, and then I walked over to the cabinet, opened the drawer, took out the gun, and shot him.

He had to pay for what he did to me all those years ago, and as I said, I was not going to be raped all over again.

"Believe me when I say that a girl never forgets certain things such as a smell, a stare, a voice, and other things like that when she is being raped. Those things stay with you and haunt you for a very long time. If you do not believe me, Jason, check his DNA, and you will see that it matches the DNA on file regarding the rape of a sixteen-year-old girl called Sally Jessop, which used to be my name before I had it changed. You may ask any questions you have for me now, Jason, if you wish."

Jason took a large mouthful of his drink and looked at Alexia with sadness that she had to go through all that at such a young age above all else.

"Why did you not tell me this from the beginning?" Jason asked as he took yet another sip of his drink.

"I did not know you and had no idea how you would react, so I thought it best to keep it to myself," Alexia replied.

"Yes, I can understand that, I guess, but what about the scratch on his face?" Jason asked.

"After I had shot him, I realized that I had to make it look like it was self-defense, which in a way it was, to me at least, so I scratched his face after he was dead, tore my dress and hit myself in the face."

"I see, and why are you telling me this now?" he asked.

Alexia took a very deep breath, looked at Jason then kissed her index finger before putting it onto his lips. She then gave him a very big smile before finally speaking.

"Because not only did you save me from going to jail, but I also do really like you, Jason. Not only would I love for you to continue being my slave, but perhaps even allow you to become one of my special personal slaves that I allow to visit me here in my private home. However, before I can do that, I need to know if I have your complete obedience, and this is a great way for me to find out. Now, what are you going to do with this information, Jason?" Alexia asked him.

Jason took another sip of his drink, looked deep into Alexia's eyes, and then asked her, "Do you know what client privilege is, and do you understand the whole concept of it?"

"Yes, Jason, I know all about client privilege and that, as my lawyer, you cannot reveal anything I say to you. Besides, there is no proof that I have admitted anything to you, but that is not the point. Forget whether or not you can legally say anything about this; I am asking you as a person and as my slave if you want to do anything with this information I have given you. You sit there for a while and think before giving me an answer, and I shall be back shortly," Alexia said as she got up and left the room.

Jason took this time to think about everything she had said to him, but deep down in his heart, he knew that he would not say anything. He had become so infatuated with Alexia that all he could think about was seeing her as his mistress as much as possible, and that would never happen if he said anything. Besides, he had broken the law himself to get her acquitted. There was no way that he would have gone to all that trouble and then turn around and tell anyone about her confession, especially regarding the death of a lowlife rapist such as Morley.

No, Jason had already decided that he would not say anything and simply waited for Alexia to return so he could tell her, but he also wondered what would happen next.

Chapter Forty

After a short while, Alexia returned, dressed in nothing but a pair of red high-heeled shoes.

"So, Jason, have you made up your mind yet?" she asked.

"Yes, Alexia, I have no wish to say or do anything," Jason replied as he got up from the couch and knelt down in front of her, unable to take his gaze away from her naked body. As far as I am concerned, what happened was self-defense, plain and simple. I want to be your slave and please you whenever you want me to," he said, getting back up after he had finished speaking.

"Very good, Jason, and now let's talk about you becoming one of my personal slaves, shall we? Just listen very carefully to what I am going to say, and do not interrupt me. Is that clear?"

"Yes, Mistress," was his reply as he eagerly waited to hear what she had to say to him. He had prayed and hoped that this day would come from the moment he met her, and he could hardly believe that this was now really happening.

"Apart from your obedience, before I can allow you to serve me as one of my personal slaves, I need to know that you have the commitment it takes to become one. You may have to do things that you will not enjoy or even want to do, but will have to do them anyway. You will have to obey my every command, whenever I want you to, day or night, without question and hesitation. I will push your boundaries to the limit, and at times, you may even question who you are or what you have become, but you will obey my commands regardless. The time could arrive when you may even regret becoming one of my personal slaves, but that will be your problem to deal with because I will not hesitate for one minute to release you from my servitude should you refuse anything I say. At times, you may feel loved by me, and at other times, you may feel let down or discarded by me. Again, this is something you will have to learn to deal with, as you will not be my only personal slave. Do you think you have what it takes to become one of my personal slaves, Jason?"

Jason thought long and hard about what Alexia had just told him before asking her, "Exactly what will I have to do, and how will it impact my life and work?"

"You will have to do exactly what I tell you to do, whatever that may be. As for your life or work, well, I appreciate that you do have a life and a job to do, but you also have a mistress to serve. I will not do anything that will cause problems with your work, as you do have to earn a living after all, nor will I do anything to cause problems within your marriage. I will expect you, however, to come to me whenever I want you to, even if that is in the evenings or at weekends when you are home with your wife. I am sure you can make some excuse, just like I am sure you made one for tonight. There may be times when I would expect you to stay overnight, which, again, I am sure you can think of some excuse to give your wife. My terms are non-negotiable if you are to become one of my personal slaves, and it is up to you to ensure you are available for me when I want you to be. As I said, I will not cause your marriage any problems, but if you want to be one of my personal slaves, then there will be times when I expect to take priority over your wife. Are there any other questions, or are you ready to submit to me?"

Again, Jason thought about what Alexia was saying and wondered if he could do all that was being asked of him, but he really wanted this. He thought about his wife cheating on him, thinking that he had no reason to be faithful to her, and even if she found out, it would not be too much of a problem as long as he had Alexia. Even if he had to leave his job, he was sure he could quite easily get another job working as a lawyer.

Without giving the matter any more thought, he said, "Yes, Mistress, I am ready to serve you in any way you want."

"Very well, but before I show you my playroom, where you will spend many hours pleasing me, whether it's by you pleasuring me or me punishing you, I want to test you out to see just how compliant you will be."

"Whatever you want, Mistress," Jason replied, sounding both eager and worried.

"That's correct, Jason; it *is* whatever I want. You may start by kneeling in front of me."

Jason did exactly that and knelt down in front of Alexia, anticipating what was about to happen next.

"Now we will see just how far you are willing to go, Jason. But before you begin, I want to tell you that I did not take a shower this morning and, in fact, have not showered since yesterday morning. I left myself nice and dirty just for you."

Jason looked at her, feeling quite shocked at what she had just told him, unsure of how he was meant to respond to that comment.

Before he could even think about replying, as she sat down on the couch, she said, "Take my shoes off and kiss my feet."

Jason took off her shoes and began to kiss her feet as was commanded, thinking to himself that this was not what he expected, but, in a way, it turned him on quite a bit.

"Do they smell, Jason?" Alexia asked.

Unsure how he should answer that question, he looked up at her and replied, "Yes, Mistress, but I don't mind if they do."

"Very good answer, Jason, but I know they smell quite a bit. But that's ok as you are going to wash them for me ... with your mouth. Now suck each one of my toes in turn and wash them well, my good slave." she demanded.

Jason complied with her demand. Even though he was not enjoying it, he knew that it was a test, and so did it anyway, sucking the toes on both of Alexia's feet.

"Very well done, Jason. First test passed, and now for the next test," she said as she got up, turned around, and knelt on the couch.

"Now lick my ass, Jason, and I can assure you that the smell there is far worse than my feet."

Jason paused for a very brief moment, surprised and disgusted at what he had been told to do, when Alexia suddenly snapped at the top of her voice, "NOW, SLAVE!"

Jason quickly leaned forward and began to lick around her very smelly, sweaty asshole, holding his breath as much as he could while doing so.

"That's it, my slave, wash my ass really well," Alexia said with a big grin on her face.

"Push your tongue inside my ass," she commanded.

Jason, feeling very uncomfortable at this very moment, knew that if he did not do so, then his dreams of being one of her slaves would be over. Taking a deep breath, he then slowly pushed his tongue inside her now wet asshoe, and then continued to tongue fuck her.

After a few minutes of doing this, Alexia told Jason to stop, telling him that he had passed test number two. Then she turned around and sat back down on the edge of the couch with her legs as far apart as they could go.

"And now for the third test, Jason," she said.

Jason was looking forward to this part, as he knew by the way she had perched her body on the edge of the couch that he was about to give her a pussy a good licking. He was looking forward to doing this very much, even if it was to smell a little bit.

"Now, Jason, you are going to lick me until I come, but before you do so, I want to let you know that Henry fucked me earlier today, without a condom, and he shot his jizz inside me. Now, lick me till I come, my obedient little slave."

Jason looked up at Alexia in total horror and disgust and then began to reply, "But, Mistress-"

However, before he could say anything else, Alexia sat up and slapped him hard around the face and said, "Get your fucking head down there and lick my dirty cunt, if you want to become one of my personal slaves, you worthless piece of shit. Or if not, get the fuck out of my house."

Jason's first instinct was to get up and leave, as this was not what he was expecting, and it was certainly nothing like what he had done with Selene. But then he realized that he had an almighty throbbing cock and was, in fact, turned on so much more than he had ever been before. He could not believe the way she had just spoken to him, or the way he was feeling at this very moment, especially as he himself was such a dominant man, or at least thought he was. Still, right now, he had no choice. Suddenly he realized that being submissive to Alexia was so pleasurable that without thinking any further, he did as she commanded. He buried his face between her legs and licked her dirty, smelly pussy until she began to moan in ecstasy.

"Oh yes slave, that's it make me come, yes faster, yes oh god I'm going to come, yeeesssss," she screamed out as her hips girated and her juices began to flow.

After Alexia had come and finished squirting all over Jason's face, she looked down at him with a very big smile.

"Very good, Jason; I am impressed. I shall forget the fact that you hesitated this time, but know that in the future, any hesitation at all will end in punishment. If you continue to hesitate too often, you will cease to be my slave, and you can go back to your wife. Do I make myself clear?"

"Yes, Mistress, I understand, and I am sorry," he replied, feeling sick at the thought that his mouth had just been where Henry had creamed earlier that day.

"Good, now let's take this to the next level. From this moment on, any hesitation will be met with punishment. Any time I have to tell you something twice, will be met with punishment. Any time you fail to please me sexually, will be met with punishment," she said as she stood up.

Alexia led Jason through to another part of the house and opened a door that led into a very large room that was filled wall-to-wall with equipment ranging from whips, clamps, strap-ons, chains, cages, uniforms, masks, and a whole variety of other sex toys. Over a hundred items were hanging from the walls, and as Jason turned to look at the various items, he saw a naked man chained to one of the walls. Jason then turned and looked at Alexia in amazement and also with a hint of fear as he began to realize what she meant about pushing his boundaries to the limits. Alexia walked over to the man that was chained to the wall, picked up a whip, and began to strike the man on the back with it. Three times she brought the whip down on his back before reaching over and rubbing her hands over the area she had just whipped.

"This is Charles, and he did not please me enough last night, so this is his punishment," she said as she brought the whip down on his butt this time.

"You won't disappoint when pleasuring me, will you, Jason?" she said as she whipped Charles's butt one more time.

"No, Mistress, I won't," Jason replied, worried and wondering if he had made the right choice.

"Good, and now it's time for your real training to start," Alexia said as she told Jason to take his clothes off, then walked over to the door and closed it, leaving the world outside.

"Ok, Jason, let us begin!"

The rest is for another time!